Beloved Hope

Books by Tracie Peterson

www.traciepeterson.com

*with Judith Miller **with Judith Pella ***with Kimberley Woodhouse

HEART OF THE FRONTIER · 2

Beloved Hope

TRACIE
PETERSON

BETHANYHOUSE

a division of Baker Publishing Group
Minneapolis, Minnesota

© 2017 by Peterson Ink, Inc.

Published by Bethany House Publishers
11400 Hampshire Avenue South
Bloomington, Minnesota 55438
www.bethanyhouse.com

Bethany House Publishers is a division of
Baker Publishing Group, Grand Rapids, Michigan

Printed in the United States of America

Library of Congress Cataloging-in-Publication Data
Names: Peterson, Tracie, author.
Title: Beloved hope / Tracie Peterson.
Description: Minneapolis, Minnesota : Bethany House, a division of Baker
    Publishing Group, [2017] | Series: Heart of the frontier ; 2
Identifiers: LCCN 2016049065| ISBN 9780764213427 (cloth : alk. paper) |
    ISBN 9780764213281 (trade paper) | ISBN 9780764213434 (large-print trade
    paper)
Subjects: LCSH: Frontier and pioneer life—Fiction. | GSAFD: Christian fiction.
    | Love stories.
Classification: LCC PS3566.E7717 B46 2017 | DDC 813/.54—dc23
LC record available at https://lccn.loc.gov/2016049065

Scripture quotations are from the King James Version of the Bible.

This is a work of historical reconstruction; the appearances of certain historical
figures are therefore inevitable. All other characters, however, are products of the
author's imagination, and any resemblance to actual persons, living or dead, is
coincidental.

Cover design by LOOK Design Studio
Cover photography by Aimee Christenson

17 18 19 20 21 22 23   7 6 5 4 3 2 1

To Calvin Braaksma—
You are an amazing attorney
with a great sense of humor and heart for God.
Thank you for being you!

Chapter

1

OREGON CITY, OREGON
MAY 1850

Y ou can't be serious." Hope Flanagan looked at the man who
sat opposite her at her sister and brother-in-law's kitchen
table. "You expect me to testify in the Cayuse trial."

Only weeks before, the five Cayuse men deemed responsible
for the Whitman Massacre had been turned over to the army
and were now in Oregon City to stand trial. Hope twisted her
skirt in her hands, thankful the table hid her actions.

For the last two and a half years, she had worked to forget
that awful day in November when the Cayuse attacked the
Whitman Mission. Then, in a single moment, this man brought
it all back to her. She remembered the kitchen at the mission
on that day. Sitting beside John Sager, the boy she'd hoped
to marry. She had thought life perfect. She'd never wanted to
come west to Oregon, but when she fell in love, everything
changed.

It changed again when Tomahas and Telokite—two Cayuse chiefs—showed up at the mission house.

There had been trouble with the Cayuse for weeks. Measles had followed the white settlers into Oregon Country, and many of the Cayuse had died. The chiefs blamed the whites in general at first, but when Marcus Whitman—a doctor—failed to save their sick while seeming to revive his white patients, the Cayuse were convinced he was killing them on purpose.

The Cayuse were angry that day. They demanded help, demanded medicine. But all the while they had planned to kill Whitman. Hope trembled, remembering the murderous look in Tomahas's eyes. Even prior to the attack, his people called Tomahas "the Murderer," and rightly so. His temper was short and his actions swift.

Hope remembered John tensing beside her. He'd been working with twine and put it to one side in a very slow, casual manner. When Telokite and Tomahas began their attack, John reached for his pistol, and Tomahas shot him. Hope had fallen to the floor with John and cradled him as he died. His blood had soaked her dress as she pleaded with him to live.

"Miss Flanagan, I know this is difficult."

The attorney's voice brought Hope back to the present. She fixed him with a look that made him grimace. He knew nothing of what had happened except what he'd been told.

As if reading her mind, he quickly focused on his empty coffee cup. "I mean to say that I've been told what you and the others went through. I understand that it won't be easy to come forward and testify."

"And that's why I won't do it."

He looked up and shook his head. "But you must. Witnesses are vital in this trial. Generally speaking, Indian massacres do

8

not have survivors. You were there, and you have vital information to offer."

Grace, Hope's older sister, brought the coffeepot and poured the man another cup. "Mr. Holbrook, a great many women and children survived the massacre. Why must Hope testify?"

"As I understand it, your sister was in the kitchen when the Indians entered and began their attack. She witnessed Marcus Whitman's murder. Few can say the same. We need her testimony to ensure the guilty verdict."

Grace was unimpressed. "Why should there be any question of their guilt? You've known the identities of the men since we arrived in Oregon City. The victims saw those responsible cut down the men at the mission. They witnessed it firsthand, and their testimony has never wavered. Furthermore, as I understand it, Telokite and Tomahas have boasted of their deeds. They take full credit for ridding their people of Dr. Whitman."

"Yes, they did, but that isn't the case now. They deny any participation. They're entering a plea of not guilty and are hoping for a complete acquittal."

Hope studied the stranger. Amory Holbrook had been appointed by the president to be the United States Attorney for the Oregon Territory. He would prosecute the Cayuse. He was young—perhaps too young for the job he held. Hope had her doubts about his abilities. She didn't like him but couldn't exactly say why. It might only be what he represented. On the other hand, she found the beard that edged his jawline and barely covered the end of his chin annoying. He was otherwise clean-shaven. It was a look Hope had never cared for.

"Miss Flanagan, I know this is difficult—"

He'd said it again. Hope gritted her teeth and tightened her hold on her skirt. She could barely force out her words. "You know nothing. You weren't there, and you can't possibly understand, no matter how many people tell you the story or give you the ugly details. You will never know what your request is costing me."

"Of course, you're right, and I did not mean to imply a first-hand knowledge of events. However, I do understand that the event described to me by other witnesses was a heinous, unforgivable act of indecency, and I want to see those men hang for what they did."

Hope drew in a deep breath to calm her spirit. "So do I."

"The trial will hopefully conclude in that. However, some feel a goodwill gesture might be called for."

"A goodwill gesture?" Grace asked.

Holbrook nodded. "There has been talk that pardoning the Indians would show the various tribes that the white man understands their plight and concerns and forgives what happened because of them. However, I do not adhere to that thought. It would be one thing if they had committed a single murder. Perhaps even multiple murders might be overlooked, but what they did in taking helpless women and children hostage is unforgivable. I believe we need to send a much stronger message to these Indian nations. In hanging those guilty of murdering Dr. Whitman and the others, we put it in clear, unquestionable terms: 'If you continue to harm the settlers, we will prosecute you and punish you to the full extent of the law.'" He paused for a moment. "The entire United States is watching to see how we deal with the Cayuse. And not only the whites, but the Indians as well. They are waiting to see if we pardon the murderers. Mark my words, it will spell disaster if we do."

Hope had never once considered that anyone would think it reasonable to pardon murderers. The very idea of Tomahas—the Cayuse who had killed the man she loved, taken her virtue, and left her to bear his unwanted child—walking the streets as a free man left her sick inside.

"So you see, we need witnesses such as yourself to tell your story of what happened on the day of the massacre, as well as what happened to you during captivity, and how those events affect you even today. If the facts are unknown—if the victims fail to speak out and give a detailed account of what happened, they'll have no one but themselves to blame if those savages are freed."

Silence hung over the kitchen. Hope knew she had little choice. She couldn't let the Cayuse get away with what they had done. She owed that much to Johnny.

"Very well. I will testify."

Holbrook nodded. "Thank you. I'll need you to come by my office, and we'll take down a detailed account of what happened, since you weren't one of the women who helped us get the grand jury indictment." He got to his feet and gave Grace a nod. "Thank you for your hospitality."

Grace exchanged a glance with Hope. "You're welcome, but I have a question to ask. Will you also need my youngest sister to testify? She's not yet fifteen. She was only twelve when the attack took place."

He looked at his notes. "Mercy Flanagan, correct?"

"Yes."

"I don't believe we'll need her testimony, Mrs. Armistead. She was in the school at the onset of the attack, as was Eliza Spaulding. We have Miss Spaulding's deposition. She acted as interpreter for the Cayuse during the days of captivity, so she had a clearer understanding of what the Cayuse intended. There should be no reason for your young sister to have to testify."

Hope saw the relief in Grace's expression. They had talked about the possibility ever since the Cayuse had been caught and the victims started being interviewed. Mercy was extremely tenderhearted, and they both feared testifying would be too hard on her.

Mercy was also of a mind that as true Christians, they should forgive the Indians and move on. It was a mentality Hope could not understand. After all, Mercy had witnessed the horrors of the massacre as well, although she might not have understood all that happened to the women. Mercy was small for her age, and the Cayuse had considered her a child. Hope had tried to shield her from the worst of it, but even so, Mercy had to remember how terrifying it had been. John Sager's brother Frank had been shot down right in front of them. Each day they had lived with the threat of being murdered. When they closed their eyes at night, none of them could be sure of ever opening them again. No one could be sheltered from that.

Grace saw Holbrook out while Hope returned to the fireplace in the front room and sat down at her spinning wheel. Spinning was a soothing task that restored peace to her soul. She picked up the wool roving and gave a gentle tug to draft out the fibers.

"I'm sorry about that," Grace said, coming into the room. "I told Holbrook that if it was at all possible to exclude you, he should do so."

"Thank you." Hope didn't look up, instead starting the wheel spinning.

Grace pulled up a footstool and sat across from Hope. "Will you tell them about Faith?"

Hope thought for a moment of the half-Cayuse baby she'd given birth to—a baby born out of an act of violence. It seemed so long ago, and yet it hadn't even been two years. She and Grace had done everything in their power to keep the secret between themselves and Eletta and Isaac Browning—the couple who'd taken the baby to raise as their own. Eletta and her husband were missionary friends of Grace. They had all met on the journey west to Oregon Country. Other than the Brownings, Hope knew that Grace had told her husband, Alex, but had otherwise remained silent on the matter. Not even Mercy knew about the child.

Hope shook her head. "I don't think so. It would serve no purpose. I doubt anyone here knows the real reason I went to California with Eletta and Isaac." She let the yarn she'd twisted earlier catch into the fibers of the roving.

"No, I shouldn't think so." Grace watched the yarn wind onto the bobbin. "Hope, I'm sorry you have to go through this. It's not fair."

"Life has never been fair." Hope stopped pedaling the wheel. "It wasn't fair that Johnny died. It wasn't fair that innocent lives were taken. It's not fair that those guilty of the murders still walk the earth and claim innocence. If it were left up to me, they'd already be dead. Without a trial."

"I can understand that. I have to admit I feel the same. I want to have a charitable heart, but toward those men . . ." Grace fell silent.

"I don't think anyone will rest easy until they're dead. I know I won't."

In truth, Hope wasn't sure she'd ever feel safe in this wild territory, despite the new regiment of soldiers that had come the year before.

At her sister's movement, Hope glanced up. She could tell Grace was preparing to leave. "Are you going shopping after you take Alex his lunch?"

"Yes. Is there something you need?" Grace pulled on her sunbonnet.

"Mrs. Reynolds offered me some of their beets from last fall.

She said they were dried out and she was going to feed them to the pigs, but I told her I'd like some for dyeing my yarn."

"I'm taking her some vinegar anyway. I'll check with her and see if she has them ready. I might stay in town long enough to give Mercy a ride home from school so she doesn't have to wait around for Alex or walk."

"That's fine. I don't mind being here alone."

And she truly didn't. Ever since the massacre, Hope had done everything in her power to avoid people. When John McLoughlin, the man who had once been factor of Fort Vancouver, had offered to sell Alex and Grace this property three miles from town, Hope had been excited. The previous owner had come to the area five years earlier. He had done a great deal with the land, and it already had a log house and a small barn for animals. His focus had been on raising horses, and he had fenced off a large section of open pasture. A difficult feat by any standard. This, along with some smaller pens and additional acreage, made it the perfect place to raise sheep.

Hope had never seen a more beautiful setting. A large creek ran through the land to empty below the bluff into the Willamette River, so water was always available for their needs. There was also prime forest that in time would be cleared away for various building projects, including a grand new house that Alex and Grace had planned and more fencing. Already a large number of felled logs were stacked and ready for use.

The farm stretched out over one hundred and forty acres all told, well away from prying eyes. It assured that Hope wouldn't have to see anyone if she didn't want to. For the last year, the only time she'd gone to town was for church functions, and she only did that to keep from shaming Grace with questions from the other parishioners.

Grace admonished her to make friends, but Hope wanted no

friends. She didn't want to care about anyone—not as she had before the massacre. It hurt too much to lose them.

"I'll be home in time to start supper, so if you would make sure the stove is hot, I'd really appreciate it," Grace said, opening the door. She didn't wait for Hope's affirmation.

Hope followed her sister outside and waited until Grace had mounted her horse and headed toward the road that would take her into town. Everything was so lush and green. The trees were flowering. Come fall there would be apples aplenty.

At times like this, when everyone else was gone, Hope pretended she lived alone without any cares in the world. She would sit and sew, or spin yarn, or tend to their small herd of sheep. There was such peace out here away from town. It was as if the rest of the world had forgotten about her—passed her by without so much as a thought. And that was exactly how Hope preferred it.

And should anyone come to cause problems or take advantage of her, Hope had her own revolver. If Indians or anyone else tried to do her harm, she would simply shoot them dead. Never again would she be anyone's victim.

∞

Grace made her way to the sawmill that her husband and uncle, Edward Marsh, co-owned. Alex had given up his life of trapping to take on logging and milling instead. He routinely commented that the latter required muscles he hadn't used in trapping. Often when he returned after a particularly grueling day, Grace would rub him down with some of her herbal oil. At first he had protested, not caring for the scents, but he eventually admitted the remedy went a long way toward easing his misery.

Thoughts of Alex always made her smile. When they had first met, he thought her snobbish and bigoted, and she thought him arrogant and brash. Grace had never anticipated falling in love with the rugged trapper.

Spying her uncle atop the roof of the mill, Grace called out, "Hello, Uncle Edward. How goes the rebuilding?"

The mill sat on the Willamette River, as did several other mills. Unfortunately, heavy rains had caused flooding a few months back, and many of the mills were damaged or destroyed. The Marsh Mill was no exception. Her uncle and Alex had been working feverishly to get things back in order, but it was slow going.

"Well, hello there!" her uncle called down from the roof.

"I thought I'd stop by to bring Alex lunch, since I had to come into town. It looks like you're making good progress."

"We're working steadily. Alex and I think we can probably start up again in a couple weeks." He came to the edge of the roof. "There's still plenty to be done, but if we don't start cutting lumber again, we won't make any money. We'll have to wait until delivery of the circular saw I ordered to really get up and running, but for now, we'll use the up-and-down method. At least that way we'll be back in business."

"Is Alex inside?"

"Yes. I have him hard at work restructuring the housing for the blade. Don't distract him for too long."

"A man has to eat." She smiled. "In fact, I have enough food here to feed you as well."

"No, but thanks. One of us has to keep working. Besides, I just got back from eating at home."

She laughed. "And there I was starting to feel sorry for you."

Grace made her way inside and found Alex at the top of a ladder. Hammer in hand, he pounded nails into the side of a wooden structure, completely oblivious to her presence. For a moment she just watched him work. He had shed his coat and rolled up the sleeves of his shirt, and never had she thought him more handsome.

She smiled and called out to him. "I've brought you something to eat." She went to a small table nearby and began to take things out of her cloth sack. "I hope you're hungry."

Alex put the hammer aside and wiped the sweat from his brow. "I'm famished." He slid down the sides of the ladder, making Grace gasp.

"You should be more careful. You could break your neck."

He ignored her protest and pulled her into his arms for a long kiss.

Grace could have stayed there forever, but she had far too much to accomplish. Pushing him back, she grinned. "You won't get proper nourishment that way."

"You'd be surprised." He gave her a look of mischievous amusement. "How is it possible that you grow more beautiful each day? I can hardly believe you're mine."

"Well, I am. You're stuck with me. Now, come on. I have some bread, cheese, and ham, as well as some cookies. Oh, and apple cider." She went back to the sack and finished producing the food, including a small jug.

Alex picked up a piece of ham. "What have you been doing with your day?"

"Plenty. Amory Holbrook rode out to the house."

Alex raised a brow. "To talk to Hope?"

Grace frowned. "Yes. He insists her testimony is needed at the trial. He said since she was actually in the kitchen and witnessed the attack on Dr. Whitman firsthand, it is her duty to tell what she saw."

"That couldn't have been easy." He picked up the cheese. "Is Hope going to do it?"

"She says she will. She didn't want to, but Holbrook mentioned the possibility of the Cayuse going free without proper witness identification. Apparently there has been talk about letting them off as a goodwill gesture to win over the Indians and secure peace."

"The governor doesn't feel that way. I heard him just yesterday declaring that he will see them hanged. He says the only way to get the Indians in line is to use force. It's not looking good for anyone of native blood. My guess is that the government will do what they did back east and start rounding up the tribes and putting them on sanctioned land with military guards to ensure they stay there."

She pulled up a stool and sat. "I know you have many friends who are native. I feel so conflicted when it comes to figuring out solutions."

He focused on the food for a moment, and Grace wondered if he would say anything at all. She knew he loved his friend Sam Two Moons and the other Nez Perce who had taken him in as if he were one of them. Alex even had good friends among the Cayuse.

"I worry about Sam and his family," he finally replied. "His band moved north, but I don't know if they remained there. They might well have joined up with one of the other bands to consolidate their strength. I haven't heard anything about them in over a year."

"I hope they're safe."

Grace didn't know much about the Nez Perce, but Sam had been a good friend to her. When the massacre at the Whitman Mission took place, she had been at another mission some seventy-five miles away. The news had sent her hurrying back to Weyiletpa, as the Indians called Whitman's mission area. Sam and Alex had urged her not to go, knowing she might well be killed or taken hostage with the others, but she had slipped away from them in the night. They caught up with her before she reached the mission, and only after Sam threatened to tie her up did she agree to let him go on alone. He risked his life for her and her sisters, knowing that the hostile mood of the Cayuse might cause them to overlook their ongoing friendship with the Nez Perce.

"I worry about Hope." Grace's statement seemed to take Alex by surprise.

"What?"

She shook her head. "I worry about Hope having to testify. I worry that the strain will be too much. She's only just started to let down her guard. This trial may ruin all the progress she's made."

"She's made of stronger stuff than you give her credit for. She made it through the attack and the shame she felt. She bore a child that she wished dead. And she came back here when she might have gone anywhere to start a life unknown. Hope will get through this just fine. She won't like it—none of us will—but once it's settled, I believe she and the other women will feel this nightmare is finally over."

Grace hadn't considered it that way. The death of Telokite and Tomahas might well set Hope free.

"You are a very great and wise man, Alex Armistead."

He shrugged and gave her a lopsided grin. "I know."

She laughed. "And so humble."

Chapter 2

Hope tended the last of the new lambs as best she could. Alex had arranged for a man to come on Saturday to dock their tails and castrate the males, but in the meantime it was her job to see that the ewes were safely delivered and to keep a record of the new births.

The sheep were used to her now. They recognized her as their mistress, and when she walked among them, they remained at ease. They were funny animals. They seemed to know her moods and in their peaceful manner offered comfort. Of course, the ram was a different story. He was a cantankerous soul who liked to assert his authority, which garnered him his own pen and isolation unless needed for breeding.

There were now thirty good breeding ewes in their flock. In the two and a half years since they'd arrived in the territory, the ewes had lambed twice. This would be their third year, and already two dozen lambs had been born. Some of those had been twin births, and many were males. The males would be raised until late fall, when they'd be sold for meat, while the females would be kept for breeding. In time, they would buy another ram or two, but Grace felt there was no need at the moment. There was even talk of getting a dog to help with herding as the flock grew.

After checking the pen fence to make sure there were no problems, Hope inspected the shelter Alex and Uncle Edward had built. It was a long, large lean-to with multiple stalls where the ewes could be separated during birth. With a pitchfork and wooden wheelbarrow, Hope cleaned up and made sure there was plenty of fresh straw. Outside in the large enclosure, the bleating of hungry lambs caught her attention. Their mothers were easily located and the babies satisfied as they settled in to nurse. Hope paused a moment just to watch. It gave her great peace of mind to see this orderly contentment. Would that every part of her life could be just as well arranged.

She drew water from the creek and began to fill the trough. The distance between the pen and the creek was only about fifty yards, but it would take at least twenty trips to ensure the animals had enough water. Uncle Edward and Alex planned to dig a well, but that would take time, and for now the creek served. It was laborious, but with help it worked well enough. Right on time, Mercy appeared to lend a hand.

"Grace said to tell you that the beets Mrs. Reynolds sent are on the porch." Mercy squatted down and reached through the fence to stroke a sleeping lamb. "They're so little. I just love them."

"I do too." Hope couldn't deny that the animals held a special place in her heart.

Mercy straightened. "In school today they talked about the trial for the Indians."

Hope stiffened. She had hoped to avoid the topic. "Did they?"

"Everyone wants the Indians to be hanged. They really hate

them." Mercy took one of the wooden buckets from Hope's hand. "I'll help you bring up the water."

She started toward the creek, and Hope followed, hoping the conversation would turn to something else. It didn't.

"I thought it was terrible that they were so excited to see them hang. After all, those Indians are human beings just like we are. No one should take a human life."

"Well, many of them were held hostage by those human beings." Hope was unable to keep the sarcasm from her tone. She filled her bucket with water.

Mercy was such a gentle soul that in spite of all that had happened to her, she was ready and willing to forgive and let the matter go. There were obviously others who felt the same way, if Mr. Holbrook was right.

Mercy dipped her bucket in the creek then followed Hope back to the trough. "I was one of those hostages too. I don't think we have to kill people who commit murders."

"An eye for an eye." The words were out of Hope's mouth before she really thought about them.

"But Jesus said that was the old way. He said to turn the other cheek—to pray for those who use you."

Hope poured her bucket of water into the trough. "Jesus wasn't at the Whitman Mission."

"Of course He was," Mercy countered. "I'm not saying that the men who killed at the mission were in the right. They should be punished, but I don't think they need to be killed."

"What do you know? You were a child. You're still a child."

Mercy frowned. "I'll be fifteen in the fall. That's old enough to know the truth."

Her words caught Hope by surprise. "What do you mean?"

"I mean that I know what happened to the women there. I'm not a fool. I knew then that the men were . . . were . . . violating the women." She shook her head. "I know what they did to you and what you did for me—how you kept me safe. I'll always love you for the way you cared for me."

Hope was surprised by Mercy's words. Her little sister suddenly seemed years older. "I'm glad you weren't hurt by them—in that way."

"And I'm sorry that you were, but I don't think you really want to see them dead. Do you?"

Hope couldn't hide her hatred of the Cayuse. "I do. I would gladly take my gun and do the job myself."

"Oh, Hope, you couldn't really kill another person."

Mercy's belief in Hope's goodness was unfounded. "When I think of those men—when I remember how gleefully they killed and raped—I want revenge."

"But revenge belongs to God."

"So it does." Hope headed back to the river, knowing it was futile to continue the conversation. She'd never meant for it to go on this long. Neither of them would ever convince the other.

She dipped the bucket into the cold water and fought back the urge to cry. She hated moments like this. It had been two and a half years since that fateful day, but when people talked about it, it felt like yesterday. Just talking about it brought back the smell of Tomahas and the feel of his touch. She shuddered.

Mercy joined her at the edge of the water. "I'm sorry, Hope. I didn't mean to upset you. Please forgive me."

Hope straightened and drew a deep breath. "There's nothing to forgive. You're entitled to your opinion." She forced a smile. "You are, as your name suggests, full of mercy."

They finished filling the water tank in silence. Hope tried to keep her thoughts to herself. She couldn't expect Mercy to understand the depths of her misery at the hands of Tomahas. Mercy knew nothing about the pregnancy Hope had endured—

the nightmares she had about giving birth to a hideous creature, the baby she'd given away. Hope's scars weren't visible ones. If she could show the world what Tomahas had done to her spirit, to her peace of mind, then maybe they'd understand.

When the water was taken care of, Hope and Mercy made sure the confined ewes had plenty of feed. Once all the lambs were born, docked, and castrated, Hope would move them out to graze on the pasture land, but for now they were completely dependent on their owners.

Mercy picked up a lamb and snuggled it close. "Have you named them yet?"

"No. Would you like to help me?" The offer might smooth things over between them.

Mercy smiled and kissed the lamb on the head. "Yes. Shall we do it now?"

Hope glanced at the cloudy sky. "Looks like rain."

"It always looks like rain," Mercy said with a smile. "At least a good portion of the time." She nuzzled the lamb again. "I think we should call this one Beth, after my friend."

"Speaking of which, how is Beth? Grace said you two are working on a sewing project."

"Yes." Mercy put the lamb down. "We're helping each other make things for our wedding chests."

"What kind of things?" Hope knew very well what went into a wedding chest, but at least with Mercy focused on that, she wouldn't be talking about forgiving the Indians.

"All sorts. We're embroidering dishtowels right now. Beth's mother and Grace each gave us a few flour sacks. We bleached them and then made our own design. Mine is a basket with flowers, and Beth is making a hen and chicks."

"I bet they'll be beautiful when you finish."

"Have you made things for a wedding chest?" Mercy asked.

Hope didn't even stop to think about it. "I don't ever intend to marry, so no." What man would want her after an Indian had touched her? Had left her with a baby to bear?

When Mercy didn't reply, Hope forced a smile and put aside thoughts of the past. "Let's go help Grace get supper on. I don't know about you, but I'm famished. After that, we can start thinking of names for the lambs."

~~~

Hope would just as soon ignore Sundays, but living in a small community, it was expected that you would be in church unless you were sick.

So Hope faithfully attended services with her sisters and Alex. She didn't mind the sermons or the singing. In fact, she loved to sing. Grace said she sounded just like their mother, who had often sung to them at bedtime, and for some reason that comforted Hope. She missed her mother dearly—especially after the massacre. Hope missed Da as well. When she was little and afraid, her father always made her feel safe. Now she never felt safe or without fear. And while she knew other women from the massacre probably felt the same way, Hope avoided any interaction with them or discussion of what had happened.

But Sundays, they all came together. No one spoke about what had happened or asked each other if they were still having nightmares about it. Instead, they watched her, she watched them, and everyone pretended not to care about the past.

Few people in town didn't know or at least have a good idea of which women had been victims of the attack on the Whitman Mission. It was understood that what had happened to them was unspeakable. No one would have ever confronted Hope with the truth, but she couldn't help feeling judged. Even though what had happened wasn't her fault.

Sometimes, when she caught sight of someone who had been there, she saw acceptance and understanding in their eyes. But even then, little was ever said. It was as if speaking about it might somehow bring it all back to life.

Some of the women had remarried or even married for the first time, and they definitely didn't want the reminder of what had happened. Hope couldn't blame them, but neither could she seem to forget. She had convinced herself that once the Indians responsible were killed, she would finally be free. If only they could be hanged tomorrow, then maybe the nightmare would finally be gone for good.

As she sat alongside Mercy and Grace, Hope tried to focus on the pastor's words. She had made her peace with God, but their relationship was still fragile. She no longer felt anger toward Him, although anger toward the Indians continued to course through her. But even with her anger toward God abated, she still felt that He had somehow betrayed her. It was hard to acknowledge that in His almighty power, He had stood by and allowed all that had happened that November in 1847.

With the sermon concluded and the final hymn sung, Hope waited while the pastor prayed a blessing over the congregation.

"May the Lord bless and keep you throughout the week, and give you courage to face the things that you must face. May He give you strength of mind and body to do your duty and care for your families. Amen."

"Amen," most of the congregants murmured in unison.

This was the time Hope hated most of all. "The fellowship of believers" was what the pastor called the gathering of friends and family after the service, and he encouraged people to remain at the church as long as they liked and speak encouragement to one another. It required an intimacy that Hope would just as soon avoid. Nevertheless, she smiled and nodded to one person and then another, mentally counting the minutes until they could leave.

"I trust you got the beets," Mrs. Reynolds said after greeting Hope.

"I did. Thank you."

Mrs. Reynolds was diverted to answer a question from another woman, mercifully cutting the conversation short.

"Hope?"

She turned to find Lorinda Bewley—no, she was Lorinda Chapman now. Hope hadn't seen her since she moved to Yamhill County. "Lorinda."

"I wondered if we might have a private word."

Lorinda had been horribly misused by the Cayuse after the attack. She had been taken from the mission grounds and given to an Indian chief whose village was some distance away. They had also killed her brother Crockett, who had been sick at the initial massacre and wasn't murdered until days later.

"All right." Hope moved to the far side of the room, not wanting to discuss anything related to the Indians but knowing it was what Lorinda had in mind. "I presume this is about the trial?"

"Yes. We came to stay a few days since the trial starts Tuesday." Lorinda lowered her voice. "Have they asked you to testify?"

"Yes."

Hope could see by the misery in Lorinda's expression that she had been asked too. "I thought because they had my sworn statement that it wouldn't be necessary to appear in person. At least I won't have to face Five Crows."

Hope nodded. She'd heard that the chief had died and was no longer a concern. "Does it help?"

Lorinda looked puzzled. "Does what help?"

"Knowing that he's dead. Does it end the nightmares—give your spirit back the freedom they stole?"

The young woman looked at the floor. "No. I wish it did. I suppose what has helped is the love of my husband."

Hope couldn't see how that could possibly help.

"William has been my rock. I've never had the courage to tell him everything that happened." She looked across the room toward a young man. "Although he knows the worst and suspects there are other things, he doesn't care. He loves me, and that gives me healing."

"I'm glad you have him." Hope meant it, even though she found it difficult to believe a husband would heal the wounds of what had happened at the mission.

"I don't know if I have the strength to testify in front of all those people," Lorinda added. "It was hard enough to give them the sworn statement. I just don't know if I can stand the embarrassment of speaking on the witness stand."

Hope didn't know what to say. She had nothing but the utmost respect for the pretty young woman only a few years her senior. All of the women at the mission had thought it appalling that Lorinda should be taken from them. At least those at the mission remained together. They were able to encourage each other and sympathize. When Lorinda was taken to be wife to Chief Five Crows, she had no one.

"I suppose we shall have to do our part." Hope's words were barely audible. "Although it seems unfair. I know the men do not mean it as such, but it feels as though we're having to live the attack all over again."

Lorinda put her hand on Hope's arm. "I know." She drew a deep breath and let it go. "We shall simply have to endure."

Hope nodded. "Just as we did then."

Chapter 3

Company D of the Mounted Rifle Regiment had been in Oregon City for a little over seven months. Lieutenant Lance Kenner had served in the Mexican War and now found himself in the middle of the Indian conflicts and keeping peace in the West.

Tall and muscled, Lance was the epitome of a well-honed soldier. His commanding officer told him he would go far if he stayed in the army. With his looks, bearing, and ability to communicate, he might very well work his way to the top. But Lance didn't want a military career. In fact, the only reason he had joined in the first place was to get away from New Orleans and the pain of losing his father. Now he was weary of soldiering and felt it was time to go home. In New Orleans he could take charge of the plantation he'd inherited and pursue his interest in practicing law.

"Here's the roster, sir," his good friend Eddie Wilson said as he entered the room. He glanced around the room as he placed the paper on Lance's desk. "So have you settled the matter?"

"What matter?"

Eddie rolled his eyes. "You know very well, Lance." With no one else in the room, he reverted to their casual friendship rather than that of officer and subordinate. "Have you settled things with the captain—for resigning your commission?"

"I have. After this Indian matter is resolved, I'll muster out and return to New Orleans."

"Wish I were going with you, but I just signed on for another hitch." Plopping into a nearby chair, Eddie shook his head.

"That certainly hasn't stopped a number of our men from deserting for the goldfields. Giving their word means nothing to some people." Lance shook his head. "I heard you were down at the jail. Were you making sure the Cayuse were still in chains?"

"I was trying to straighten out the thinking of a couple of our soldiers. Henry and Robert think the Cayuse are being treated unfairly. They figure they're just five men picked out of their tribes to be sacrificed on behalf of the guilty."

"Maybe Sergeant Crawford and Corporal Mahon should keep their opinions to themselves. They are posted to guard the prisoners, not defend or judge their case."

"I heard the captain say the same. I figure the only good Indian is a dead one."

"While I understand that's the general consensus out here, you and I were both raised to have a little Christian charity."

"I have some of that, but it means very little in the face of an attack. Charity will just get us killed. Besides, those Indians aren't exactly offering us trust in return."

"Well, we've taken their land and reworked treaties until they no longer bear the original terms. You can hardly blame them for not trusting us."

"Captain says power should be in the hands of the white

man. We're the ones coming up with new inventions. We're the ones bringing proper civilization and religion to these wild lands. He thinks if the Indians are going to be kept around, we should make them slaves as we have the Negroes. It makes sense to me. After all, they're uneducated and childlike, and they've proven themselves incapable of living without conflict. If they were slaves, they'd work for us and be taken care of. Seems to me it would work well for everyone."

Lance shook his head. They'd been friends for a long time, but Eddie's bigotry was something he didn't tolerate very well. "Well, as one who owns slaves, I've never felt comfortable with the institution. Neither did my father. He had plans to do things differently—to pay his people a small salary."

"And what about you?"

"I'd just as soon set them free to make their own choices. If they want to work for me, then I'll employ them."

Eddie rolled his eyes. "And how are you going to make a profit doing that?"

"There's more to life than money, Eddie."

His friend nodded with a grin. "I reckon so, but it surely helps to have it."

Lance decided the conversation had gone on long enough. He'd probably never change Eddie's mind nor any of his Southern neighbors'. As his father had once told him, all that mattered was that he stay true to his convictions.

They remained momentarily silent as Lance considered the roster. After seeing that everything was in order, he filed the papers away. This signaled Eddie to take up the conversation once more.

"I still wish you'd stay on. As I hear it, we're heading north in the weeks to come. Going to settle into Fort Vancouver as those Hudson's Bay Company folk head farther north. We're taking up residence there with the other regiments. Captain says it'll be a regular army fort."

Lance had heard as much but had very little interest in it. He would be a civilian by the time the move took place. All that really interested him was a ship to take him to New Orleans.

"It's a well-positioned fort, to be sure. I'm sure it will make a strong post, and no doubt a city will grow up around it. It'll probably be the final destination for many of the westward travelers." Lance glanced at his pocket watch. "I have a meeting with the captain." He jumped to his feet and shook his head when Eddie remained sitting. "You won't have it as easy with your next commander."

"Don't I know it," Eddie replied glumly.

Lance laughed, took up his cap, and headed for the door. He was going to miss Eddie in spite of his flaws. Besides, his sergeant's feelings were hardly different from those of most of the men he knew. There was an ongoing conflict of opinions in the East regarding slavery as well as the undeclared war on the Indians. No matter where Lance turned, if the color of a man's skin was other than white, he was on the losing side of the battle.

The captain welcomed Lance and immediately urged him to sit and be at ease. "There's trouble brewing, and I want to be certain that we're on top of the matter," he began. "The citizens of this town are up in arms about numerous issues, not the least of which is this Indian trial."

Lance nodded but said nothing. He shared a comfortable relationship with his captain but certainly not one as casual as he kept with his sergeant.

"We're tightening the guard on the prisoners. I thought that by positioning them on Abernathy Island at the foot of the falls there would be little to concern ourselves with, but last night there was another attempt by several local men to take the law into their own hands.

"Now, I'm not without sympathy to their desires. Many of the women molested during the massacre ended up here and married Oregon City men. I'm sure the need for revenge is great. However, we must see that the law prevails." He paused for a long moment then resumed his concerns.

"I'm putting you in charge. You have proven yourself to be even-tempered, and your honor and obedience to orders is well documented." He fixed Lance with a piercing look. "I need to make certain those Indians remain alive for trial, or there will be the devil to pay from our superiors and the locals."

Lance doubted the locals would worry overmuch if the Cayuse prisoners were put into the hands of a lynch mob. To hear the talk about town, the people would be only too happy to see the matter laid to rest rather than worrying about the formalities of a trial.

The captain opened his humidor and offered Lance a cigar.

"I don't smoke, sir."

The captain frowned then nodded. "Of course, I knew that." He chose one for himself and then returned the humidor to its place. Lance said nothing as he cut off the tip of the cigar and then lit it. The captain did his best thinking with a cigar in hand.

"I wish you'd change your mind and reconsider staying in the army." He took several puffs on the cigar before putting it aside. "You're an excellent soldier. You proved that from the first. I need more men like you, Lieutenant. In fact, I've been in discussion with my superiors. I believe you should be promoted."

"I'm honored, sir, but my mind is made up. It's time for me to settle down and take up my own work."

"And what will that be?"

Lance shrugged. "My desire before joining up was to practice law, sir. My studies were in law, and I had started work in the practice of a family friend. I hope to renew that arrangement while I run my family's plantation."

The captain smiled. "I can imagine you being quite accomplished as a lawyer. Better still, a judge. I've seen you settle many a dispute with equal satisfaction to both sides. You might even find your way into politics."

Lance felt a surge of pride at his captain's compliment. "Thank you, sir."

The captain picked up his cigar. "Getting back to the matter at hand, you will assume command at the prison immediately and oversee the appointment of the guards and the condition of the prisoners. The trial starts tomorrow. I can't imagine it will last long. We both know it's more a formality than anything. Those men, whether or not they were the actual men who led the massacre, are condemned men."

Lance nodded. "Yes, sir."

"You and your men will present the prisoners to their lawyers at eight thirty. Court is set to begin precisely at nine. We don't want them there too much ahead of time, but the lawyers insist on time to go over the proceedings and get them settled in before the trial actually starts." He drew on the cigar and exhaled. Hazy smoke filled the air with an unpleasant odor. Lance had never cared for any kind of smoking, but cigars were his least favorite.

"The courtroom is bound to be packed—standing-room only, as I see it. Governor Lane and other men of import will be on hand, as well as other Cayuse and Nez Perce Indians. These so-called friendlies are to be treated with respect. In fact, several are to give testimony, although I'm not sure why. You and your men will stand guard throughout the proceedings. You will affix a line across the front of the courtroom behind the bar. Your men will face the spectators and be alert for any sign of trouble."

The captain was smart. Any trouble at the trial was far more likely to come from angry spectators than the defendants.

"My intention is to have every man searched before admission to the courtroom. We have already put out the word that guns will not be allowed, but this precaution will ensure it."

"Yes, sir." Lance wasn't sure that would eliminate the problem, however. "And what of the women?"

The captain's eyes narrowed. "What of them?"

"We can hardly search them. It wouldn't be proper."

"I seriously doubt any woman would come armed into court. It isn't in their nature."

"May I speak openly?"

"Of course." The captain rolled the cigar between his fingers. "I give you leave."

"Well, since most of the witnesses are women who were held hostage and . . . harmed, they might be more of a danger than their menfolk." If anyone came armed, Lance imagined it would be one of the abused women. And if one of them did pull a gun and attempt to shoot one of the Cayuse—what would he or his men be able to do but step in front of the bullet? They certainly couldn't fire upon a woman.

The captain shook his head. "I seriously doubt that. Women are frail creatures, and although they might defend themselves in the absence of their men, I have yet to see one feel the need in mixed company. The courtroom will be filled with men, soldiers, and even the marshal and his deputies. We needn't worry about the women."

Chapter 4

D r. McLoughlin." Grace smiled at the white-haired gentleman as he entered the room. He had aged so much in the last year, and his complexion was pale.

"Mrs. Armistead, how nice to see you." He turned to where Hope stood beside Grace. "And you, Miss Flanagan. Come and sit by the fire. I find myself rather chilled today."

They made their way through the elegantly appointed vestibule and into the parlor, where a cheery fire had already been laid in the hearth. The McLoughlin house was one of the finest—if not *the* finest—residences in Oregon City. It bespoke the money and refined taste McLoughlin had, which was surprising, given he had lived most of his adult life in the middle of the wilderness.

"I apologize that my wife cannot join us. She's feeling under the weather."

"I heard that and felt I should come and see if there was anything I could do. I realize you're a fine physician, but I wondered if perhaps her troubles might be of a female nature," Grace replied.

He shook his head. "It's more to do with having overtaxed herself. Spring cleaning and that sort of thing. You understand." He smiled. "I will give her your regards. Now, please have a seat. I've ordered tea, and my servant should have it here shortly."

Grace and Hope took seats on the settee while the doctor pulled up a large stuffed chair covered in a striped fabric that looked like silk. Once they were settled, McLoughlin's servant arrived with tea. She served each of them tea in a fine china cup, and after seeing they had all that they needed, exited the room as quickly as she'd come.

The delicate china captured Grace's fancy. She hadn't seen such finery since living back east, and even then it certainly hadn't belonged to her family.

"This china is quite lovely."

"I had it brought from England for Marguerite. She enjoys pretty things, and they come at a premium here in the West."

"Indeed. My mother and da never had the funds for such delicate pieces. Mrs. McLoughlin is most fortunate to have a husband who cares about such pleasures."

"My wife has been my mainstay. I doubt I could manage without her." He sampled his own tea then set it down before continuing. "I suppose you'll both be at the trial."

Grace nodded. "Yes. They've asked Hope to testify. I can't say that I want to be there, but I do want to support my sister. I know it won't be easy for her or any of the other women."

"No. I'm certain it will be an arduous task for them."

"Doctor, I understand you will be at the trial tomorrow." Grace looked at Hope. It was clear she was troubled by the conversation. Her face had gone pale, and her head was bowed, as if studying her tea was of utmost importance.

McLoughlin nodded. "I will be there. I'm to testify as well. The defense has called me. They feel it's important to note

40

that I warned Whitman from settling in the area of his mission. Somehow, because the doctor was told of the dangers, the defense believes this should allow their clients to go free."

"I hope you won't give any testimony that might help those animals," Hope said, her head snapping up. "They attacked without provocation, blaming the measles. In truth, they hated Whitman for many reasons. They saw their life and culture being imposed upon. They needed very little encouragement or excuse to attack."

McLoughlin gave her a knowing nod. "Still, the defense feels it's important to state for the record that Whitman had been forewarned of the possibility he could be killed, along with his family."

"It's just legal nonsense to allow guilty men to go free. I know the dangers of a cookstove, but if I burn myself, it's my fault and no one else's. But if someone forces me to put my hand upon the stove, then they have imposed the danger—that is their responsibility." Hope crossed her arms. "Rest assured, if they go free, some of us will take the matter into our own hands."

Grace startled at the tone in her sister's voice. For a moment she could believe Hope capable of usurping the law and seeing the Cayuse die for their deeds.

"I'm sadly certain you speak the truth, Miss Flanagan. Believe me, I hold no love for those men nor what they did. They deserve death. However, I won't lie. I'll answer their questions as best I can and pray God sees justice served."

Hope got to her feet. "One way or another, justice will be served." She looked down at Grace. "If you'll excuse me, I need some air." She left without waiting for Grace to respond.

Grace turned to McLoughlin. "I apologize for my sister's rudeness."

"Nonsense. She was greatly wronged by those Indians. I do

not blame her for her anger, nor her desire to see them dead. Were I in her shoes, I would feel no different."

"I must admit I want them dead as well. For her peace of mind—if nothing else."

McLoughlin gave her a sad smile. "I've seldom seen relief come in such a manner. I fear your sister will be disappointed."

Grace nodded and gave a heavy sigh. "I fear it as well."

Hope wanted only to return home and be done with the town and its people. Everywhere she turned, there was someone talking about the trial. There were even sales going on, as storekeepers knew this event would bring in people from hundreds of miles around.

"I only need to stop a moment at the mill," Grace told her as she directed the horse down Main Street.

Along the river, the mills were in various stages of repair. The flooding had wiped out most of them, and rebuilding had been of the utmost importance. This was a river town, and its life depended on the Willamette for the salmon, for the power of the falls, and for transportation.

Grace gasped and drew the horse to a stop in front of the Marsh Mill. "Sam!"

She jumped from the wagon, but Hope could only sit and stare. Sam Two Moons was Alex's Nez Perce friend and had been a good friend to Grace too. If Hope were honest, he'd been a friend to all of them, but right now she had little desire to see an Indian. Even a friend.

Grace embraced him. "I didn't know you were here."

"Came for the trial. Some of the Nez Perce chiefs have come. Others too. Some are to testify. I came on behalf of my people, knowing I'd have a chance to see you and Alex."

Alex came out of the mill. "I see you've found Sam. I was going to bring him to the house and surprise you."

"When did you get here?" Grace asked Sam.

"This morning. I asked Joe Meek where I might find Alex." Marshal Joseph Meek was a longtime trapper before becoming involved in the politics of the Oregon Territory. He'd also lost a daughter at the Whitman Mission. She had died from measles in the days of captivity due to a lack of medical attention. As far as Hope was concerned, the Cayuse had killed her all the same. She wondered if the marshal felt the same way.

"I told Sam he could stay with us, but he declined," Alex said. "He wants to stay with his people and interpret for those who can't understand English. He did say he'd come for supper sometime, though."

"Oh, Sam, it's so good to see you again. Hope and I were . . ." Grace fell silent and only then seemed to remember Hope. She looked at Hope, and the others did as well.

Hope wanted nothing more than to slap the reins and set the horse and wagon in motion. She wanted to be home, where she could hide from the world and all its sorrows.

Sam smiled and nodded. "Miss Hope, it is good to see you again."

She stiffened but nodded in return. Sam had never caused her harm. In fact, he'd come on her behalf and Mercy's when they'd been captive at the mission. Even so, he was still an Indian, and Hope had no desire to deal with him. She looked toward the river, hoping they would understand that she couldn't be part of their conversation.

"Hope has been asked to testify at the trial," Grace said, as if to offer explanation.

"I am sure that won't be easy," Sam replied.

Alex joined in. "None of this will be easy. A lot of hatred

has been stirred up again. It's only been two and a half years since the massacre, and people haven't forgotten."

Nor should they, Hope thought. The details of that horrible day of death and the month of captivity that followed would forever be burned into her memories. No matter how hard she tried to forget, the nightmares still came.

"The tribes long for peace to be reestablished," Sam said. "That's why the Nez Perce and others pushed the Cayuse to give up the guilty men. There would never be any peace with the whites until this matter was dealt with."

Hope couldn't help herself and turned back to face Sam. "And why should there be? Would you not have them bear the responsibility of their actions?"

"No. They deserve to die for what they did. No man has the right to kill another and . . . do the things they did." He met her gaze and didn't look away. "I would have killed them myself if the opportunity had presented itself."

Hope knew he'd hated seeing her and Mercy held hostage. He'd risked his life to ask Telokite to free them. So why couldn't she accept that he cared—that he was a good man?

Because he's still an Indian.

She knew it was wrong to hate someone for the color of their skin, their ancestral heritage, but her heart was hard where the Indians were concerned. If it were up to her, they would all be taken off the face of the earth, never to harm another person again.

"We should probably get home," Grace said. She gave Alex a kiss on the cheek then turned to Sam. "You're welcome to eat with us anytime you choose." She glanced quickly toward Hope then turned back to the men. "You're always welcome."

Alex helped Grace back into the wagon. "I'll be home by six."

She nodded and waited for him to step back. "We'll pick

up Mercy on the way home." She snapped the reins, and Alex moved away. "Get along," she called to the horse.

Hope was relieved when they were finally in motion again. She was certain Grace would bring up her attitude toward Sam, but to Hope's surprise, she didn't.

"It looks like they've made good progress in restoring the mill, don't you think?"

"I suppose so."

"Uncle Edward told me that he ordered another circular saw blade back in February, so it should arrive soon. Until then, they're going to use the old up-and-down method. It doesn't produce nearly as much lumber in a day as the circular saw can, however."

"You don't have to do this."

Grace looked at Hope and smiled. "Do what?"

"Make small talk so I can forget about Sam and the trial."

Her sister's expression sobered. "I just want you to heal—to forget all the bad and move forward with the good."

"I'd like that too, but I don't think it will happen any time soon. Not with the trial bringing it all back in detail."

Grace reached out to take hold of Hope's hand. "You won't face any of this alone."

But Hope knew that part of the experience would always be hers to bear alone. No kindness of her family, no trial to declare guilt, would ever take away what had been done to her. The recollection of those heinous acts, those terrifying days, could not be expunged by words. Maybe not even by deeds such as hanging the guilty. Her biggest fear was that nothing would ever take those memories away—that she would bear them until the day she died.

"Show me again, Hope." Mercy narrowed her eyes at the spinning wheel. She was determined to figure this out. "I just can't seem to make it all work at once. You make spinning look so easy."

"It isn't really that complicated. You just need to practice. In time you'll become much better at it."

Mercy shook her head and looked at the sorry bobbin of yarn she'd just made. "Mine isn't even at all. Some of the yarn is thick and some as thin as thread. I just can't seem to draft out the wool in a consistent manner. And then when I think I have that under control, I put too much twist in the strand, and it curls up."

With the infinite patience that Hope usually reserved for the sheep, she showed Mercy again how to pedal and coordinate the wool. "You must slow down your pedaling. It isn't a race. Just let your foot move in a slow, steady manner. As for the drafting, I have an idea."

Hope turned to the bag of carded roving. She held up a long strand and divided it down the middle. "Try using this. It won't require quite as much drafting." She handed the piece to Mercy.

"I really appreciate you teaching me this. I love the way you make money by selling your yarn. I know it'll be years before I can do the same, but maybe by then you'll be married and won't have much time for spinning."

Hope frowned. "I told you, I don't ever intend to marry."

"But why? Even Lorinda has married. Good men don't care about what happened. They know you were forced to . . . well . . . it wasn't what you wanted."

Hope shook her head. "It doesn't matter, Mercy. I don't intend to marry. I can't. There's nothing but bitterness in my heart where such things are concerned."

"But . . ." Mercy paused to choose her words carefully. She

was glad Grace and Alex had gone for a walk. "Hope, God can take that bitterness away. He can send you someone who will love you."

"Will that man also be able to take away my regrets, my anger, my nightmares? You don't know what you're talking about, Mercy, so just forget about it and pay attention to your spinning. I don't want to discuss this anymore."

Mercy knew it was useless to force the issue. She'd talked about it with Grace, who reminded her that neither one of them could fully understand all that Hope had gone through. Not only had she been molested continuously during their month of captivity, she had also seen the boy she loved killed by the same man who violated her.

But there has to be a way for Hope to get better. Lord, please show her the way. She won't listen to any of us.

Tears came to Mercy's eyes, but she kept her face bent toward the spinning wheel so that Hope wouldn't see. Mercy didn't want to make her sister feel any worse than she already did. Talking about the massacre had helped Mercy get over the worst of it, but it only seemed to make things worse for Hope.

I just want her back the way she used to be. You can do that, can't You, God?

Chapter 5

OREGON CITY, OREGON
MAY 21, 1850

Hope sat in the middle of the courtroom with Grace and Alex. Around her were women she recognized from her days at the mission. There were others in the room as well. Men from Oregon City who had married some of these women, as well as others just fascinated by the trial itself. It was the biggest event ever to come to Oregon City, and it seemed no one intended to miss it.

Packed as it was, the room soon became very warm and left Hope feeling crushed from all sides. She thought more than once of running out the door, but Grace held her hand firmly, as if knowing Hope might bolt at any moment.

They'd arrived early, admonished by Mr. Holbrook to do so in order to have a proper place to sit. He'd reserved two rows of chairs for his witnesses but still had to post soldiers to keep others from taking their seats. Rows of wooden benches had been made to accommodate the crowd, but many people had to stand.

Mr. Holbrook was already seated at his table, along with another man Hope didn't recognize. Across the room, the grand jury was assembled. There would be another jury to consider the actual trial. These men were simply there to bear witness to the indictments they had prepared after hearing initial testimony and determining there should be a trial.

A noise from behind and the gasps of several women made Hope stiffen. She knew without being told that the defendants were being brought in. She closed her eyes, uncertain that she could endure seeing them again. She tried to pray, but the murmurings of the audience and the sound of prisoner chains forced her to open her eyes. Marshal Meek led the way. This was personal for him, just as it was for so many. Had his daughter Helen received proper care during the captivity, she might still be alive.

Hope had already seen Indians among the viewing crowd, including Sam Two Moons. She knew that some of them were going to testify, while others had been encouraged by the governor to attend so they could report back to their people. Their nearness made her nervous, and when Telokite appeared behind Meek, she had to fight back the bile in her throat. She didn't look away, however. She was determined to look them in the eye and make clear that she was no coward.

Tomahas was next. He walked proudly and arrogantly, as he always had. He glanced at the people around him, unafraid and unashamed. When his gaze reached Hope, she couldn't help but cringe, causing him to smile. Dressed in his breechclout, buckskin leggings, and an elaborately decorated shirt, he commanded everyone's attention. They all did, but the fierce, hard look of Tomahas coupled with his haughty nature drew most of the stares. All were dressed in their native clothing intermingled with that of the whites, except Tomahas. Where the others wore a white man's styled shirt, Tomahas wore fringed buckskin. He was pure Cayuse. Fierce, mean, and full of hate. Here was a man who knew he was soon to die, yet he glared at the people around him as though he were in charge.

After Tomahas came Kiamasumkin. Hope didn't recognize him as one of the Cayuse who had participated in the massacre, but she didn't really care. He was an Indian and of the same tribe that caused her such misery. Behind him walked Clokomas, who stood a whole head shorter than the others. Last was Isiaasheluckas. Hope knew the latter two only by sight and name, as told to her by Johnny Sager.

The prisoners were led to the defense table while uniformed soldiers took their place facing the crowd from just behind the bar. Hope felt reassured by their presence. If the Indians tried anything, the soldiers would be able to contain them.

She bit her lower lip to keep her jaw from quivering. It had been madness to agree to bear witness. Hope knew she could never do it. She would never be able to speak with Tomahas in the room. She drew her hand away from Grace and clutched her large reticule against her stomach. The heavy feel of the pistol inside helped allay her fears, but only a little.

As the Cayuse settled beside their lawyers and interpreters, another appearance drew everyone's attention. Governor Lane came down the aisle to take his place in the front row behind the prosecutor's table. He was accompanied by several men, most of whom Hope had seen at one time or another but hadn't bothered to know.

The court clerk, George Curry, took his place at a table near the judge's bench along with his deputy clerk. They would record all that was said and done at the trial. The two men were barely in their chairs when the judge entered the room and everyone was ordered to rise. The clerk announced, "Court is now in session. The Honorable Orville C. Pratt presiding."

There was some confusion at the defense table as the interpreters explained the custom and instructions to the defendants. Reluctantly, the Cayuse got to their feet and looked around. All looked puzzled, except Tomahas. Even the aging Telokite seemed to lack any understanding of the tradition.

The crowd was instructed to take their seats after the judge took his. Hope eased back in her chair, hoping the judge would deal swiftly with the legalities. Mr. Holbrook had said that the trial would be handled with the same formalities and requirements as any court back east. To Hope, that only meant one thing—long, tedious hours of legal ramblings.

"Mr. Holbrook, as United States Attorney, do you have any business for the court?" Judge Pratt asked.

Holbrook stood. "I do, Your Honor. Indictment Number Eleven: United States versus Telokite, et al."

Hope listened as the deputy clerk rose and read the indictment. The words were phrased in such a way that it seemed a waste of time. Why didn't they simply state that on November 29, the Cayuse tribe attacked and killed the men at the Whitman Mission, along with Mrs. Whitman, and then took everyone else hostage, beating, raping, and degrading any and all who remained? It seemed straightforward to Hope. There was no need for legal ramblings from men who normally spent their days keeping a store or farming.

The reading went on for some time, the Indian interpreters speaking rapidly to keep up. Hope heard some of the translation but didn't understand a word. She'd never wanted nor attempted to learn the Cayuse language.

The clerk concluded reading and sat down. Hope stiffened. The legal papers had only mentioned Marcus Whitman. Why?

Those savages had killed her Johnny and eleven others, including poor James Young and Andy Rogers. All had died at the hands of the same murderers. What about them and Mrs. Whitman? Those heathens had shot her and then, on the pretense of taking her elsewhere to be cared for, they dropped her in the mud outside the mission house, clubbed her with axes, and shot her additional times. Hope had seen it all and knew those images would never leave her no matter how many years passed.

The defense lawyers were formally assigned by the judge. Hope listened as they requested and received a very short continuance that would allow them time to familiarize themselves with the indictment and list of witnesses. It seemed completely unnecessary to Hope, but it meant that once they recessed, she would be able to return home and not have to be present until the trial resumed. It was a small thing—only a delay—but it gave her a great sense of relief. It would give her even more relief if someone—anyone—would just kill the Cayuse and put an end to the need for a trial.

She again felt for the reassurance of her gun. Tomahas's penetrating sneer ignited a flame within her soul. She might not be able to put an end to the trial, but she could put an end to Tomahas.

Standing guard with his men in the courtroom, Lance noticed a small, pretty woman sitting several rows behind Governor Lane. Her brown hair had been pinned atop her head in a simple, no-nonsense style that added to the severity of her expression. She was no doubt one of the victims, as she sat in the area reserved for them. He might not have thought twice about her, but her brilliant blue eyes had narrowed in almost tangible hatred when the Cayuse were brought into the courtroom. While others had looked away, this young woman had made it her business to face her attackers. He admired that.

After assigning the lawyers, court was recessed. Four hours later they came back together without the defendants and most of the spectators, including the pretty woman. The grand jury resumed their seats, along with the clerk and his deputy, and Judge Pratt took his place at the bench. He looked down at his papers then commanded Holbrook to continue.

Only Lance and two of his men had returned to the courtroom in case there was any ruckus, but he didn't expect anything to go amiss. He could have sent someone else, but his love of law had been stirred by the morning's formalities, and he found himself longing to return.

Holbrook stood. Familiar with court trials, Lance wasn't surprised when he announced additional indictments. Eleven people had been killed at the mission on November 29th. Two more had been killed a few days later.

Once the entire list had been given and the foreman of the grand jury swore them to be true, Judge Pratt discharged the jurymen with thanks for doing their duty. Lance in turn dismissed his men to resume their regular duty and headed out himself.

The skies had grown heavy again with rain, although it hadn't yet started to fall. Lance hated nothing more than the feel of a wet uniform and hurried to report to his captain.

Once that was accomplished, he went to the jail, crossing the narrow bridge that connected to Abernathy Island. He heard a report from Eddie, who was on duty, then made his way to check on the Indians.

The one called Telokite approached him and, to his surprise, spoke in fairly good English. "You come to take us back to that place?"

"No." Lance looked past the old man to the one called Tomahas—the Murderer. If Lance were his lawyer, he would have heartily objected each time the name was used—even though he felt certain of the Cayuse's guilt.

Tomahas's dark eyes held Lance's gaze. Here was a dangerous man. Among the five, Tomahas was definitely the one to be watched.

Lance looked back at Telokite, who watched him with a sense of anticipation. "I've only come to check on you and the condition of your cell."

Telokite frowned and moved away, as if confused. Lance didn't bother to explain. He'd seen what he'd come to see. His men were treating the prisoners fairly.

Returning to Eddie, Lance gave him a nod. "I'll trust you to keep things under control."

"Sir, yes, sir!" Eddie gave him a smart salute, and Lance smiled and returned his own.

Lance walked back to the riverbank and for a moment watched the falls. They were beautiful. While many bemoaned them for the barrier they formed to river traffic farther upstream, others praised them for their usefulness to the various industries that lined the banks.

The noise of the water crashing down over the rocks was almost musical to Lance. He'd grown up with the Mississippi River as a vital part of his life, and there was something about a river that spoke to the very heart of him. He doubted he'd ever want to live far from the water. Hopefully the trial would conclude quickly, and then he could be on his way home.

New Orleans was a world away, and Lance had no idea what it might hold for him after an absence of over four years. After his father died, there had been nothing to keep him there—nothing but the holdings of his family. Once he returned, he would no doubt be expected to take a wife, continue the family line, and increase those holdings as his father and grandfather had done.

But was that truly what he wanted to do? There was surely need for good attorneys in this part of the country. Maybe even more than in New Orleans. As for the family plantation and other holdings, they had operated smoothly in his absence so far and would no doubt continue to do so.

The young woman from the courtroom came to mind. He wondered who she was, where she'd come from. Was she married? Did she have children? What had happened to her that day at the Whitman Mission?

He knew a lot about the massacre and the aftermath. Although it had been over two and a half years ago, plenty of people were still willing to talk about it. Of course, most of the discussion happened amongst men—none of whom had been there. The women were completely silent on the matter, as if ashamed that it was somehow their guilt to bear.

Heading back toward the hotel where he and other soldiers were bivouacked, Lance spied the handsome woman who had sat beside the blue-eyed woman at court. She looked enough like the blue-eyed woman that Lance figured they were sisters. As he approached, the woman smiled, but a man called to her from inside the open mercantile door.

"Are you coming in, Grace?"

She turned and hurried inside without bothering to answer. Lance would have liked to follow her—to ask about the woman who'd been at her side in the courtroom—but proper etiquette taught to him by his mother dictated that this was neither the time nor place.

Besides, he'd no doubt see the blue-eyed woman again.

Chapter 6

Hope walked among the sheep, content to be rid of the trial and town, if only for a short while. The ewes fed on the grass while their lambs nursed. Outwardly all was calm, but within her small frame raged a war.

Seeing Tomahas had made Hope think of Faith. When she'd found out that the Cayuse brave's child grew within her, Hope had longed only to be rid of it. She thought of the unborn baby as a thing of terror akin to the Devil himself. She would rather have died than give that child life, but then her heart had changed.

The woman who adopted Faith, Eletta Browning, had reminded Hope that the baby was innocent of wrongdoing. She was just as much a victim as Hope. Then Eletta pointed out that if Hope killed her baby, she would be forcing her will upon the child just as Tomahas had forced his will upon her. It was more than Hope could bear.

But giving the infant life and raising her were two different things. Hope wanted nothing to do with Faith. She knew the child would only serve as a constant reminder of what had happened. Thankfully, Eletta and her husband had wanted the baby, and because they lived hundreds of miles away, it was easy to forget Faith even existed.

At least it had been until today.

Now Hope not only remembered but felt as if she owed the child something. The conviction and death of Tomahas would fulfill that debt, just as Hope was certain that ending his life would end her nightmares.

"But what if the court doesn't find them guilty? Or what if it does, but sets them free?" Hope murmured to the sheep. She'd heard more than one person comment on the possibility of the Cayuse being let go as an act of goodwill between the whites and the Indians.

She felt the weight of the revolver in her pocket. She knew the answer to her questions. She would never allow Tomahas to go free. Even if the others were let go, Tomahas could not have that privilege. If need be, she'd put a bullet in him—just as he had done to poor Johnny.

Hope waited for a sense of guilt or horror at the thought of ending a man's life, but it didn't come. Tomahas wasn't a man. Men didn't act like he had. He was a beast. A rabid, loathsome animal who needed to be put down.

She noted the darkening skies and decided to lead the sheep back to the pen. She found the belled ewe close at heel and prodded the animal with her crook toward the pens. The sheep bleated in momentary protest then casually walked to the pen, her bell calling the others to follow. Hope had just managed to get them all to the safety of the fenced enclosure when the rain began to fall.

She secured the gate and hurried across the yard to the house, barely reaching it before the skies opened up. Leaving her crook by the door, she burst into the house as if being chased.

"Are you all right?" Grace asked, looking up with wide eyes from where she was busy with mending.

"Yes. I was just ahead of the rain." Hope ran her hands down the sleeves of her dress to rid herself of excess water. "The sheep are penned for the night."

Grace smiled. "I'm glad you've taken such a liking to them."

Looking around the large, open room, Hope cocked her head. "Alex in the kitchen?"

"No. He's ridden to town to see Sam Two Moons. They had a lot to say to one another, and I encouraged him to stay as long as he liked. I would have invited Sam here, but I didn't want to make you uncomfortable."

Hope nodded and moved to the hearth to warm herself by the fire while Grace went back to her sewing. For a long while, neither sister spoke. Hope had little desire to talk, but Grace would no doubt have much to say about the day. She sighed.

"I'm surprised you haven't asked me my thoughts on the trial."

Grace looked up again and shrugged. "I figured if you wanted to talk about it, you would. You've made it clear to me in the past that I shouldn't pry."

Hope pushed aside a feeling of guilt. "Thank you." She sat down at the spinning wheel. "But I know this matter will not go away. I know it must be discussed."

"In your own time, Hope. It's going to be hard enough that they're demanding you testify. I can't deny I'm curious about your thoughts, but I can also see how troubling this all has been. I don't want to add to your miseries. Home should be a refuge from all that."

Hope was deeply touched by her sister's kind words and by her thoughtfulness in keeping Sam away. She wondered if Grace would be shocked that Hope had contemplated killing

Tomahas. And, if it came to that, would her sister ever speak to her again once the deed was done? Would she still allow Hope to live with them?

Weary from the day, Hope yawned. "I think I'm going to go to bed. I know it's still early, but I want to take the sheep out before we go to town tomorrow." She got to her feet and waited for Grace to protest. When she didn't, Hope smiled.

For all that had transpired between them, Hope knew she was loved. Whether she took the law into her own hands and ended Tomahas's life or not, Hope knew she could always count on her sisters' love, even if no other love was ever afforded her.

~

The next day, the trial started with the defense filing a motion. A Plea in Bar declared that the defendants were native-born and their land lay west of the Rocky Mountains. Therefore, they were not subject to the jurisdiction of the Courts of the United States.

Lance had expected this. It was exactly what he would have done had he been forced to defend the Cayuse.

Holbrook had anticipated this move, whether because it was what any decent lawyer would do or because he'd been informed in advance. Either way, he countered with a Replication to Plea in Bar stating to the contrary that in 1834, Congress had passed a law that declared all parts of the United States west of the Mississippi and not within the states or territories to be Indian country. For a moment it seemed he was proving the defense's point, but then he quoted from the Indian Trade and Intercourse Act of 1834. The act cleared up the matter nicely by detailing that the laws of the United States regarding crimes were in effect for any land under the jurisdiction of the United States.

Agreement rose from the audience, but Judge Pratt quickly

pounded his gavel and brought order. He also very quickly rejected the Plea in Bar.

The Indians' lawyer jumped to his feet to take exception to the ruling. It was a necessary move in order to later appeal the court's decision—even though everyone knew there would never be an appeal. Just as everyone already knew what the outcome of the trial would be.

The judge noted the exception and moved on to register the defendants' plea of guilty or not guilty. Again, one of the lawyers for the defense got to his feet to file a Petition to Change the Venue.

Lance knew this would be coming too. He looked around the room at the puzzled spectators who grew less confused as the lawyer declared his reasons.

"The petitioners cannot have a fair and impartial trial," he began then continued to declare that not only had there been death threats against his clients, but the people of the town were quite vocal about their desire to see these Indians hanged. He declared them both biased and set upon revenge.

This caused an outcry in the courtroom. No one was willing to sit by and accept that they were being cast in the role of unfair and corrupt.

Lance watched the young woman with the blue eyes. She said nothing, but the look on her face spoke volumes. It was a mix of fear and anger.

The judge quickly brought the room to order. He denied the request and declared that the trial would continue as planned. Lance thought it strange that the defense lawyers didn't take exception to this, but then, it wasn't important that the people in this area were hostile toward the prisoners. All whites were hostile when it came to Indians massacring settlers. If Lance had been defending them, he would have filed the motion based on the fact that the trial was being held in Clackamas County, several hundred miles west of where the attack had taken place in Clark County.

The petitions caused a great deal of concern amongst the spectators. Lance and his men stood ready with their rifles in case further protests should get out of hand, but to his surprise, things calmed almost immediately. Judge Pratt moved matters forward quickly, allowing Holbrook to bring out two of the additional indictments that had been filed the day before. These focused on the killing of Mrs. Whitman and Luke Saunders, the schoolteacher.

The Indians' lawyers asked for more time to prepare their defense on those indictments, just as they had with the first one, and Judge Pratt granted it. But Lance felt confident those indictments would receive no further consideration. The court was focused on the Marcus Whitman murder, and there was little doubt that the Indians would be convicted and hanged for that alone.

It was raining when the judge adjourned the court for the day. Lance quickly dismissed his men to return the prisoners to the jail. He turned back to see the young blue-eyed woman was already gone. Strangely, the people she'd come with remained.

Hope knew what had to be done. With all the legal nonsense and objections being bandied back and forth, she had the dreadful feeling that the Cayuse would be set free. She had never thought of herself as a murderess, but she couldn't risk Tomahas getting off. Nothing would be worse than knowing he was still out there somewhere. Over the last two years, it had been all she could do to imagine herself safe. Only the knowledge that the army and other volunteers were actively searching for the guilty Cayuse gave her any relief at all. Now, however, if they set those men free, Tomahas could come and go as he pleased.

She shivered and looked down the bank of the Willamette River at the island where the Indians were being jailed. She couldn't let that happen.

A battle raged within her, however. She knew killing another person was wrong, but surely there was some sort of forgiveness in this situation. And even if there wasn't, she wasn't overly concerned about it. Forgiveness didn't matter in light of what she felt. If they put her to death for killing the Cayuse, then so be it. At least her nightmares would finally end.

She moved the gun from her purse to her pocket. The soldiers would probably search her purse, but they wouldn't be likely to go any further. Of course, most likely they would simply forbid her entry.

But as she approached the jail, she could hear the guards arguing about something. Neither one paid her any attention as she watched them for a moment. Seeing this as God's way of approving her actions, Hope snuck around the back of the jail and entered while the soldiers were still deeply engrossed in their discussion.

The smell of the room nearly sent her fleeing. It was the same one she couldn't seem to wash from her body after the attack. She fought back the urge to vomit and forced her steps forward.

Tomahas seemed to be expecting her. He stood a short distance from where the others sat on the ground. His lips curled into a sneer as he assessed her from top to toe. Hope found it impossible to speak. The other Cayuse watched her with looks that wavered between disbelief and curiosity, but not Tomahas.

She returned her gaze to the proud warrior. When he gave a laugh, she felt her body stiffen. He found this amusing. She felt for the revolver in her pocket. The weight of it brought a renewed sense of assurance. She pulled the gun from her pocket and smiled when Tomahas's eyes narrowed and his face grew sober.

"I've come to kill you," she whispered.

"Good. It's not right to hang an honored warrior like a dog."

"There's nothing of honor in you. You are worse than a dog. You're a snake."

He laughed again, shattering her nerves. Hope felt her hand tremble but wouldn't give him the satisfaction of acknowledging her fear.

She had memorized what she would say to him, but now the words seemed unimportant. He knew why she was here. There was hardly any need for words. In a matter of seconds, it would all be over.

Once the courtroom was cleared, Lance made his way outside. He could see many of the folks who had been watching the trial gathered in groups. No doubt they were discussing the events of the day despite the rain. He made his way through them, hearing their comments.

"Well, if they intend to let those Injuns go free, we'll give 'em our own kind of justice," one man declared.

"I can hardly believe anyone would defend them. What in the world is Mr. Pritchette thinking? He may very well be Secretary of the Territory, but that doesn't give him call to say we're prejudiced and unfair," another man argued.

Lance knew the lawyers responsible for the defense would face a certain amount of ostracizing from their friends and neighbors for their role in the trial. Folks didn't care if the Indians had fair representation. They were, after all, savages, and the benefit of white laws didn't apply.

As Lance neared the jail, he heard the argument before he even rounded the corner.

"You take it back," one private said. He'd squared off with his fists drawn up. "If you don't, I'm going to wallop you."

"You couldn't wallop my sister," the other private countered.

"Attention!" Lance commanded.

The men immediately straightened and offered wide-eyed salutes.

"What's the meaning of this?"

"It's a personal matter, sir," the first private said.

"This is hardly the setting for personal matters, is it?"

"No, sir."

Lance opened his mouth to further chastise them, but the clear voice of a woman came from inside the jail. The two privates seemed just as surprised as he felt. "Who's in there?"

The two men shook their heads and shrugged.

"See to your posts," Lance ordered.

He rushed inside and found the blue-eyed woman with a Colt pocket revolver in her hands. She stared down the tallest of the five Indians, who stood grinning at her in a sadistic fashion.

"I won't give the court a chance to let you go," she said. Her voice was even and steady.

"Shoot me then—if you can," Tomahas replied, still smiling. He moved toward her as far as his chains allowed, causing her to back up several paces. She stopped only when she bumped up against Lance.

Startled, she turned to face him. Lance pushed the pistol aside but didn't attempt to disarm her. He raised a brow and smiled. "I hope that isn't intended for me."

Her eyes widened. "No. It's for him." She jerked her head toward where Tomahas still stood leering.

Lance put his hand on her shoulder. "He's not worth the effort."

Seeing her relax, he took the revolver from her without protest and led her from the jail. Outside, the sentries jumped to attention, unable to hide their surprise.

Looking at each man for a moment, Lance admonished them. "It would seem your personal matter interrupted your duties and caused lives to be endangered. I'll see both of you in my office when you come off duty."

"Sir, yes, sir!" their voices sounded in unison.

He fixed them with a hard gaze. "I want your word that neither of you will speak of this incident. It wouldn't bode well for any of us if the citizens of this town knew someone could just sneak past our sentries."

"No, sir . . . I mean, yes, sir," one of the men responded. The other nodded.

Lance shook his head again, wondering at the quality of men protecting the country. He took hold of the woman's elbow and moved toward the bridge. He didn't speak until they were across and back on shore.

"I can hardly blame you for desiring to see them dead, but if I allowed you to shoot that man, it would be murder."

"I don't care. He needs to die."

"And he will."

She looked at him, fire in her eyes. "You heard what they said in court—the lawyers say we don't have the right to put them on trial. And there are rumors that the judge intends to let them go as a gesture of goodwill."

Lance felt sorry for her. She was terrified. He could feel her trembling. "May I walk you home?"

"You're not turning me over to Marshal Meek?"

He laughed. "For trying to do what everyone in town wants to do?" He looked down at her and saw the dark lashes that lined her crystal blue eyes. "No. I figure you have a reason for hating that man."

She drew in a deep breath and nodded. "I do."

"If you promise me you won't try this again, I'll keep it to myself."

She stopped and turned. "I don't know if I can make that promise."

"Well, why don't you think about it while I escort you home?"

"Home is several miles outside of town."

He nodded. "Then I'll get my horse and borrow one for you. Better yet, I'll borrow a carriage or wagon, since you're hardly dressed for riding, Miss . . ."

"Flanagan. Hope Flanagan."

He smiled. "I'm Lieutenant Lance Kenner."

Chapter 7

Hope found it impossible to still her trembling even after they were well on their way to her house. She still couldn't believe she'd actually gone to shoot Tomahas. She couldn't believe it had been so easy to get to him.

Would I have pulled the trigger?

Now that the panic that drove her to the jail had faded, Hope could scarcely believe what she'd done. Her sisters would be appalled. The lieutenant said he wouldn't say anything, but how could she explain him bringing her home? She'd told Grace that she intended to stay in town and spend the night at Uncle Edward's. They wouldn't expect her back, and they would assume something was wrong. At least Grace would. She always had a sense about these things.

"How long have you lived here?" Lance asked, breaking through her deep thoughts.

"Since we were rescued and brought here from the mission." She held on to the side of the wagon seat to keep from bouncing into the soldier. She would have jumped down and bolted for home, but something told her this man would just chase her down. Besides, he was being kind in overlooking what she'd done.

"That must have been a terrible ordeal. I've seen what the Indians are capable of." He gave her a sidelong glance, but Hope found it difficult to meet his gaze.

"I . . . well . . . thank you for not turning me in to the marshal. I felt justified in what I was doing, but . . ."

"I'm sure you were," the lieutenant said when Hope failed to continue. "And even if you had fulfilled your task, I'm fairly confident no one would have wanted to see you prosecuted for murder. Still, it would have been a difficult thing for someone as gentle as you to live with."

She shook her head. "I don't know why you think me gentle." She felt her strength returning and turned to face him. "I was set to kill that murderer."

"But you didn't, and you won't." He spoke in a serious tone, yet he offered her a hint of a smile.

"You seem quite sure of me, and yet you know nothing about me."

"But I'd like to."

Hope was surprised by his boldness and turned her attention back to the road. She steadied her voice. "Why?"

The lieutenant laughed. "Because I admire you. Because you intrigued me even in the courtroom before you went to the jail. Because I could use a friend."

"A friend?"

"Yes. A friend. Just a friend." He smiled. "I don't really know anyone here. The townsfolk aren't exactly in favor of the army, and no one ever extends invitations to us. There have been a few gatherings with some of the men in charge, but otherwise nothing."

"I see." Hope looked down on the Willamette as the road rose higher. "I'm sorry to disappoint you, but I neither need nor want friends."

For a while Lieutenant Kenner said nothing, and Hope feared she'd offended him. How could she explain that she'd refrained from even making friends among the women of Oregon City, much less the men?

"How did you get your hands on a Colt pocket revolver? They're a very new design."

She nodded. "I know." There was no harm in telling him the truth, and it might ease her guilt over dismissing his friendship so quickly. "I just wanted to feel safe, so I talked to Dr. McLoughlin. He used to be the factor at Fort Vancouver, and he has steady shipments to his store in Oregon City." She cast a quick side-glance at Lance, and when he nodded, she continued.

"His friend came with one of the shipments late last year. He brought a couple of the new revolvers and suggested McLoughlin sell them to women because of their light weight and . . . the need for protection on the frontier."

"Sounds reasonable."

"I spin yarn and sell it to the women in Oregon City and had put aside quite a bit of money. I begged Dr. McLoughlin to sell me one and show me how to use it, and he did."

"Are you any good?" the lieutenant asked, grinning.

Hope nodded but couldn't bring herself to smile. "Good enough. Especially when my target is just five feet away."

She thought he might admonish her about the dangers of firearms and the importance of the court system and letting justice run its course. It was what she would expect from a soldier.

To her surprise, however, he took the conversation in a different direction. "Do you like it here?"

"I do, to a degree. It's peaceful, and because it's such a large settlement, there isn't any real fear of the Indians attacking. At least not lately. Knowing the difficulties between them and us, I doubt it will stay quiet for long."

"I've only been here for a short time, but it seems quite nice. Unless the river floods. We—that is, the army—were alarmed at how rapidly the water rose and the destruction it caused last December."

Hope nodded. "It wasn't so bad the first year we were here. Last year was the worst it's been in several years. We used to live in a cabin right on the river, but thankfully we were on higher ground when the floods came. The cabin withstood the flood, but it was damaged and filled with mud and debris. It belongs to my uncle and hasn't been lived in since. He also owns a sawmill, and much of that was destroyed too. He's still working with my brother-in-law to rebuild it."

"Was that the man I saw sitting with you in court?"

"My brother-in-law?"

He nodded.

"Yes, he's married to the woman who sat beside me. My sister, Grace." She was surprised at how calm she felt. This man had a strange ability to put her at ease.

Lieutenant Kenner chuckled. "I figured you two must be sisters, even though her eyes are green."

"We have a third sister, Mercy. She's not yet fifteen, so she's been in school."

He sobered. "Were your sisters also at the mission when it was attacked?"

Hope drew in a long breath and let it go before replying. "Mercy was. Grace was off helping a friend at another mission."

"So at least you had each other."

"Yes, but I cannot say that made the captivity any better. I feared what the Indians might do to Mercy and worried constantly about how I might protect her." Hope could scarcely believe she was saying all of this to a virtual stranger. She hadn't spoken with such open candor to anyone—not even Grace.

"But they left her alone?"

She looked up to see the concern on the lieutenant's face. "Yes."

"But not you." There was only tenderness in his words. No judgment or condemnation.

"No."

"I'm sorry. No woman should ever be treated in such a manner."

Hope didn't know what to say. She was puzzled by this man's interest and gentle nature. She'd only agreed to let him take her home because he was in a position of authority, and after what she'd done, she was afraid to refuse him. But now she found that she actually felt safe in his company. It was a strange and unexpected feeling.

Lieutenant Kenner maneuvered the wagon down the narrow lane to the farmstead, letting the silence of twilight wrap around them. When he brought the horse to a stop, Hope hurried to jump down before he could offer to help her.

"Thank you for bringing me home." She turned to go.

"Hope?"

She stopped and drew a deep breath. "Yes?" She turned back around.

"You might want this." He held out her revolver.

"Yes, thank you." She went to the wagon and took the gun. Placing it in her pocket, she felt she should say something more, but words wouldn't come.

She glanced up and found him watching her. He smiled and tipped his cap. "It was a pleasure meeting you, Miss Flanagan. I hope we will meet again very soon."

That evening Grace was surprised when Alex returned to the homestead with Sam. They had expected Hope to stay in town with Uncle Edward, so Alex must have felt it was all right to bring his friend to the house. Grace had no chance to warn him, but to her surprise, Hope actually welcomed the Nez Perce brave without any animosity. She even joined them for dinner, though she left before dessert to tend to the sheep.

Grace could see how happy Sam's return had made Alex. The two were longtime friends and had spent many years trapping with their friend Gabriel. Alex had even lived with Sam in his village for a while.

"I have apple crumble if you're of a mind to eat dessert." She put the baking dish in the center of the table. "It's still warm."

"You don't have to ask me twice," Sam said, grinning. "The love of sweet food is one pleasure I've easily picked up from the white man."

"Better that than alcohol," Grace countered.

Sam laughed and reached for the spoon. He helped himself to a heaping portion then offered Alex the spoon. Alex didn't need any more encouragement and followed Sam's example while Mercy excused herself to tend to her homework.

Grace brought the pot of coffee to the table and placed it alongside the crumble. "I'm going to see if Hope needs any help and then tend the rest of the animals. You two enjoy a nice long chat."

Alex caught her hand and drew it to his lips. He placed a kiss on her palm then smiled up at her with such love that Grace felt her heart skip a beat. "You're a good wife," he said. "The best west of the Rockies."

"Just west of the Rockies?" she teased.

The men laughed, and she left them to discuss the affairs of the world. She made her way outside, glad that the drizzling rain had stopped. There was still plenty of light, and far across the field she saw Hope walking with the flock. To her surprise, Hope was singing, something Grace had not heard her sister do voluntarily since their days at the mission.

She decided to investigate and walked through the wet grass, thankful she wore her high-top boots. The hem of her gown soaked through up to her knees, but at least her feet were dry.

"I heard you singing," Grace said as she approached Hope. "You always remind me of Mama when you sing."

Hope seemed almost embarrassed. "The sheep like it."

"I'm sure they do. It's soothing." Grace stopped to pet one of the curious lambs. "I want to thank you for your kindness toward Sam."

With a shrug, Hope stared off across the field. "I know he's been good to you."

"He cares deeply about you as well. I remember how upset he was when he came back from seeing you and Mercy after the attack. He was so distressed that Telokite wouldn't let him take you with him."

Hope looked at Grace. "He tried to reassure us that all would be well, but he knew just as we did that there was no guarantee of that happening."

"No. I suppose we all knew that."

"I thought for sure they would kill us. God knows there were times I wished they had." Hope shook her head. "How strange it is to have it all back in front of us again. I knew the trial would be hard, but . . . seeing him . . ." She fell silent.

Grace closed the distance and took Hope's arm. "I wish I could keep you from having to return."

"I do too," Hope admitted. "A part of me wants to see Tomahas and the others get what's coming to them. I just don't want to have to relive the details of why they deserve to die."

"Alex said the governor told him the trial would most likely conclude tomorrow. At least your part of it."

Hope's brow furrowed. "Will it really be that quick?"

"The governor doesn't want it stretched out. He believes it would be too hard on you and the others. He said tomorrow would be testimony, and then the matter would be in the hands of the jury. He doubts they will need much time to deliberate."

"No, I don't imagine so. I hope the governor has no intention of pardoning them."

Grace squeezed her arm. "I don't see how he can. Not now. Too many people have demanded those men pay for what they did."

Hope sighed. "I hope you're right. I've been so afraid they would be let go on the basis of some undeserved charity to show how forgiving we are. I feel no forgiveness where they're concerned."

"It would be to your benefit if you did."

Her statement clearly surprised Hope. "Why?"

Grace dropped her hold and crossed her arms as the chill of her damp gown began to make her shiver. "Because forgiveness is more beneficial to the one forgiving than to the one being forgiven. A tremendous burden is lifted when you're able to forgive those who've harmed you."

Hope looked at Grace as if she'd grown a second head. "Forgive? You want me to forgive that animal? I'm not going to forgive him."

"But if you don't forgive him, he continues to hold you hostage."

Hope gave her a blank stare. Grace knew there was no sense in belaboring the point. It would take Hope time to process the past and all that it had cost her.

After tending to her chores, Grace made her way back to the house, desperate to feel the warmth of the fire. She spied a horse tied to the post outside and realized they had company. Entering the house as quietly as possible so as not to disturb the men, she heard the unmistakable voice of Governor Lane.

"I need you to do this, Alex. It's important and might very well be the difference between peace and war."

"I'll have to speak to Grace about it. I can't just take off for several weeks, even months, and not consult her."

"Once she sees the importance of the matter, I know she'll agree."

Grace eased closer to the fire, which just happened to take her nearer to the kitchen, where the men were seated around the table. Where did the governor want to send Alex? And why now?

"The Indians of that region know you and trust you," Governor Lane stated. "I believe they'll listen to you, especially since Sam will be with you. When their chiefs return to tell of the trial and hanging, it will be important that you offer my desires for a peaceful future. They should know that we don't plan further bloodshed or retribution. We must convince them that it's in their best interest to make peace with the settlers. I can't speak to all of the details, but there is a bill before Congress even now that deals with the Indians and this land. If it passes as it is expected to do, they will find everything changed."

"That hardly seems reassuring," Alex countered.

"Better that they know and understand from someone they trust."

Sam spoke up. "It's true, Alex. I know my people will listen to you."

"They'll trust their own people first, as they should. Let them tell what has happened and what you want for the future."

"Alex, I know the people will be less inclined to listen to anything a white man has to say, but you have lived among them. They know you from experience to keep your word and speak honestly to them. If you go as my representative, then you can help them understand that white men want peace."

"I'm not against going," Alex replied. "I just doubt the impact I can have. I think you give me too much credit for being a peacemaker."

"But all of the Cayuse chiefs know you. The Walla Walla and many others as well. You lived among the different tribes for a great many years. I believe you're the only man who can go, and I feel confident of the impact you'll have."

"Well, I'll speak to Grace tonight. If she agrees, then I'll do it. I'll go after the hanging, when the chiefs return to their villages. That way we can discuss it on the journey and figure out the best way to tell their people."

Grace turned to face the fire, her mind in turmoil. She wanted Alex to do the things that were important to him, but this would take him away for a long time—probably the entire summer. That would put an end to their plan to build a bigger house this year, despite the land having been cleared and the logs set aside and waiting.

She touched a hand to her flat stomach. There was another reason she wanted him to remain close to home. She hadn't told him or anyone else, and now she felt she couldn't. Alex would never go if he knew she was pregnant. Even if it meant the hostilities increased between the Indians and the settlers. He would feel completely obligated to Grace and their unborn child—just as he should.

The men were concluding their business. Grace heard chairs scraping on the wood floor as they rose and knew they'd soon join her in the front room. She didn't want them to know she'd been eavesdropping and quickly moved to the front door. Opening it, she stood there as if she'd just arrived when the men entered the room.

"Grace, look who's come to pay us a call," Alex said, coming to her side.

"Governor Lane. How nice to see you." Grace smiled. "I was tending to chores."

"Looks like you're soaked," Alex said before the governor could speak.

"Yes. I went out in the fields to speak to Hope. The grass is very wet."

"I'll not keep you any longer," the governor said, taking up his hat. "Mrs. Armistead, your husband offered me some of your crumble. It was quite delicious." He didn't wait for her response but turned to Alex. "I'll need your decision tomorrow."

Sam came to Grace. "I'm going to ride back to town with the governor, but I wanted you to tell Hope how much I appreciate her allowing me to be here."

"I'll tell her." Grace gave Sam a hug. "I'm glad you're here. I know Alex has missed you terribly."

"I have. Are you sure you won't just stay the night with us?" Alex asked.

Sam pushed back his long black hair and shook his head. "No. The chiefs will need me to interpret for them, and I don't want Hope to feel uneasy. She's going through enough already."

"If you're ready," the governor said, stepping through the open door, "we'd best get on before we lose the light altogether."

Once they'd gone, Grace turned to her husband. His expression made it clear he was wrestling with some matter, most likely the governor's request. She would do whatever she could to assure him that all was well . . . that she wanted him to go. The baby wasn't due until December, and Alex would be home long before then.

She smiled and put her arm around his waist. "So what decision do you need to give the governor?"

Chapter 8

Lance headed toward his meeting with Tom Claiborne, one of the defense lawyers for the Indians. Claiborne was a brevet captain with the Mounted Riflemen and had been one of the men who escorted the Cayuse to Oregon City. He was a man of temper and opinion, and most of the soldiers in the regiment disliked him. For some reason, he had summoned Lance to come see him as soon as possible.

"Come in, Lieutenant," Claiborne said, opening the door to his dwelling. "I was just transcribing some notes from the trial."

"I came as soon as I received your note, sir." Lance removed his cap and took the seat Claiborne pointed to.

"Would you like a drink?"

"No, thank you, sir."

"Let's dispense with the formalities. You'll soon be a civilian, and I'm much too busy and tired to care." Claiborne sank into his chair and picked up a glass containing amber liquid. "I have a task for you." He tossed back his drink.

"Sir?"

"In regard to the Cayuse prisoners. I have an idea to get them treated more fairly."

"I understand you believe them innocent." Lance wasn't sure why he'd said this, but now that it was out there, he could hardly take it back. Hopefully Claiborne wouldn't feel Lance was challenging him—even if, in a sense, he was doing exactly that.

Claiborne seemed unconcerned. "I do. I think the Indians chose five scapegoats, hoping to put an end to the army's harassment. I'm not the only one who feels that way, either. Governor Lane has assured me that should they be found guilty, he will stop any death sentence." He put his empty glass aside.

"It seems to me the governor is speaking out of both sides of his mouth. I overheard him tell a group of folks that he was confident of a guilty verdict and a quick and proper hanging."

Claiborne frowned. "He has to keep peace with the townsfolk. Once the verdict is reached—and even I realize it will be a guilty verdict—he will make his plans known. Try as I might, I cannot convince my associates of anything but the Indians' guilt and will surely have no influence over the jury. Even though the prosecuting attorney himself told me he believes in the innocence of those men."

"Holbrook believes them innocent?"

"At least some of them. He pointed out that the witnesses can't agree as to when the attack started or even where. Some say it started in the house, some swear it was by the gristmill, and still another version is that it started in the yard between houses. Then there's the issue of which Cayuse were truly there. The witnesses admit there were a great many more than the five sitting in the courtroom, but even so, they can only agree to the presence of Telokite and Tomahas. However, because the defendants are being tried as a group rather than individually, it's a point he won't raise. It's madness, to be sure. The governor knows that hanging the Indians will only lead to more uprisings. He'll have to overturn the sentence in order to keep the peace."

"I'm not so sure of that. The people of this town will lynch those men if the court doesn't." Lance thought of Hope Flanagan for the hundredth time that night. He couldn't tell Claiborne of her attempt to kill one of his defendants, even if his duty required him to. He wouldn't betray her trust, and nothing about the incident would change the outcome of the trial.

"That's where the army comes in. We'll see the prisoners adequately protected and removed to a safer location. The people here clearly hate them."

"That reminds me, why didn't you approach the change of venue from the angle of location rather than the temperament of the people? The massacre clearly took place in the Clark County District, so it would seem that's where the jurisdiction lies."

"I forgot you were a man of law. I told Pritchette that very thing, but he refused to use it. He doesn't want a change of venue any more than Judge Pratt did."

Lance chose his words carefully. "You mentioned why the prosecutor believes some of the defendants are innocent, but why are you so sure? As I hear it, there are witnesses who know for a fact that those men were responsible for what happened. Women who were raped. Women who watched those men kill and mutilate their husbands."

"You know as well as I do that witnesses are fallible. They see what they want to see and remember what they want to remember. It's been over two years. None of those women can be sure of what they saw."

Lance knew better. Hope Flanagan had no trouble remembering. She remembered every detail, of that Lance had no doubt. She didn't strike him as the type of woman to risk her life trying to kill a man who had never wronged her. She had suffered a great deal at the hands of Tomahas. She'd seen him kill firsthand. Lance had no doubt about that and no doubt that other women from the massacre would try what Hope had attempted as well if they had the opportunity.

He put aside his thoughts and pressed Claiborne for the reason he'd asked Lance to come in the first place. "You said you had an idea for helping the defendants?"

"I want them to look their best tomorrow. I've obtained proper clothes and want them to put aside their Indian trappings. If they look more presentable, I believe we can make the jury see them in a different light."

"You mean if they look more white?" Lance shook his head. "These men aren't going to put aside their culture and way of dressing. Even if I forced them into those clothes at the jail, they'd be naked by the time they made it to the courtroom. They're a proud people, and rightly so. If I were one of them, I'd feel no different."

"There's no place for pride in this. I'll speak to them. I'll tell them it's in their best interest."

Lance approached it from a different angle. "Captain, as you've already stated, no one but you has any concern for their best interest. Clothes aren't going to change the opinions of the jury tomorrow after those women get on the stand and tell what they saw and what those Indians did to them. You know it, and so do I."

Claiborne swore and got up so fast he knocked over his glass. "Fine. Let them dress as heathens." He spewed out a stream of profanities.

Lance got to his feet but remained silent. He couldn't offer anything that would calm the raging captain. It was a concession that he'd been allowed to speak as freely as he had.

"This is the fault of those missionaries. Spaulding and the

others. They think that because they come on holy missions, the rest of the world should just bow at their feet. I told Spaulding he and Whitman had no right to impose their will on free men. No right! And if they hang those men, there will be the devil to pay." Claiborne went to the door and opened it. "You might as well go now, Lieutenant. It's obvious I cannot change the inevitable."

Lance moved toward the door, but he couldn't refrain from speaking. "Sir, I know of at least one woman who was raped and abused by Tomahas. She isn't lying about it, nor is her memory incapable of clear thought. She deserves justice."

Claiborne shook his head and calmed. "This trial isn't about justice. Those men are already condemned, and it grieves me that the good citizens of Oregon City are content to go through the motions of giving them a fair trial. We know perfectly well that they would have lynched them without a second thought had we allowed it."

"Yes, sir." Lance stepped outside and pulled on his cap. He turned to bid the brevet captain good evening, but he had already closed the door.

Lance muttered, "He's right on one account. This trial isn't about justice. It's about revenge."

Hope sat in the courtroom on Thursday morning, wondering how she would ever endure the day. Lieutenant Kenner stood just a few rows ahead with his soldiers. He offered her a nod when their eyes met, but otherwise held his attention on the courtroom.

Most of the morning had been consumed by the jury selection. Some men were more than eager to serve, and a few would just as soon have been left to their own devices. Several were rejected and sent on their way, but it wasn't long before the jurymen were all selected. Judge Pratt issued the oath and then directed the prosecution to begin.

Holbrook got to his feet and glanced at the massacre victims seated behind him. He gave them a confident smile, then related to the jury the information that had been read in Indictment Number Eleven. He concluded his speech by assuring the jury that he would provide enough evidence to leave no doubt in their minds.

"I am confident that once you good gentlemen of the jury hear what these poor victims have to say, you will have no choice other than to find the defendants guilty of all charges." He turned back to his table and glanced down at his papers. "I call Mrs. Eliza Hall to the stand."

Hope watched as the mother of five made her way forward. She remembered Eliza in the aftermath of the attack. Her husband, Peter, had not been among the men killed on the mission grounds, so she felt confident that he had gotten away to get help. They later learned that Peter had made it to Fort Nez Perce but found little help available and immediately set out for Fort Vancouver. He was never seen again and was presumed to have drowned in the Columbia River.

As Mrs. Hall was sworn in and took her seat, Hope felt her stomach clench. Now would begin the descriptions of that day so long ago. That day when the world had gone mad.

"Mrs. Hall, please tell the court where you made your residence in November of 1847," the prosecutor began.

"My husband, Peter, and I, along with our children, lived at the Whitman Mission in the Emigrant House. We'd come from Illinois, and because my husband was an architect and carpenter, Dr. Whitman wanted him to stay and help with some of his building projects."

"And so you were both there on November 29th when the attack took place."

"Yes . . . we were." Her voice quivered.

"And where exactly were you when the trouble started?"

"I was in the Emigrant House."

"And where was this house?"

Hope startled when Judge Pratt interrupted. "Mr. Holbrook, I presume this witness's testimony will take some time, so it is my opinion that we should adjourn for lunch." He looked at the jury and the marshal. "Marshal Meek, take charge of the jury. Jurymen, you will not speak on this matter to anyone, nor amongst yourselves. The army guards will remove the prisoners back to the jail. We will recess until two o'clock this afternoon." He pounded his gavel and rose. The audience got to their feet as well.

Meek rounded up the jury members and led them away while the soldiers ushered the defendants and their lawyers from the courtroom. After that, everyone filed out, off to see what they could get in the way of lunch.

Thankfully, Grace had planned for this. She told Hope they could either eat in the wagon or go to Uncle Edward's house. Either way, she had a picnic basket with supplies in the wagon. Hope followed her and Alex from the courtroom, but she had little interest in food.

"I can't believe they spent all morning just figuring out the jury," Grace said, shaking her head. "It seems this thing just drags on and on."

"Alex!"

Hope looked up to see Uncle Edward approaching. He gave her a quick embrace and then did likewise with Grace.

"Always good to see my lovely nieces."

"I was glad Mina and the boys could stay at the farm with

Mercy today," Grace said, smiling. "Since they closed school for the day, I didn't want her to be there alone."

"The boys were beside themselves at the prospect of playing with the lambs. They figure life is a grand adventure on the farm," their uncle replied.

"Well, I appreciate that your sweet wife would give up her day to help me out. Why haven't we seen you at the trial?"

Edward chuckled. "Purely selfish. I was afraid they'd stick me on the jury. When they got rid of that first bunch and Marshal Meek was instructed to wrangle up more men, I figured it was best if I lay low."

"But you would be a good juryman," Grace said, surprised by his answer. "And it's your civic duty."

Edward sobered. "It is, but I'm afraid if I got up there, that close to those Indians, I might not be able to hold my temper, knowing what they did to my nieces." He shook his head. "I don't think I could ever give them a fair hearing on account of that."

Hope was touched by his words. She had never spoken to Uncle Edward about what happened, but she was sure Grace had.

"Given your association," Alex threw in, "I doubt the defense would have found you unbiased and allowed you on the jury."

"I couldn't take that chance. There's no possible way I could have found them anything but guilty as charged," Uncle Edward replied. When no one offered anything more on the matter, he continued. "Alex, I need your help, if you can pull yourself away from the trial. I'm having some trouble reinforcing the joists."

Alex looked at Grace. "Can you manage without me? I don't want you or Hope to feel you haven't got proper protection."

"We'll be fine. Most of the people around us are friends. Dr.

McLoughlin is sitting just behind us, and you know he would take charge should anyone act untoward."

"I can well imagine John brandishing his cane like a knight of old."

Grace smiled. "I can imagine it as well. But what about your lunch?"

Alex kissed her on the head then turned back to Uncle Edward. "I can eat later."

"I have a better idea. Why don't you have lunch with us, Uncle Edward? Court is adjourned until two, and since Mina is helping me out, I can surely return the favor by feeding you."

Their uncle heartily agreed. Since the skies were threatening to resume raining, Grace decided it would be best to eat indoors, and the sawmill was closer than Uncle Edward's house. They took the picnic basket and made their way through the muddy streets and down the river to the mill.

It had rained all morning, and the heavy clouds muted the sun so that it cast a dull shadow on everything. It did nothing to help Hope's mood despite the flowers in bloom and the landscape colored a deep emerald green. This place could be so beautiful, so lush, but that came at the price of regular rain.

The lunch recess passed much too soon, and before she knew it, Hope found herself back in the courtroom. Holbrook returned Mrs. Hall to the stand, where Judge Pratt reminded her she was still under oath to tell the truth.

Holbrook began to question Mrs. Hall. Hope tried to let her mind think on something other than the testimony, but it was impossible.

"I heard gunshots and went to see what was going on," Mrs. Hall said. She related how she helped Narcissa Whitman carry her mortally wounded husband into the house.

Hope could see it all in her mind. She had crouched against

the house, terrified of what might be happening to Mercy, who was in the schoolroom. She could hear the hideous war cries, see the Indians chasing down unarmed men and attacking them without the slightest restraint.

The questions continued, Eliza Hall answering them in a clear, steady voice. When Holbrook finished with her, the defense was given a chance to cross-examine, but they had no questions.

Next Holbrook called twelve-year-old Elizabeth Sager to be sworn in. Hope was unsure why the prosecutor felt the need to call the young girl. He already had Eliza Spaulding's sworn testimony. Surely that could be entered in, or she could even be called to testify. She spoke the Cayuse language and had been called to interpret for them during that long month of captivity. To Hope's way of thinking, she would surely know more than Elizabeth.

"Now, Miss Sager, would you please explain how you came to be at the Whitman Mission?"

The girl nodded, her eyes wide with fear. "My folks died when we were coming west, and Father and Mother Whitman took us in."

"And when you say 'us,' to whom are you referring?"

"My brothers John and Frank and my sisters."

Holbrook nodded. "And how old were you when the attack took place?"

"Ten."

The prosecutor walked back to his table and picked up a piece of paper. Hope felt a growing sense of fear. It started deep in her belly and rose steadily, making her chest feel tight. After Elizabeth gave her testimony, the prosecutor would expect Hope to take the stand. Her face grew hot. She reached into her reticule, her hand brushing the pistol that Lieutenant Kenner had returned to her. She pushed it aside and found her fan.

"Now, Miss Sager, tell me in your own words what happened on the day the defendants brutally killed Marcus and Narcissa Whitman and the others."

"Objection," Pritchette declared from the defense table.

The judge nodded and looked at Holbrook. "You know better."

"I apologize, Your Honor." Mr. Holbrook didn't look sorry. "Miss Sager, tell us about the day when the Whitmans were killed." He glanced at Pritchette and then Judge Pratt and, hearing no further objections, continued. "In your own words, tell us what you saw and heard."

Elizabeth squirmed. Hope fanned herself and bit her lower lip. "The Indians came to the house to ask Father for medicine. Mother was giving me a bath."

"Who demanded his help? Can you point to them?"

Elizabeth pointed to Telokite and Tomahas.

Mr. Holbrook nodded. "Let me make it perfectly clear for the jury and the record, you're talking about Telokite and Tomahas." He walked to the defense table and pointed to each man as he said their names. He looked back to Elizabeth for confirmation.

"Yes, sir."

"What happened after they asked for medicine?"

"There was loud talk and then shooting. It scared me bad. Mother and the ladies started crying, and they brought Father into the house. He was bleeding badly, and Mother tried to bandage him. Then Mother went to the window and someone shot her."

"Did you see who shot her?"

Elizabeth shook her head. "No, but she was yelling at Joe Lewis. I think he might have done it."

The questions continued, and Hope felt the churning in her stomach grow stronger. She knew she was going to be sick. She bolted from her seat and all but climbed over the other people in her row. When she reached the aisle, she ran for the door, pushing through the crowd that stood at the back of the room.

She fled from the building, having no idea where she'd go. All Hope knew was that she couldn't testify. She couldn't. The bile rose in her throat, and with no other choice, she doubled over and expelled her lunch.

Her vision blurred, and Hope felt her knees giving out, but before she fell headlong into the mud, strong arms wrapped around her waist.

Chapter 9

"Try to relax," Lieutenant Kenner said. "Breathe deep."

Hope was too weak to fight off his hold. She felt another wave of nausea and bent over again. She was mortified that anyone should see her in such a state, but there was nothing she could do about it. When she'd emptied the contents of her stomach, she struggled to straighten.

"I'm . . . I'm . . . sorry." She could barely breathe the words.

"Hope?" Grace called.

"She's here," Lieutenant Kenner replied.

In another moment, Grace was at her side. "I'm her sister. What happened?"

"I can't go back there," Hope said, shaking her head. "Grace, I can't do it. I can't."

Grace looked at the lieutenant. "What can we do?"

"Is your wagon nearby?"

"Yes, just over there." Grace pointed up the street.

Without warning, Lieutenant Kenner swept Hope into his

arms and carried her to the wagon. Hope couldn't bring herself to look at him. She was far too ashamed.

"Just put her here," Grace said, motioning to the back of the wagon.

Kenner placed her gently into the wagon bed. "Stay here with her," he said to Grace. "I'll go speak to someone and let them know she's collapsed. They can hardly expect her to testify if she's sick."

Grace nodded. "Thank you."

Hope curled into a tight ball, unable to stop reliving the massacre. She could see the blood and hear the screams and cries of her friends. She could feel Tomahas's hands on her body.

"Hope?" Grace was beside her, pushing the hair back from Hope's face.

"I can't go back. I can't go back."

"Shhh, you don't have to. Lieutenant Kenner is going to let them know you're too sick." She gently stroked Hope's hair. "I won't let them take you back in there."

Hope felt her fear abate a little. "Why can't they just hang them? They're guilty. I was there, so were a lot of those other women. It isn't fair that we have to go through all of this again. The Indians nearly destroyed us the first time, but now it's our own people. It's not right. It's just not right."

"I know. It isn't right at all, but it's how things are done."

Grace continued stroking her hair and speaking in a soft tone. For a moment, it was as if Hope were back in her mother's care. Mama had offered the same soothing comfort, and Hope was almost certain that if she opened her eyes, she'd find her mother there.

Oh, Mama, I wish you were here. I need you so.

Lance wasn't at all sure who to speak to. He could hardly interrupt the court. He'd already left his post and would no doubt have to answer for it. But he knew when he'd seen Hope run from the room that he couldn't leave her to face her demons alone.

He stepped inside the courtroom just as the prosecutor ended his questioning of Elizabeth Sager. Again the defense waived their right to question the witness. Lance took that moment to rush forward to the bar. Holbrook glanced his way, and Lance motioned to him.

"Judge Pratt, could I have a moment?" Holbrook asked.

"Very well."

Holbrook joined Lance and listened as he quickly related the problem. "There's no possibility of her returning at this point."

"It's all right. I have enough without her. I'll let the judge know what's happened. Thank you for trying to bring her back."

Lance nodded then went to Eddie, who stood guard with the rest of the soldiers. "Take over here."

Eddie nodded but didn't have a chance to reply before Lance was gone.

When Lance reached the wagon, he offered the ladies a comforting smile. Hope was curled up beside Grace and didn't open her eyes or move. "You don't have to testify. Holbrook says he has other witnesses."

He saw relief in Grace's expression. "Thank you. I know she couldn't have managed."

"No, I don't imagine so."

"I'm Grace Armistead. I appreciate what you did for my sister."

Lance's throat went dry. Armistead. That wasn't a name for which he held any affection. "It was my pleasure to help."

To his surprise, Hope opened her eyes and sat up. She met his gaze briefly then looked at Grace. "Lieutenant Kenner is the one I told you about. He drove me home."

Grace beamed at him. "It would seem you've come to our rescue more than once. I'd love to repay you. Perhaps you'd like to come to dinner. I know my husband, Alex, will want to extend his thanks as well."

And then it all fit together. Alex Armistead. The man who killed Lance's brother was here in Oregon City. There couldn't be two men with that name. Thinking back to the dark-haired man who'd sat with Hope and Grace in the courtroom, Lance felt as if he'd been gut-punched. He'd thought there was something familiar about him but figured it was just from having seen him in town rather than the memories of a twelve-year-old boy.

"Are you all right, Lieutenant?"

He looked at her in confusion for a moment then nodded. "I'm sorry. I have to get back to the courtroom. You'll have to excuse me."

He returned to his post, but his mind was flooded with memories of long ago rather than the courtroom.

"Your brother Justice has been killed in a duel," he remembered his father telling him and his brother Marshall. Lance was only twelve and just two years earlier had lost his mother and little brother to yellow fever. Death seemed a constant companion.

Friends of his brother had flooded the plantation house with reports that it hadn't been a fair fight, that Alex Armistead had murdered Justice. His father and Marshall had sworn revenge, and Marshall had taken matters into his own hands and set fire to the Armistead family home.

When word came that the fire had claimed the lives of Alex's mother and father, Lance had been appalled. It was one thing to destroy property, but Marshall had killed those people the same as if he'd put a gun to their heads.

Their father immediately made plans to spirit Marshall away, but the law had shown up much too quickly, and despite their father's protests and assurances that Marshall would remain in the area, they arrested him and took him to jail. Lance had never seen him again. He had been convicted and sentenced to a dozen years but had died before his release.

Lance grew up an angry young man. He often talked to his father about how they might get justice for their family, when in truth he meant revenge. It drove him to study law, thinking that one day he might actually see Alex Armistead tried for murder.

For years his father shared his desires, but then sickness took hold of him, and some of the people who had sworn Alex had murdered Justice admitted to lying. His father's views changed.

"Your brothers are gone, and soon I will join them. You have to put this all behind you, Lance," his father had told him years later. *"You must accept it as God's will and move forward with your life."*

And Lance had tried to do that, but now the past had come back like an enemy who'd been stalking him all along.

Lorinda Bewley Chapman was called to testify, followed by Josiah Osborn. He was the only man who could bear witness to what had happened on the day of the massacre. After he was sworn in, the prosecutor immediately began.

"Tell the court where you were on the day of November 29, 1847."

Lance did his best to pay attention to the proceedings and forget his personal issues. There was absolutely nothing he could do about Alex Armistead right now, since he was responsible for keeping peace in the courtroom.

"Mr. Osborn, was your family with you?" the prosecutor asked.

"Yes."

"Would you tell the court where you were when the attack began?"

Osborn explained that he and his family had taken sick with the measles. Lance listened as Osborn told of hearing the commotion first and then seeing the Indians attacking. He identified the Indians he'd witnessed and continued to answer Holbrook's questions with relative ease.

"How is it you escaped being killed, Mr. Osborn?"

"I hid with my family under the floorboards of the house. There'd been some work going on in the house, and the boards hadn't been nailed down yet. I pulled them up and helped my wife and children underneath, and then I joined them. We hid there until nightfall."

"And what, if anything, did you see or hear while you were hiding there?"

"Murder."

There were murmurings throughout the courtroom, but the judge did nothing to still them. Holbrook continued his questioning and then finally turned it over to the defense.

The defense posed questions related to the appearance of the Indians. Osborn admitted there were a great many Indians milling about the grounds and that the Whitmans had arranged to have a steer butchered that day. The meat would be shared with the Indians. They were also grinding grain for the Indians at the gristmill.

"Were there other reasons for the Indians to be present?" Pritchette asked.

"Yes, a large number of Indians were sick—their families too. They came to Dr. Whitman for medicine."

"And did he give it?"

"Yes."

The testimony continued, but Lance could only think of Alex Armistead. Why had he reappeared in Lance's life? For years, Lance had wrestled with his anger and sorrow over all he had lost, and now without warning the cause of his misery was living only a few miles away.

It was late in the afternoon when Holbrook announced he would call no further witnesses, and Lance fully expected the judge to recess until the next morning. Instead, Judge Pratt announced that the proceedings had gone on long enough and he wanted the defense to call its witnesses immediately. They did, beginning with John McLoughlin.

Mr. Pritchette began by asking the doctor to explain who he was, even though there wasn't a man in the room who didn't already know. Even Lance knew of this great man and all he'd done. The point of his testimony, however, was quickly proven when he said he had warned Dr. Whitman against settling in Indian country.

"The Cayuse have a practice of killing their medicine men when they fail to provide healing. It's not at all uncommon among many tribes to take that attitude."

"So when the measles epidemic raged on and many of the Cayuse died, they would have perceived Dr. Whitman as responsible for the deaths?"

"Aye. They would have."

Pritchette asked McLoughlin a few more questions then offered the prosecution its chance to cross-examine. To Lance's surprise, Holbrook waived his right, and the defense called its next witness. This time, an Indian named Chief Istachus, or Stickus as he was called by the settlers.

The spectators were shocked by a Cayuse chief being called as a witness, but the judge instructed him and allowed the defense to begin questioning.

Stickus knew Whitman and had hosted the doctor at his village some miles to the south of the mission on the day before the attack. He testified that he had warned Whitman that the Cayuse at his mission would kill him. He told the doctor he shouldn't return, but Whitman insisted on going home.

Holbrook had only one question for the chief, and that was how Stickus knew the doctor was in danger. Stickus shared that he had been told this by another Indian who frequented the mission.

The last defense witness came to the stand to be sworn in, the Reverend Henry Spaulding. Spaulding and his wife had come west with the Whitmans. He had known Marcus Whitman perhaps better than anyone else. He had also been with the doctor at Stickus's village the day before the massacre.

Lance listened as the defense attorney asked about that day and the advice of Stickus to remain in the village.

"Reverend Spaulding, did you leave with Dr. Whitman when he departed the village?"

"No. I stayed the night and left the next day. I feared for my life and wanted to return to my own family and home in Nez Perce country."

The defense witnesses seemed to be there purely to prove that Whitman had ample warning that his life was in danger. It hardly disproved the intent of the defendants and, if anything, strengthened the prosecution's case, as far as Lance could see.

Pritchette rested his case, and a hush fell over the courtroom as people waited for the judge to recess for the day. Instead Judge Pratt surprised them all.

"I want to end this today. I'll call a thirty-minute recess, and then I want the closing arguments from both sides."

It hardly seemed worth the effort to recess. Lance and his men took the defendants out a side door while the crowd poured out the back of the room. The soldiers hurried the Indians back to the jail.

"This over now?" Tomahas asked Lance. His scowl reflected his anger.

"No," Lance replied, trying not to be unnerved by the brave's piercing eyes. He couldn't help but think of Hope at the mercy of this man. He was twice as big as she was and seemed to take delight in intimidating his opponents. His hate-filled expression had caused more than one of Lance's soldiers to take a firmer grip on their firearms.

"When it over?" Tomahas asked, narrowing his eyes.

Lance looked him in the eye. "When you're dead."

Chapter 10

Hope sat at her spinning wheel, trying not to think of the trial going on in town. It was the fourth day, and she wasn't sure what would take place. After getting sick the day before, she was relieved to be dismissed as a potential witness.

The carded wool roving was soft and smooth. As she pulled the strands apart, Hope thought of how her life was much like this wool. It had started out in a completely different form. Then it went through a shearing process. It had been washed, dyed, and carded, and with each process, it was altered just a little bit more, refining it to become what it was now. It had to go through all that in order to be useful. Was God processing her as she had the wool? Were all those horrible things she'd gone through part of that refining process?

It was hard to imagine that a loving God would subject His children to such atrocities in order to make them into something new. Grace had said that what happened wasn't what God desired for His children, but because the world was in a fallen state of sin, these things happened at the hands of willful men. However, she had also reminded Hope that God could take evil and turn it into good. So far, Hope didn't see how that was the case. She doubted the women at the trial saw it that way either.

Yesterday, Alex had gone back to the courtroom to hear the rest of the testimony after helping Uncle Edward at the mill. Meanwhile, Grace accompanied Hope home. They had said very little on the wagon ride, for which Hope had been grateful. When Alex returned that evening, he shared that Lorinda Bewley Chapman had testified for the prosecution, as had Josiah Osborn. After that, Holbrook turned it over to the defense, who called several witnesses, including Dr. McLoughlin, who shared that he had warned Dr. Whitman against remaining amongst the Cayuse. For some reason, the defense seemed to think that because Whitman was warned he could be attacked and killed, it negated the actions of the five men on trial.

The testifying for both sides had concluded almost as quickly as it had started. Grace and Alex had gone into town that morning to hear whether the jury had reached a verdict, and if so, what was to be done. There were still plenty of rumors about what would happen after the verdict was rendered. No one truly believed the Indians would be found innocent. The worry was that even if the judge sentenced them to death, the governor would pardon them. Talk went back and forth that this would never happen—that Lane only made the suggestion as a way to calm the defense and encourage them to keep their arguments and witnesses at a minimum. Nevertheless, it terrified Hope to imagine Tomahas as a free man. If he remained alive, she knew she'd never feel safe again.

And so she worked at the spinning wheel, trying to forget. There was something cathartic in the rhythmic pace of the pedal. She felt a sense of accomplishment as the yarn wound onto the bobbin. It wouldn't be long before the sheep were sheared for the summer and she'd start the process of washing and carding the wool all over again. That aspect was more of a chore, but spinning was purely pleasure.

Hope startled when she heard a rider approaching. She looked at the mantel clock and saw it was nearly four. Somehow the day had escaped her. Had it not been for Mercy calling her to lunch hours earlier, Hope might have remained at her wheel all day.

Grace and Alex planned to have supper with Uncle Edward and his family, so Hope had no idea who might be coming to the farm. She frowned and tried to decide how to handle the situation. The farm was a refuge to her, but when strangers came and no one else was around to offer protection, Hope felt some of the old fears building within.

Getting to her feet, she started to pull off her apron then decided against it. The pocket of the apron made a good hiding place for her revolver. Mercy had been out in the fields, tending the sheep, since after lunch, so Hope knew that no matter who their visitor was, she would have to deal with them alone.

She put the Colt in her pocket and went to the window. The gun gave her a sense of protection, but after her encounter with Tomahas, she wondered if she could ever pull the trigger. Hopefully the mere appearance of the Colt would scare off anyone who thought to harm her.

She pulled back the curtain but couldn't see the visitor thanks to the horse that he was tying up. She put her hand around the butt of the gun and drew a deep breath. Why couldn't she just be left alone?

Squaring her shoulders and drawing a deep breath, Hope knew there was no choice but to greet the visitor. Opening the door while he was still busy with his horse, Hope breathed a sigh of relief at the sight of Lieutenant Lance Kenner.

He stood by his mount and offered her a smile. "I wanted to come give you the news—the Indians were found guilty, and Judge Pratt sentenced them to hang on the third of June."

Hope slumped against the doorjamb for support. "Thank you for letting me know." She was touched that he cared enough to ride out to the farm just to deliver the news. "Do you suppose they'll really go through with it?"

"I do." He stepped away from his horse. "Could I come inside and tell you about it?"

"Of course." She walked into the house, knowing he would follow. "Would you like something to drink?"

"Just some water would be great."

Hope nodded. "We boiled a fresh batch just this morning, and it's had plenty of time to cool off."

He looked at her oddly. "Boiled?"

Hope was used to people's surprise. "My sister Grace is a healer. She learned from our mother and grandmother that boiling the water is good for the health."

"What an interesting thought."

She motioned him to the kitchen. "Have a chair." She went to the cupboard and took down a glass. "This family is full of interesting thoughts. Grace also makes us take vinegar every day. She believes it to be an all-purpose commodity. She says it keeps us healthy and aids digestion, and it also cleans better than soap." She poured water into the glass then set it on the table. "Are you hungry? We have fresh bread and butter. Oh, and some berry jam."

"Sounds delicious." He remained standing by the chair, hat in hand. "I'd love some, but only if you join me."

Hope brought the items to the table. "After yesterday, I've been rather hesitant to eat." She figured it was the best way to bring up her embarrassment from the day before.

"Your nerves got the best of you. It happens to the bravest of men. I've seen soldiers in my regiment do likewise before battle. You mustn't let it bother you in the least."

He sounded so sincere that Hope could only smile. "Well, it was rather like being in battle." She reached out to take his hat. "Please sit." She put the hat on the sideboard then joined him at the table. "I appreciate you coming to tell me what happened. Grace and Alex plan to spend the evening with my uncle and his family." He looked concerned, and Hope hurried to ease his conscience. "If you're worried about what they'll think if they find you here, don't fret. Mercy is here, and besides, I think they've come to think as highly of you as . . ." She fell silent.

"I think you were just about to say you think highly of me." He grinned and took up the knife to slice a piece of bread.

Hope felt her face grow warm. "I suppose I was. It's just . . . well . . . I don't want you to get the wrong idea."

He paused and met her gaze. "What idea?"

"That . . . well . . ." She sighed. It wasn't in her nature to be silent with her feelings. "I don't want you to think I'm playing coy or trying to flirt."

He chuckled and went back to cutting the bread. When he finished, he slathered on butter then handed one piece to Hope and kept one for himself.

"I didn't think you were flirting. I thought you were being very kind. I want you to think well of me."

Hope took a spoonful of berry jam and smeared it atop the butter on her slice. "That's my concern, however. I don't want you to read more into my thoughts than is intended. I'm not looking to be romanced. I'm not even looking for friendship, as you suggested once before."

He said nothing, making the situation all the more uncomfortable.

Setting her bread aside, Hope shook her head. "I wouldn't flirt with anyone, is all I'm trying to say. I'm not foolish enough to believe that what happened to me could be overlooked by decent men. I lost more than my innocence in that attack. They took my dreams of love and a family. They took my ability to feel safe. They took everything. That's why I carry this." She drew the revolver from her pocket and put it on the table.

Lance had put down the jam spoon to study Hope with great intent. "And does that make you feel safe?"

She considered his question. "Not exactly, but it does help me realize that I can defend myself, and being able to do that makes me feel better."

"I can understand that. What you went through should never have happened. I'm sorry you had to endure it, but at least the men responsible are going to hang for it. Maybe then you'll finally feel safe again."

Hope shook her head. "I'd like to think so, but I have my doubts." She gave a harsh, brief laugh. "I have a great many doubts. My future is the biggest one of all."

"Why?"

"Because as I see it, I don't have much of one. I'm at the mercy of my sister and her husband unless I can make enough money to support myself. Then there's this territory. I hate it. I don't fool myself into believing that the Indian conflict won't escalate. The Indians aren't simply going to yield their land to us. There will be more massacres—more women like me." She forced a smile. "I'm sorry. Grace says that in time I'll feel better, that I'll learn to put my trust in the Lord and even marry." She paused. "I'm learning to trust in the Lord, although His ways are confusing at times, but I'll never marry. I can't expect any man to overlook what I've gone through." She looked away. This man had a strange ability to draw information from her. He put her at ease, but for the life of her, she couldn't understand why.

"Hope." Lieutenant Kenner took hold of her chin with infinite tenderness and turned her head to face him. "No decent man would ever hold that against you."

"He doesn't have to." She pulled back, forcing him to let go. She didn't care for the intimacy of his touch. "I hold it against myself."

"I wish you wouldn't, but I understand that these things take time. Still, might we at least be friends? I'm not looking for romance either, but I could use a friend."

She tried to sound unaffected by his gentleness. She didn't want to argue, and if she tried to explain her fears, it would no doubt lead to that. "We could be friends. But nothing more."

His expression was solemn for a moment, but then he smiled. "I think being friends is quite enough."

His nearness made her uncomfortable. It wasn't that he made her feel unsafe, but rather that he made her feel anything at all. She'd tried so hard not to for the last two and a half years.

She straightened and fixed him with what she hoped was an all-business expression. "Now, please tell me what happened in court."

He frowned but nodded and picked up his bread once again. "The jury didn't consider the matter for long. Not even two hours. They returned a guilty verdict against all of the defendants. There was some question about one of the men—Kiamasumkin—and whether he participated, but in a strange turn of events, the judge called Mrs. Chapman back to testify that she had witnessed his participation."

"Why was that so strange?"

Lance shrugged. "The defense had rested, as had the prosecution. The judge had sent the jury out to deliberate, and yet he allowed them to come back posing that concern. It's not generally how things are done."

"You seem to know a lot about it." Hope nibbled at her bread.

"I suppose I do. I studied law in college. I plan to take it up again once I muster out. I intend to return to New Orleans, where I'm from. I started practicing law there with a family friend before joining up."

She'd never thought of him as a learned person, but reflecting on his manners and speaking, it made perfect sense.

"But the verdict was guilty?" she asked.

He nodded. "They were all found guilty. Remember, they were tried as a group, not individually."

The back door opened and closed with a resounding thud. "Hope?"

"I'm here in the kitchen."

Mercy popped into the room. "The sheep are in the pen." She stopped at the sight of the lieutenant.

"This is Lieutenant Kenner," Hope introduced. "Lieutenant, this is my sister Mercy."

He got to his feet. "I'm pleased to meet you, Miss Mercy."

She smiled. "I'm pleased to meet you, Lieutenant Kenner."

"Please, call me Lance. Both of you. I'm mustering out after the hanging."

Mercy frowned. "So they're going to hang those poor Indians?"

Hope saw the surprise on Lance's face. "My sister is of the mind that forgiveness is due everyone, no matter how heinous their crime."

Mercy plopped down at the table. "Well, it doesn't say anywhere in the Bible that only certain people get to be forgiven by God."

"I think a person ought to repent and ask for forgiveness,"

Lance replied, reclaiming his seat. "I'm afraid the Cayuse do not believe they've done anything wrong. They aren't in the least ashamed or concerned by what they did."

"Killing them isn't going to change what happened," Mercy replied, sounding years beyond her age. "It won't bring Dr. Whitman and the others back to life, and it won't change what happened to the women and children who were taken hostage."

Hope got up so fast her chair fell over backwards. "Mercy, you can forgive who you will, but don't expect me to do the same. I do well to have just a few minutes of sleep where I don't relive that horror."

She stormed out of the room, unable to continue. She knew Lance would understand. She just wished her sister might afford her the same compassion.

Lance considered going after Hope, but something held him in place. He ate his bread, uncertain whether he should stay or go.

"She isn't like that all the time," Mercy said after a long silence. "She was getting better until the trial."

"It'll probably take a long time and a lot of patience on your part."

Mercy nodded. "I know. I've been praying for her."

"I'm afraid that the trial has taken its toll on your sister. It's actually made her sick at times."

Mercy considered this. "I think it's the hate that's making her sick."

"What do you mean?"

"Grace helped me see that when you hate someone, it's like a chain wrapped around your heart that reminds you of all the ugly, bad things that person did to you. Holding a grudge takes a great deal of strength. You keep carrying it, and it wears you out. You can hate so much and get so worn out from it that it makes you ill and ruins your life. It's better to let bad things stay in the past and put the chain down. Leave it to rust. You don't have to carry it and be reminded of what happened . . . and you don't have to get worn out and sick."

The words permeated deep into Lance's heart. Learning that Hope's brother-in-law was Alex Armistead had been hard. The past had never been easy to forget, but it was less intense before this new revelation.

"You look sad."

He nodded. "Sometimes the past makes me that way. Hearing you talk about hate making a person sick made me think of some things I'd hoped to forget."

"Sometimes talking about them helps."

He smiled. "I was thinking of my family."

"But surely you don't want to forget them."

"No, but I do want to forget some of the tragedies and pain that surrounded them. See, my mother died when I was just ten."

Mercy nodded. "I was eleven when my mama died. Da was already dead, so losing her was really hard."

"I know it must have been, because it was for me. Although my father was still alive."

"Do you have brothers and sisters?"

Lance tried not to betray his feelings. "I had two older brothers and a younger one who died around the same time as our mother. It was a yellow fever epidemic. They're all gone now."

She frowned. "It must have been hard to lose them all to sickness."

Lance didn't bother to correct her. There was no sense getting into the details of his older brothers' deaths.

"So you have no one?" she asked.

112

"No." He shook off the memories and met Mercy's turquoise eyes. He smiled. "You have very pretty eyes. They aren't like Hope's or Grace's."

"No." She shook her head. "Hope's eyes are blue like our mother's. Grace's eyes are green like our father's. Mine are a mix of both. Mama always said I was the tie that bound everyone together."

He smiled. "What a wonderful way of looking at it."

Mercy nodded but said nothing more.

The silence prompted Lance to ask a question. "Do you really believe that everyone deserves to be forgiven?"

"No. I don't think anyone deserves it." She shrugged. "The pastor says everybody has sinned and gone astray. He read that to us from the Bible. He said that no one deserves grace. I remember that because Alex teased Grace, saying that when she's difficult, he's going to remind her of that." She smiled, and it seemed to light up her entire face.

Lance nodded with a grin. "I've met your sister Grace. She seems very nice."

"She is."

He didn't want to dwell on Grace or Alex, so he said, "But you've decided to forgive the Indians who took you hostage even though they haven't asked for your forgiveness?"

"Yes." She paused and looked down at the table for a moment. "I don't want to carry around that hate. I don't want to always live in the past." She looked up and smiled. "I want to leave the chain to rust so I can have a good life. I want that for Hope too. She suffered more than I did, though, so I understand why it's harder for her."

Lance toyed with the bread in his hands. "Maybe she can't bring herself to accept what they did."

"Forgiveness isn't about accepting anything. I don't accept

or approve of what happened. Those men committed murder and . . . other things. They deserve to be punished, but I think it's wrong to kill them."

"So they can be forgiven and punished at the same time?"

"Of course. God forgives us when we ask, and the Bible says He forgets about it as well. But, like Grace says, there are earthly consequences and laws that have to be dealt with as well. I can forgive them, but they did wrong, and the court has decided they deserve to die for committing murder. That doesn't bother me nearly as much as the pleasure so many people take in that decision. I can't bear that they look upon human life so casually. Of course, they don't believe the Indians are human."

She was so wise and tenderhearted for one so young. "I think you're an amazing young woman, Miss Mercy."

Mercy stood at the head of her class. The teacher handed her a certificate of award for her perfect grades. She held the paper proudly and returned to her seat, glad that classes were officially over for the summer. She loved school, but given all the trial talk and enthusiasm over the upcoming hanging, she wanted nothing more than to sequester herself away from town.

The teacher concluded their school year by having them stand and recite the Lord's Prayer. After that they were dismissed, and the revelry began.

"I thought he'd never stop talking," Otis Banks said, leaning closer to Mercy than she liked. "Want to take a walk by the river with me?"

"No, thank you," Mercy replied. "I have chores and need to get home."

Otis shrugged and turned away to discuss the hanging with

some of the other boys. Mercy hurried to collect her things. Beth Cranston, her dearest friend in all the world, came to stand beside her.

"I heard Otis ask you to walk out with him." Beth smiled. "I think he's very nice-looking, and his father is very wealthy. He plans to buy a steamship."

"I don't care about that." Mercy stacked some books as the teacher had asked her to do earlier. "Otis may be very nice to look at, but there's a meanness to him that I can't abide."

Beth shrugged and gave her long blond hair a casual stroke. "I don't think he's mean—he's just older."

"Only a year, and at sixteen, he ought to know better than to bully the younger boys and tease the girls." Mercy was about to say more about the way Otis showed the teacher disrespect as well, but his voice rose above the others in the room.

"My pa says I can go to the hanging with him." The pride of his father's decision was clear in Otis's expression. "What about you, Toby?"

Toby Masterson was the preacher's eldest child. This was his last year of schooling, and Mercy would miss him.

"I don't know." He glanced at Mercy. "It seems like bad form to talk about it in front of the ladies."

"I'm gonna be there," another of the older boys declared, ignoring Toby's comment. "I ain't never seen a hangin', but my pa has. He says they deserve worse than hangin' though. He says they ought to be dragged behind a horse over rocky ground then left for the buzzards to eat."

"My pa says that if they don't hang 'em just right, they'll twist and kick until they strangle to death," still another boy offered.

Mercy thought she'd be sick. She no longer cared about her things and bolted for the door. She hadn't intended to continue running, but that was what happened. She ran until her sides ached and her legs began to burn. The road home was three miles, mostly uphill, as it rose away from the river. She usually waited and rode home with Alex, but not today.

Grateful for the cover of tall firs, oak, and ash, Mercy veered off the muddy road and made her way into the quiet depths of the forest. When she could go no farther, she collapsed on a fallen log and had a good cry. She might have stayed there indefinitely, but a sound to her left caught her attention.

"Mercy?"

It was Toby Masterson. The tall, blond-haired young man took a seat beside her.

"Why are you here?" She wiped at her eyes with the back of her sleeve.

"I was worried about you. I saw how upset you were at what those boys were saying."

"They made it sound like they were preparing for a party instead of the killing of human beings."

Toby stretched out his long legs. "They're fools. I'm really sorry they upset you."

"You are?" She looked at him as if seeing him for the first time.

"I think the Indians have some valid complaints. I think the settlers have caused them so many problems by taking their land that the Cayuse felt they had to do something. Of course, it wasn't right that they killed the folks at the mission. That surely wasn't the way to handle it, not that I know what the answer is. Like most of the other settlers, I want my own land too." He shrugged. "Maybe the government could pay them for it. I don't know."

"I don't know either. I don't know if such different people can live side by side, but I hate the ugliness. I was at the mission,

Toby. I know how horrible it was. I was scared to sleep for fear they'd kill me, but then I was just as afraid in the daytime. I still have nightmares sometimes."

His expression was sympathetic as he reached out and took her hand. "I'm sorry you had to go through that."

His kindness encouraged Mercy to continue. "I saw the dead bodies. I even saw a boy killed right in front of me. They forced us to cook and help them and they . . . well . . . they forced the older girls and women to be their . . . to . . . ."

He gave her hand a pat. "I know what they did, Mercy. I'll be eighteen in November, and my pa talked to me about it. He said we should never belittle or blame the women for what happened."

"No, you shouldn't. I didn't have to go through it, because Hope protected me and because I've always been small for my age."

He smiled. "I think you're the perfect size."

She smiled and looked at the ground. "It served me well at the mission, but so many others were hurt. I wish it had never happened, but I don't think hanging the Indians is going to make anyone feel better."

"Maybe not, but that isn't the point. The laws were broken. Killing is against the law, and if the Indians are to be treated like the white man, then they have to understand that there is punishment for breaking the law."

Mercy nodded. "I know. I just wish people weren't so happy to see other people die. To me, that makes them just as bad."

Toby stood and held his hand out to her. "It's wet and the temperature's dropping. You should get home. I'm going to walk with you, if that's all right. I don't want anything to happen to you."

Mercy took his hand and felt warmth spread through her

when he continued to hold it tight. She had always thought him a fine-looking young man but had no idea he'd ever noticed her.

"I want to ask you something," he said as they began to walk toward the road.

"What?"

"Would you be willing to take a walk with me Sunday? After church, of course."

"A walk?"

He smiled and nodded. "My ma told me that she invited your family to eat with us after church, and that your sister accepted. I thought maybe we could take a walk after lunch while they visit."

Mercy swallowed the lump in her throat and looked up. "I . . . I'd like that."

Chapter 11

June third was soon upon the town. The gallows were ready, and the townsfolk were more than happy to rid themselves of the guilty Cayuse. Hope hadn't planned to attend the hanging, but at the last minute she changed her mind. She didn't so much want to see Tomahas and the others die, but she desperately needed to feel some sort of closure to the entire affair. Perhaps watching the men face their just deserts would finally bring her a sense of safety—of the peace she so desperately longed for. And it wasn't like she hadn't seen men die before.

Oregon City was packed with people when they arrived in town. Alex and Sam Two Moons rode ahead of them while Grace did her best to navigate with the wagon. Sam had joined them just outside of town as he and Alex had previously agreed. Alex had come to talk to Hope about it the night before. He wanted to make sure she knew ahead of time and wouldn't be troubled by Sam's presence. He and Sam planned to leave as soon as the hanging was complete so that Alex could do the governor's bidding and speak to the various tribes.

That morning Hope and Grace had packed the wagon with the supplies Alex and Sam would need for their journey so as to leave their horses unburdened until the last minute. Grace had watched her carefully—almost as if expecting Hope to break into pieces any minute.

"You don't have to go," Grace told her more than once.

"I'm not as weak as you seem to think," Hope had replied. Grace hadn't looked convinced.

As they rode toward the sawmill, Hope thought of Faith. Would Eletta one day tell her about her father, Tomahas the Murderer?

Will she tell her about me?

Thoughts of Faith no longer made Hope as uneasy as they once had. She had never intended to even lay eyes on the child after giving her life, but God had had other plans. The baby couldn't take cow's milk, and Hope had been forced to nurse her until a wet nurse could be found. Now, nearly two years later, Hope had no regrets about having done it. Nursing Faith had helped her see that the baby wasn't some hideous creature. She couldn't say she had any maternal feelings of love for the child, but neither did she feel hatred toward her existence. God had at least allowed Hope peace where that matter was concerned.

Oregon City had enjoyed three days of decent weather with long hours of sunlight, and the pleasant weather had dried out the muddy streets, making passage much easier. As they came into town, it seemed the warmth and sunshine was also making the residents of Oregon City lively and playful. The entire atmosphere was more like some sort of fair than a solemn hanging, and in spite of it being a Monday, many businesses had remained closed so that their owners and employees could attend the hanging.

"I'm glad Mercy stayed home," Grace murmured as they

came to a stop in the sawmill yard. "I don't like her being there alone, but I certainly don't want her here."

"No, it's better this way." This would have been much too hard on their sister. Hope couldn't agree with Mercy's desire for forgiveness, but she certainly didn't wish to make her suffer more by imposing the hanging on her.

Alex and Sam tied off their mounts then came to help Grace and Hope. Thankfully, it was Alex who offered Hope a hand down from the wagon.

"Thank you." She meant it for more than just the help. As kind as Sam had been to their family, she couldn't have handled the Nez Perce touching her. Alex had always seemed to understand and care. Not long after the women and children had been set free from their Cayuse captivity, Hope had made him promise to end her life rather than let the Indians retake her. He hadn't liked the idea, but he understood. She loved him for that and was more than happy when her sister married him.

"You're welcome, Hope." He gave her a smile before heading over to where Grace and Sam were standing. "Everyone ready?"

"As ready as we're going to be," Grace replied. She took Alex's arm. "I hope this goes quickly. It's hard enough to watch men die, but for the people to make such a celebratory affair of it makes it all the worse."

Leaving the wagon and horses at the sawmill, they walked the rest of the way to the gallows on the banks of the Willamette near Abernathy Island. Crowds were already pressing in from every direction, so they held back. Alex and Sam disappeared for a time, leaving Hope and Grace to observe the scene. When a young boy came by selling peanuts, Grace shooed him away.

"You would think this was a party," she said in disgust.

"They should have just killed them immediately after the trial." Hope thought that would have been more sensible. "I just hope Governor Lane doesn't change his mind and pardon them. I don't know how I'll bear it if he does."

"I know," Grace said, taking hold of her hand. "But Alex feels confident he won't."

"I'm glad someone is confident. But you know as well as I do that talk has gone back and forth on whether there will be a stay of execution."

Grace nodded. "I know."

Alex returned, but Sam was no longer with him. Alex looked troubled.

"What's wrong?" Hope asked before Grace could.

"The Nez Perce and Cayuse have already started for home. They said it wasn't right to stay and watch the life go out of their brothers in such a disrespectful way. By leaving now, they offer them honor."

"Disrespectful?" Hope nearly yelled. With effort, she lowered her voice. "I would say that what their brothers did at the mission was far more disrespectful. They deserve to be dishonored."

"Where's Sam?" Grace asked.

"He's hanging back. Things could get ugly toward the native people, and it's best that he not be here in the middle of it all. I think that was the real reason the Nez Perce chose to leave."

"And what about the governor?" Grace asked. "Is he going to proceed with the hanging?"

Alex nodded. "He is. He's not even here."

"Not here? Where has he gone?"

"South to deal with the Rogue River Indians. There's been some trouble between them and the miners. Lane wants to negotiate a peace."

Hope felt only a modicum of relief. Until Tomahas and the others were dead, anything could happen. Judge Pratt might even step in to stay the execution order until the governor returned.

The very idea made Hope's heart pound all the harder.

Just before two, there was a commotion, and the throng of spectators parted as Marshal Meek and the prisoners approached. Behind them, Hope spied Lance and a dozen soldiers. All were well-armed. She'd already noticed several soldiers surrounding the gallows and wondered at this added security. Were they expecting trouble?

The entourage stopped at the base of the gallows platform long enough for a priest to administer last rites to the Indians. Hope had heard that the Cayuse had all made confession and been baptized by the priests. No mention was made, however, as to whether they'd finally accepted responsibility for what they'd done. Not that it really mattered to Hope. She knew they were guilty.

With the prayers concluded, the men were escorted to the top of the platform. Hope couldn't help but edge closer. She could clearly see Tomahas and the others. They no longer seemed like fierce, offensive warriors. Rather, they looked like defeated men—trapped animals. She stared long and hard at Tomahas, almost hoping he'd return her gaze and know that she was there—that she was exacting her revenge in the only way she could. But he never looked her way.

Gunny sacks were placed over the head of each prisoner and the nooses secured over these. Meek read off the sentence, and then before Hope even had a chance to brace herself, the rope was released and all five men were hanged at once.

There were too many people to see exactly what was happening, but the deed was done, and the Cayuse were left to dangle until it was certain they were dead. Hope heard a child crying somewhere in the crowd. She looked around and to her surprise found a great many children present. It seemed unreasonable to her that a good parent would bring them to a hanging.

"They're dead!" someone bellowed, and cheers went up.

A shiver ran down Hope's spine. Tomahas was dead. He was really and truly dead. Never again could he force himself upon her . . . or anyone else. Never again would he be able to kill the innocent.

For a moment she thought of Johnny Sager. She remembered the desperation she felt when she realized he was dead. Hope had wanted to die then. She had actually tried to end her life, and had the pistol not misfired, she would have. Tomahas had caused those feelings. He caused them again when Hope realized she was pregnant. She had wanted to die then as well. In both situations, she had felt completely helpless. She never wanted to feel that way again.

As the crowd dispersed, Grace took Hope's arm. "Now maybe we can get on with our lives and put this behind us."

Just like that?

Hope had expected some great release with the death of Tomahas, but instead she felt nothing. She let Grace lead her through the crowd as she contemplated the matter. She never need fear Tomahas again. He could no longer harm her. At least not physically.

There had to be a way, she thought as they worked their way back to the sawmill, to be free once and for all—to feel safe again. Pastor Masterson had said just yesterday that this event would settle the Whitman Massacre and allow those involved to put it behind them. Hope had prayed he was right, but at the moment she didn't see how that could be.

"Well, it's done," Grace said, looking up into Alex's face. "I suppose now you'll be on your way."

Alex nodded, his expression sober. "I won't be any longer than I have to be." He put an arm around her shoulders and continued walking. "I wouldn't do this if I didn't think it was important."

Hope followed them at a short distance. Seeing Alex and Grace walking together reminded her again of Johnny Sager. She stopped and gazed out at the river, the noise of the falls muffling some of the revelry going on behind her.

Johnny, I would have loved you for all of our days.

She sighed. She had loved him for all of their days together, but now he was gone, and Hope knew she had to move forward with her life. Her friendship with Lance had been a start, but she was hard-pressed to know where to go from here.

"Hope."

She turned and found Alex next to her. "I'm sorry you're leaving," she said. "I know Grace will miss you terribly."

He nodded. "I hope you'll take special care of her for me."

"Of course." Hope could see that he was serious. "I promise to help her in any way I can."

"Don't let her be alone too much. I know you like your solitude, but she isn't the same. It might be asking a lot of you, but please keep her company." He paused, and his expression took on a look of worry. "I once made you a promise that wasn't easy to make, and now I'm asking for one in return. If anything should happen to me, I need to know that you and Mercy will help her through."

Hope hadn't expected this. She remembered all but forcing Alex to promise he'd kill her before allowing the Indians to take her hostage again. "Nothing is going to happen to you, Alex. Grace will have you so thoroughly prayed for that nothing would dare harm you. Not man and certainly not beast." She forced a smile. "Don't worry. She'll be fine and so will you." She paused and drew in a deep breath. "But I promise."

He nodded. "Will you pray for me too?"

Over the last couple years, Hope had maintained a fragile relationship with God. She prayed from time to time and tried to read the Bible and heed the pastor's sermons, but there were still far too many unanswered questions.

"I will pray for you, Alex." She could at least offer that much.

The serious expression left his face, replaced by a warm smile. "Thank you. I'm going to pray for you too. I know this isn't over for you—not like you wanted."

She was surprised by his comment but had no desire to discuss the matter. Instead, she murmured her thanks and then nodded toward where Grace and Sam were talking by the wagon.

"You . . . *we* should rejoin them."

<hr />

On Saturday, when Grace asked Hope and Mercy to join her for a quilting bee in town, Hope wanted to refuse. She had no desire to sit amongst a group of women talking about their lives and gossiping about others. But her promise to Alex echoed in her head, and she knew she couldn't refuse.

She packed her spindle and plenty of roving as well as finished yarn she might sell. She could quilt as well as most, but by occupying herself with her wool, she wouldn't have to sit around the frame with the other women. Other women would bring their knitting and crocheting, so she wouldn't seem oddly separate.

Her Aunt Mina was hosting the event, and afterward, Hope and her sisters would eat an early supper with the Marsh family before heading back to the farm. If things got too uncomfortable, Hope knew she could slip away for a time. After all, there would be plenty of family and friends at the house to keep Grace occupied and even comfort her should she grow sad.

Mina was a consummate hostess. She had set up a side table for refreshments, which some of the women added to as they arrived. There was tea to drink, and Mina had set out her best china cups and saucers.

The women quickly settled in to work. Mina had been working on a large quilt top for some time and was happy for the help to finish putting it together. She had the frame set up in her sitting room with dining room chairs gathered around. Otherwise the furnishings had been cleared away.

"I like to never got that top finished," she told the gathering. "Baby John has kept me quite busy, and without the help of Beth Cranston from time to time, I fear I would accomplish little indeed."

Mercy and her best friend, Beth, were even now entertaining the younger children in one of the back rooms of the house.

"I'm not ashamed to say that we've hired a girl," Mrs. Masterson, the pastor's wife, declared. "She's a half-breed and works hard. She cleans well and is good with children, being the oldest of a family of ten." Since she was a mother of five with one on the way, no one faulted her for her decision. But Mrs. Masterson still hurried to add, "Besides, her family moved away, and she had no one to care for her, so it was an act of charity as well as necessity."

The talk continued on the subject of children and the difficulties in keeping their families fed, clothed, and free of sickness.

"Oh, Grace," Aunt Mina began, "I need a couple five-gallon jugs of vinegar. I have the empty jugs to trade you for them, and Edward will happily pay you. We've all been much healthier since you suggested we take several teaspoons a day."

"Vinegar is a definite gift from God," Grace replied. "My grandmother and mother used to say there was very little vinegar couldn't help and nothing that it would hurt."

The conversation moved on, and the inevitable topic of the trial and hanging came up. Hope tried to pay little attention to the discussion, but the ladies were boisterous, and ignoring them was all but impossible. Nevertheless, she took up her spindle and did her best.

Spindle spinning was an interesting art Eletta had taught her. It required a weighted dowel with a hook at the end. A piece of starter yarn was attached to the spindle and then drawn around the hook. Hope would then turn the spindle to create a tight twist on the starter yarn and add roving to be caught into the twist as she released her hold. Once a nice line of roving had been twisted into yarn, she would then tuck the spindle between her knees and wrap the yarn around it. After that, she would start the process again. It was monotonous and not at all as relaxing as being at the wheel, but it served her purpose all the same.

"My husband said a couple of the Indians didn't die right away. Their necks weren't broken, so they slowly strangled. I can't help but believe it was God's punishment for the most wicked of the bunch," Mrs. Fuestelle said in an authoritative manner befitting her nearly sixty years.

Her daughter-in-law Mary offered her opinion as well. "I think they should have forced all the guilty Indians to trial. Pity that the governor made a deal to let so many others go."

Hope was curious about this but didn't want to join the conversation. Thankfully she didn't have to, as one of the other women joined in.

"Yes, Dr. Whitman's own nephew Perrin stated for the newspaper that the governor allowed eight others who participated in the killings to go free. Apparently he felt the five we hanged were the leaders and instigators."

"Nevertheless," Mary continued, "they should have been forced to pay for what they did. I knew sweet Narcissa Whitman, and it's a travesty that anyone responsible for the deaths that day should go free."

Hope focused on her spindle. She spun the wooden dowel to tighten the twisted yarn then paused to put the spindle between her knees and allow the next section of drafted wool to be caught up in the twist.

"I can't abide the Indians," Mrs. Fuestelle declared. "I say the sooner they're eliminated, the better off we will be. They simply refuse to get along with anyone."

"That's because they're more like animals," one of the women murmured.

"It's true. They live in the most primitive manner," Mrs. Fuestelle continued. "Some of them live in structures covered with mats made out of grass. If they were an intelligent people, they would have learned to cut down trees and make log houses."

"Or collect stones," Mary added. "Rock houses can be very nice."

Mrs. Fuestelle nodded. "Or they might have made those adobe bricks. Heavens, the Israelites made bricks for Egypt. It hardly requires much skill or material."

Mrs. Masterson paused in her sewing. "My husband said that Chief Telokite made a statement when asked why he had given himself up if he wasn't guilty. He said, 'Did not your missionaries teach us that Christ died to save his people? So die we to save our people.'"

"Of all the nerve," Mrs. Fuestelle said, disgusted. "To use our Savior's name as an example." She shuddered.

It did seem strange to Hope that Telokite had made such a statement. He knew about Jesus and His death, as Dr. Whitman had taught that much every Sunday, and many of the Indians professed to accept this as truth. Still, the idea that Telokite was sacrificing himself to save the rest of his people rang hollow as far as Hope was concerned. If he cared that much, he never would have killed in the first place.

Grace took that moment to interject her thoughts. "Ladies, you must allow that not all Indians are unsaved heathens, just as not all white men are Christians. It is up to the individual heart to decide. Therefore, not all Indians are bad and all whites good."

"I don't think the heathens ever truly understand the issue of salvation," Mrs. Fuestelle countered. Her tone betrayed her irritation. "I believe it's beyond them."

"Then is it also beyond God?" Grace asked. "After all, God is the one who calls the heart to repentance and salvation. Is He not able to save the Indian?"

Mrs. Fuestelle sputtered and fell silent.

Grace looked around the room at each of the women before continuing. "I owe my life to a very good Nez Perce man who loves the Lord every bit as much as I do. He was kind to all of us, in fact." She looked at Hope and smiled. "I also know a stalwart and faithful missionary who happens to be part Indian. He has led many people to Christ."

"My husband has many Christian friends among the tribes. For years he was a trapper and shared the Word with the unsaved whenever the opportunity presented itself," Mina offered.

Hope continued to spin and listen. She hoped they would soon tire of the Indian topic. After another twenty minutes or so, they finally moved on to concerns about their sons and husbands desiring to relocate to California, where the streets were apparently paved with gold.

"My dear, I do so love your yarn. I wonder if you might have brought any for sale," Mrs. Masterson asked Hope, taking a break from the others. "With the baby due at the end of July, I want to knit a few things. Yours is such a fine, soft yarn."

"Indeed it is." Mrs. Fuestelle had to throw in her opinion. "I used to spin my own but would much rather purchase Miss Flanagan's."

The other women nodded or spoke their agreement.

Hope smiled. "I did bring quite a selection. It's in the wagon. Would you like me to bring it in?"

"Oh, please do," a chorus of voices answered.

Hope put her spinning aside and rose. She quickly retrieved the large flour sack of yarn, and as she made her way back into the sitting room, Mrs. Masterson was already staking her claim.

"I get first choice since it was my idea," she said with a smile.

Hope opened the sack and began taking out the beautifully colored yarn. Mrs. Masterson immediately grabbed up two skeins of yellow and three of white. "Oh, these will be perfect."

The other women joined them, leaving their places at the quilting frame. They exclaimed over Hope's work, and before they were done, they'd purchased all of the yarn, including the undyed skeins at the very bottom of the sack.

"I have to make John some socks," one of the women said. "This darker yarn is perfect. He can't keep anything clean."

The women laughed and one by one paid Hope for their treasures. In just a few minutes, Hope was nearly ten dollars richer.

"Mercy, can you take a walk with me?" Toby Masterson asked.

She smiled, feeling shy. "I suppose I can." She looked at Beth, who was on her left. "Beth and I were caring for the children while the women quilted. I was just walking her home. You're welcome to join us."

"Yes, please do," Beth urged.

He grinned. "I'd like that. Then afterwards, Mercy, I could take you home."

"No, I'm spending the evening here with my sisters. Uncle Edward and Mina have asked us to stay for supper."

He shrugged. "No matter. We can just walk around town, if that suits you."

Mercy nodded. "It does. Let me tell Grace. I'll be right back." She hurried into the house and found her sister. "Toby Masterson has asked me to walk with him after we see Beth back to her house. Will that be all right?"

Grace glanced at Mina, who was nursing her son. The women exchanged a knowing smile. "Of course. Just be back in time to eat."

"I will."

Mercy rejoined Toby and Beth. "Sorry, but I knew if I didn't tell Grace, she'd worry."

"It's no matter," Toby said, smiling. "I was in town to get some seed for my uncle, and when I saw you on the porch with Beth, I thought I'd better take the opportunity to ask you something."

Mercy looked at Beth and then back to Toby. "Me?"

He nodded. "I wondered if you would let me accompany you to the Fourth of July picnic."

She couldn't contain her joy. "I'd like that very much."

"There's a dance that night," Beth offered. "I'll be there."

Toby nodded. "I was getting around to that. I hope you plan to be at the dance too, Mercy."

She shrugged. "I'm not sure."

"Well, if you are, I want you to save all your dances for me," he replied with a lopsided grin.

"She can't do that," Beth protested. "There are a lot of other fellas in town who'll want to dance with her. You'll have to pick a few of the dances on her card and be satisfied with that."

Toby considered this a moment. "Well then, if that's the way it is, I'll dance half the time with Mercy and half the time with you."

Beth giggled. "I guess that might work."

Mercy shook her head at the silly look on Beth's face. Beth was far more romantic than Mercy and often talked about all sorts of ridiculous notions, like knights in shining armor coming to carry her away on a white horse. The only white horses in the entire valley belonged to old Mr. Simmons, and he wasn't even able to ride anymore.

They reached Beth's house after a few blocks, but Mercy could tell she was hard-pressed to leave them. The girl could be absolutely daffy.

"You could come inside," Beth urged. "Mama might let me serve you some cookies and buttermilk."

"No, I can't stay too long. My uncle expects me back by dark." Toby turned and offered his arm to Mercy. "We'd best be on our way."

Beth nodded, but disappointment was clearly written in her expression. "I suppose I'll see you on the Fourth."

Mercy let Toby lead her away. She liked walking out with Toby. It made her feel grown up. After all, Toby would turn eighteen come winter. Mercy didn't believe the same romantic nonsense that Beth did, but she liked the idea of having a steady beau. After all, she was nearly fifteen, and most girls her age were already spoken for.

"So, you'll talk your sisters into staying for the dance—won't you?" Toby asked.

Mercy smiled. "I'm sure I can. Even if they don't want to stay, I could come with Uncle Edward and Aunt Mina. They would let me spend the night with them."

"Good. I can hardly wait. I want everyone in town to know you're my girl."

"You do?" Mercy couldn't keep the surprise from her voice.

"Of course, you ninny." He chuckled. "Why do you think I asked you to start walking out with me?"

"Well, so we could get acquainted. Getting acquainted isn't quite as serious as telling folks we're . . . a couple."

He laughed all the more. "You women are queer creatures. Fellas don't waste time with just getting acquainted. We have the future on our minds."

Mercy swallowed the lump in her throat. The future suddenly seemed much closer than it had an hour ago.

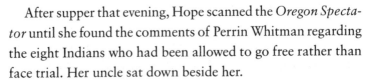

After supper that evening, Hope scanned the *Oregon Spectator* until she found the comments of Perrin Whitman regarding the eight Indians who had been allowed to go free rather than face trial. Her uncle sat down beside her.

"I bet you're reading about the Indians the governor let go."

She lowered the paper and nodded. "Dr. Whitman's nephew sounds enraged."

"What about you?"

Hope frowned. "What do you mean?"

He gave her a smile and patted her hand. "I just wondered if it was upsetting to you as well."

"I think it's wrong to let guilty men escape justice. There were definitely more than five Indians at the massacre and definitely more than five participating in the murders. The governor should never have bargained with the tribes and set guilty men free. In fact, the tribes that hid those men for so long ought to be punished as well."

Her uncle frowned. "So when is enough enough?"

"What do you mean?" Anger rose to the surface, and Hope was hard-pressed to keep from expressing it.

"When will enough people die to satisfy the debt? I just wondered. I mean, I figure there ought to be punishment for wrongdoing, just like you. But there does come a time when wars need to be settled and pardons allowed for."

"You think they should simply be pardoned, then? Maybe you think it was wrong to hang those five."

"I can't say. You told me yourself they were among the men responsible for the death of Dr. Whitman and the others. The jury, too, found them guilty, and so legal justice was done. But we can hardly go around killing every Indian. I'm saying that we need to learn to live side by side—find common ground where we can all get along."

Hope bristled. She knew he was right, but it still didn't sit well with her. How could the settlers ever learn to live with a people who were so very different? How could either side just forgo their ideals and culture to make peace with the other?

When was enough . . . enough?

Chapter 12

I think you'll work out just fine," Edward Marsh said. "You
can start Monday."

Lance breathed a sigh of relief. He was quickly running out of money and didn't have the means to get back to
New Orleans. He could send for the funds, but that would
take months. Also, something about Hope Flanagan had given
him second thoughts about leaving. With her in mind, and his
pockets empty, he'd decided to stay for a while.

He'd tried to find someone to take him on as a law partner
but hadn't had much luck finding a paying position. One man,
Mr. Davis Bryant, offered to let Lance work with him for a few
hours each evening for experience, but he couldn't offer any
pay. Thankfully, Edward Marsh had agreed to take him on at
his sawmill.

"I appreciate it, Mr. Marsh. Like I said, it isn't permanent."

"Well, with my partner away for several weeks and so many
men gone to the goldfields, I can definitely use the help. Hiring
a good man who'll stay on the job is getting harder and harder.

We're nearly back up and running to full capacity, so it's likely I'll need to hire more full-time workers. If you prove to be capable, I might want to extend your position into something more permanent."

"I promise to give you my all, but it is still my intention to return to New Orleans once I have the funds. For now, however, a man has to eat and put a roof over his head."

Edward scratched his beard. "Say, where are you staying?"

"Over at the City Hotel."

"That can't be cheap. I tell you what. I have an empty cabin on the far end of town right on the river. It needs to be cleaned up. My nieces used to live there, but when the river flooded some months back, it took a beating. It's just a little place, but if you'd like to take it on, I'll let you stay there for free."

Lance couldn't hide his pleasure. "I would be much obliged. The hotel has been eating into what little I'd managed to save."

"Well, that's settled then. Give me a couple minutes, and we'll head over there so I can show you around."

Lance waited just outside the mill. He'd been a civilian for a week, and it was still hard to get used to. He'd served only four years, but somehow it felt like a lifetime. After all, he'd been involved in a war and then made a two-thousand-mile trek across the vast American wilderness. With that part of his life behind him, Lance felt both a void and a sense of excitement. And always in the back of his mind was Hope Flanagan.

"All right, let's head out," Edward said, pulling on his coat. "I hope you don't mind walking."

"Not at all. I walked here. My horse is being stabled."

"Well, there's an area near the cabin you can use for him. You'd have to rebuild a pen or stake him out, however. I put together a rough pen for the girls, but the flood took that out."

"I'm sure I can work with whatever is available."

Edward nodded. "Oregon City has grown a lot since I first came here. In fact, the first time I laid eyes on this area, there wasn't much more than a couple of cabins, like the Portland settlement is now. But it didn't matter to me back then. I was a trapper and mostly hung out at Fort Vancouver when I wasn't up in the tall and uncut."

Lance chuckled. "I was born and raised in New Orleans, so this still seems like a tiny town to me. But there's something about it that I like very much. It's given me a sense of home, even though mine is far away."

"I can well imagine. I spent my growing-up years in and around St. Louis. There's something about a river town that gets into your blood. I suppose that's why I love it here. We haven't got the river traffic of the Mississippi, but give it time. It's coming."

A sprinkle of rain fell, but both men were so used to it that it was nothing more than a minor annoyance. Lance felt like his life was finally falling into order. He tried not to think about Hope any more than necessary, but he had to admit she came to mind quite often. He'd offered her friendship and nothing more, and she'd offered the same, but he wasn't so sure he could leave it at that.

"So that's it just up the way," Edward said.

The cabin wasn't much to look at, but once the area around it was cleaned up, it would suit just fine. Of course, he hadn't yet seen the inside. "Does the river flood often?"

"Oh, it depends on the snowmelt from the mountains and the rain, of course. It floods pretty consistently, but not like last year. Generally speaking, it might overflow the banks and come up the property ten or twenty feet, but the cabin's usually far enough back that it isn't bothered. Last year was different. We lost most everything along the river, and what wasn't lost was severely damaged."

Edward opened the door of the cabin. The smell was musty. There was mold on the logs, and mud still layered the warped wood floors.

"I'll bring over some wood to fix up the floors. Some of the furniture is still good. The wooden chairs and table didn't suffer too much. We put the bed and mattress upstairs, along with the rocking chair and settee. They're old but serviceable, if the varmints haven't gotten into them. The cupboards on the kitchen walls are fine, but the cupboards below are probably not worth the trouble of cleaning up. It'd probably be best to just pull them out and replace them with new ones."

"I'm sure I can make do." Lance surveyed the mess. "I'll purchase some supplies tomorrow and get right to it."

"Go to the Brick Store and tell them to put it on my account. Get a broom, mop, buckets, whatever you need. I'll bring a shovel over later tonight and some cleaning rags. I'll bring my boys too—at least the older two. We'll help you clear out some of the rotten wood and debris."

"Thank you, sir."

Edward let out a belly laugh. "Now that's a fine how-do-you-do. Here I thought maybe we'd be friends."

Lance chuckled. "Too long a soldier, I guess."

"Well, call me Edward and leave it at that." He pulled out his pocket watch. "Say, why don't you come over to my place right now? It's nearly supper time, and we'd love to have you. We can discuss anything else you might want to know over dinner, and then we can head back here afterward. We'll have plenty of light left to us."

"I'd hate to impose. Your wife will surely be vexed if you bring home a guest unannounced."

"She won't mind at all. My nieces are already joining us. One more isn't going to make a difference."

"A home-cooked meal does sound mighty appealing."

Lance followed Edward out of the cabin and pulled the door closed behind him. It didn't want to close all the way due to some warping. One more thing to put on the list to fix.

When they entered Edward's two-story house, they were greeted with boisterous laughter and racing children. Lance smiled at the way the three young boys chased after one another, their giggles echoing through the halls.

"My boys," Edward offered. "Well, most of 'em. We have another one not yet a year old, but give him time, and he'll be running circles around the other three. And if I have my way, we'll have another two or three in the years to come."

"Two or three what?" a beautiful brown-haired woman asked. She smiled at Edward. "I see you've brought us a guest."

Edward put his arm around her. "I did indeed. This is Lance Kenner. He's helping me out while Alex is off talkin' to the Indians. Maybe longer, if he decides to give up studying to practice law."

Lance frowned. Was Edward's missing partner Alex Armistead? He'd heard that Armistead had left town to speak to various tribes about the trial but didn't realize he was a partner in the sawmill.

"Mr. Kenner, I'm pleased to meet you. I'm Edward's wife, Mina."

Lance bowed his head then offered her a smile. "Pleased to meet you."

The boys came rushing through once again, but this time big, burly Edward swooped down and caught all three in his muscular arms. "Whoa, now. I have someone for you to meet."

The boys' legs were still moving even as their father raised them off the ground.

"Lance, this one here is Phillip. He's the oldest." Edward moved his right arm forward just a bit. "He's ten. In my other arm are Thomas and Oliver."

"I'm five," Thomas declared, holding out his hand with fingers splayed. He seemed perfectly content to dangle from his father's arm.

Lance smiled. "I'm pleased to meet you boys."

"Boys, this is Mr. Kenner. He's going to work with me at the mill."

The children seemed unimpressed, and the minute their father put them down, they were off and running. Edward and Mina shook their heads.

"Sometimes I think there are twice as many boys in this house," Mina said. She gave Lance a smile. "We've kept you standing in the foyer long enough. Please come in and let me introduce you to our company."

Lance followed her into a lovely, well-appointed sitting room to find he already knew the three visiting women.

"That there is Alex's wife, Grace," Edward said, nodding to where Grace sat with a fat baby bouncing on her knee. "And that's Baby John."

So it *was* Alex Armistead he was filling in for. Lance tried not to show any emotion. He had been going over the details of the past in his mind and still wasn't sure what he would do when face-to-face with Alex.

"Lance!" Mercy declared, getting to her feet. "Look who's come, Hope."

Hope turned from the floor-to-ceiling bookshelves where she'd been perusing a book. Her eyes widened in surprise. "Well, I must say, I didn't expect to see you here tonight."

Edward laughed. "So you know each other already?"

Mina looked at Grace. "Do you know Mr. Kenner, as well?"

"I do. He's come to our rescue a couple of times." Grace cocked her head. "But as I recall, you were Lieutenant Kenner then."

"I was, but now I'm just plain old Mister, and happily so."

"Well, you're most welcome company, no matter your title." Grace shifted the child on her lap.

"I didn't know you had a child," Lance said, smiling at the baby.

"I don't," Grace replied. "He's Uncle Edward's youngest."

Mina took the child. "And it is Baby John's bedtime. If you'll excuse me, I'll see to him. Grace, would you mind making sure our dinner doesn't burn? We'll eat when I return, so feel free to start putting the food on the table, if you like."

"I'd be glad to." Grace got up from her chair. "Mercy, why don't you come help."

They left the room, heading off in the opposite direction from which Lance had come.

"I'm going to round up those boys and get their hands washed for supper," Edward said just as the shouts and laughter started to sour. One of the boys was yelling that his brother had hit him in the ear. "Sounds like I'd best hurry."

His departure left Lance and Hope facing each other. She closed the book and waved to a chair. "You might as well make yourself comfortable."

"It's nice to see you looking so well, my . . . friend," Lance said. He chose a nearby wooden chair and eased back with his legs outstretched. "Last time I saw you, I thought you might be ill."

She frowned. "When was that?"

"At the hanging."

Her eyes widened. "I . . . well . . . I wasn't sick, but I was overwhelmed. I'm sure you understand. I did see you marching behind the prisoners."

He nodded. "One of my last official duties."

"I wasn't going to attend, but at the last minute I thought perhaps I should. I didn't see much, since the scaffolding wasn't very high and we were toward the back of the crowd. But after hearing the gossip regarding the . . . well, the way they died, I think I'm glad for that."

"It wasn't an easy death."

She nodded. "Are you glad to be out of the army?" she asked, seeming to relax a bit.

"I am. No more polishing brass or inspecting the work of others. I'm going to work with your uncle since your brother-in-law is away."

She sighed. "I wish Alex hadn't gone. Grace misses him so."

He couldn't help but ask about the man he'd long considered his family's enemy. "What's your brother-in-law like? I saw him at the trial and again at the hanging. He was with one of the Indians."

"Yes, that was his good friend Sam Two Moons. Sam is Nez Perce, and he and Alex used to trap together. They've been friends a long time." She paused and took a seat in the rocking chair. "As for what he's like, well, he's trustworthy and honorable. He's a good man—a great comfort and help to my family."

It was strange to hear such praise for Armistead. "Where does he come from?"

Hope shrugged. "I don't recall. I know he lived with his grandfather for a time in Montreal or somewhere near there. I really don't remember. You'd have to ask Grace. I think he was originally from somewhere in the South. Apparently there was some sort of trouble that sent him north. For a time we thought it might even keep him and Grace apart, but just when all seemed lost, he returned to us, having settled his problems."

Lance knew very well about the troubles that had sent him

to Canada. Even so, the man Hope portrayed was nothing like the hateful, vindictive one Lance had created in his mind. He'd always thought of Armistead as a coldhearted man who counted life cheap. But in Oregon City, Lance heard nothing but praise for him.

"He's a hard worker." Hope smiled. "When we moved out to the farm last year, he worked himself crazy putting up fencing for our sheep. He plans to put up more, but he and Uncle Edward are building a bigger house first."

"It's good of him to take you and Mercy in."

She nodded. "Like I said, he's a good man. But enough about Alex. You'll have a chance to get to know him when he returns. If you're still here."

"I plan to be. I have my home in New Orleans but figure to be here for a while. The army never paid much, and what I'd put aside is spending fast. The job at your uncle's mill will allow me to refill my coffers." He paused and offered her a big grin. "Besides, I kind of like it here, and I've already made one good friend."

Hope shook her head. "I don't know how good of a friend I am, but call it as you will."

"You don't seem to like having friends. I mean, I've never seen you with anyone but your family."

"Are you keeping an eye on me?" She watched him as if assessing him for the truth.

"I look out for my friends." He grinned. "Besides you're one of the only women in town I know."

"Well, maybe you should start attending church. You'd make a lot of new friends there."

Lance sobered and shrugged. "Never been much of a church man. In my boyhood I was, but only because my father insisted on it."

"I understand that well enough. My mother and father did as well. Since then, though . . ." She left the rest unsaid.

Lance heard something akin to regret in her tone. "But you attend services?"

She sighed and looked off toward the front window. Light was still shining through the panes despite the cloudy day. "I do. I guess since we're friends, I can be honest with you." She looked back at him and gave a slight smile. "The massacre changed everything for me. I blamed God for not stopping it and wanted little to do with Him. I'm still not entirely sure what He expects of me or what I want of Him, but I'm working on knowing Him better so I can learn."

"I could have said the same for myself. Of course, it wasn't a massacre that caused me to question."

"What did?" she asked.

He couldn't explain it to her, and he didn't want to lie. "We'll keep that story for another day."

Mercy rushed into the room. "Grace isn't feeling good and she wants to go home."

Grace joined them, looking pale. "I'm sorry for the inconvenience and sorry that we can't share dinner with you, Mr. Kenner. Perhaps we might have you dine with us at the farm soon." She gripped the back of a chair and closed her eyes.

Edward came into the room and immediately noticed something was wrong. Grace smiled and waved him off when he insisted she could take a bed upstairs.

"I'll be fine. I think I've just been sleeping poorly since Alex left. I don't want to be a bother or create a fuss. Just give my regrets to Mina and tell her the food is on the table." She let go of the chair and crossed the room.

"I could ride with you. It wouldn't take me long to fetch my horse," Lance said.

"No." Grace shook her head. Her color was a little better, but she still looked weary. "Hope and Mercy will be with me, and it's still light. We'll be fine."

"Mina won't like that I let you run off," Edward said just as one of the boys let out a banshee-like scream. He looked torn between going to investigate and staying to help Grace.

She stretched up on tiptoe and kissed his cheek. "Go. I'll be fine."

The scream sounded again, and after a roll of his eyes, Edward took off.

Lance wanted to do something more, but there was nothing he could do without making a scene and imposing himself upon the trio of women.

Hope passed him and turned. "It was nice to see you again . . . friend."

"It was nice to see you, as well." He looked at the other two women. "It was nice to see all of you."

And then they were gone, and Lance was left standing there feeling awkward and, strangely enough, lonely.

Grace asked Hope and Mercy to join her by the fire once they reached home and had cared for the horses. Hope wasn't sure what was going on, but she had her suspicions.

"I don't want either of you to worry," Grace said. "I'm truly fine. It's only that . . . well, I'm going to have a baby."

"A baby!" Mercy clapped her hands. "When?"

"December."

Hope had suspected as much and mentally calculated that her sister was a little over three months along. About the same amount of time had passed when Hope learned she was with child.

"This is so wonderful," Mercy said. "I was afraid you were sick, and I didn't know what we would do because you're the healer."

"Well, I'm just fine. I felt faint at Uncle Edward's and a little green. The smell of the pork fat was overwhelming. The night air made me feel much better, however, and I'm actually hungry now."

"I'm going to fix us something to eat," Mercy said, jumping to her feet. "You have to eat for two now and take good care of yourself. I'm going to help you and do all your chores."

Grace laughed. "That isn't necessary, Mercy, but something to eat would be nice."

The fourteen-year-old nodded enthusiastically and headed for the kitchen. Hope was more guarded with her feelings, and Grace seemed to sense this.

"I hope this isn't too hard on you."

Hope shook her head. "It comes as no surprise. And while it does bring back memories, I won't be grieved by them. This is a happy occasion, and I will do what I can to be nothing but joyous."

Grace settled back in her chair. "I know you both will be wonderful help."

"Does Alex know?" Hope asked. If he knew about the baby and had left Grace to fend for herself, Hope was going to be angry.

"No. I couldn't tell him. He would never have gone, and I think he needed to go on this journey as much as the governor needed him to. Alex loves Sam's family, and he needs to know they'll be safe."

"But you need to be safe as well."

"And I am. We're all quite safe here." Grace smiled. "Besides, he'll be home in a few weeks. We have plenty of time before the baby comes, and we'll have more than enough work to keep us busy. I'll need lots of soft yarn to make blankets and booties."

Hope nodded. "Good thing the sheep are getting sheared next week. Mercy and I will get right to washing and carding the wool."

It would be simple enough to spin yarn for her sister. What wasn't so easy was feeling confident that they would be fine without Alex in the meantime. Hope thought of Lance and how he'd been reintroduced into their family circle. Perhaps he could be useful in the days to come, should they need a man's help. Uncle Edward would continue to ride out and check on them as well.

Hope noticed Grace watching her and forced a smile. "I was just calculating how much yarn we might need. What colors do you think you want?"

Grace smiled. "I don't know. I haven't allowed myself to think on it for fear I'd give it away. You're the only people I've told, and I'd just as soon keep it a secret—for the time being, at least."

Hope nodded. "A secret is something I understand quite well."

Chapter

13

The Oregon City Bible Church suited Lance. He'd come here at Edward's enthusiastic invitation, but it was knowing that Hope would be here that sealed the deal. And, just as Hope and Edward had told him, folks were welcoming.

"Before we conclude our services," Pastor Masterson said, "I want to remind everyone that the Methodist Church is planning a citywide Fourth of July picnic this Thursday. We're all to bring food for the celebration. I was also asked to announce that there will be a political meeting at four o'clock at the City Hotel to discuss state business. Those of you interested will want to attend. I would imagine there will be some discussion on Governor Lane's resignation. Secretary of the Treasury Pritchette is acting governor in the meantime."

Lance had been less surprised by the governor's resignation than some. Governor Lane had been with the army in the Mexican War and had distinguished himself in such a way that he rose from colonel to brigadier general and won the appointment to governor of the Oregon Territory from President

Polk. It was clear to the men who knew anything about Lane, however, that he aspired to higher political office—perhaps even the presidency.

The pastor led them in a final hymn and then dismissed the congregation. Lance sat several rows behind Hope and her family despite Edward inviting him to join them. He didn't want to impose himself on the family. He did, however, plan to greet them and waited until they began to make their way down the aisle before he stepped out.

"There you are," Edward said, coming toward Lance with his arm extended. They shook hands. "Mina thought you might like to join us for lunch."

Lance wondered if Hope and her sisters would be joining them as well, but before he worked up the nerve to ask, Edward offered up the information.

"And don't worry about whether there's plenty to eat. My nieces were going to come, but Grace is still under the weather and begged off. So you might as well eat their share."

"With the way your wife cooks, I could very well see myself doing just that."

"So it's settled then." Edward turned as his five-year-old tugged on his coat. He bent low, and the boy whispered in his ear. Edward nodded and turned his son toward the door. "The call of nature," he whispered as he passed Lance. "See you at the house."

Lance greeted others around him but noted that Hope, as usual, had avoided the crowd and instead made her way to where the family horse and wagon waited. Politely excusing himself, Lance followed her outside.

"Hope, I wondered if we might talk a moment?"

She turned at the sound of his voice and nodded.

Lance caught up to her in two long strides and smiled. "I must start by saying you look lovely today."

Hope blushed and looked away. "Thank you, but surely that isn't what you stopped me for."

He laughed. "Always to the point. I wondered if we might . . . that is, if you would accompany me to the Fourth of July events. I'd like to attend, but I don't really know anyone."

"What about Uncle Edward and his family or your army buddies?"

"Your uncle and his brood are a family and should be allowed to enjoy the festivities together. I don't want Edward thinking he has to entertain me or take time away from his boys. As for my army friends, there weren't that many. My sergeant and I were friends, but he's been relocated to Fort Vancouver, and soon the rest will follow."

She nodded. "I suppose there is sense in that, but honestly, you've been here for months. It seems you should have made friends with someone."

"I have." He grinned at her.

Hope narrowed her eyes and cocked her head slightly. "You haven't forgotten that we're just friends, have you? I'm not at all interested in romantic notions, and I'm certainly not looking for a husband."

"Nor I a wife. You are quite free of emotional entanglements with me." But even as he spoke, Lance wasn't completely convinced of his words. He liked Hope very much—perhaps too much. He felt he'd seen her at her worst and would like to witness her at her best.

"I suppose it would be all right, then. I doubt Grace will feel up to going, so would you be opposed to Mercy accompanying us?"

"Not at all. I hope she'll soon be a friend to me as well. In fact, I think she already is. She's congenial with most everyone."

"That's true. Probably far too congenial," Hope replied.

"Mercy and I will drive in on Thursday morning around nine. We'll have food to add to the picnic, and after that we'll be free to walk around with you. I understand there are going to be games and even a play."

"That sounds wonderful, but are you sure it wouldn't be better for me to ride out to the farm and help you in? I could leave my horse and just ride back and forth with you and Mercy. I heard there's to be a dance, and I wouldn't want you to have to head home in the dark, alone."

Hope considered that a moment. "I hadn't figured on staying for the evening dance, but I know Mercy has her heart set on it. I was going to suggest she just stay in town with Uncle Edward and head home early the next day."

"But you might be surprised at how much fun the dance will be."

She shrugged. "I used to like them well enough."

He could see she wasn't convinced. "Look, if you stick around and come with me to the dance, we can keep an eye on Mercy. We don't have to dance if you don't want to."

For several seconds she seemed to consider this. Finally, she looked up and gave him a nod. "Very well. If you want to ride out to our place, be there by eight thirty."

He nodded and smiled. "I will be delighted to do exactly that." Grace and Mercy arrived at that precise moment. "Good day to you both." He still held his hat in one hand and gave a slight bow.

"It's nice to see you, Lieutenant—Mr. Kenner," Grace corrected. "I'm afraid I'm feeling a little tired and must be on my way."

"Let me help you up." Lance took hold of Grace's waist as she started to climb into the wagon. He made certain she was seated before he turned to Mercy. "May I assist you as well, milady?"

Mercy laughed. "Why, thank you, fair knight." She gave a deep curtsy and let Lance lift her into the back of the wagon.

He turned just in time to see Hope roll her eyes. She hiked up her skirt and climbed up into the wagon seat without waiting for him to help her. He might have laughed at her expression had he not known how sensitive she could be.

"I'll see you Thursday," he said to her.

Grace frowned and looked at Hope. "Thursday?"

"I'll explain on the way home," Hope said, then snapped the reins.

Fourth of July arrived a little overcast but dry. Hope finished loading the wagon by herself while Mercy tended to the sheep. Grace had been sick most of the morning, so Hope had insisted she go back to bed. She'd even offered to stay home with her, but Grace wouldn't hear of it, reminding Hope that it was just the way of her condition and would pass soon enough.

When Lance arrived, Hope felt her own stomach give a flip. She wasn't exactly queasy, but his appearance did disturb her system. Throughout the night, she'd thought about his accompanying them today. She'd wondered how she might react if he should forget his promise of friendship and press her for more.

"Is there more to load?" he asked, jumping down from his mount.

Hope shook her head. "No. You can put your horse over there. He'll have plenty of water and grass." She motioned to the pen, and Lance's gaze followed.

"Very well. I'll be right back."

Hope used the opportunity to return to the house one last time. She took up her sunbonnet and knotted the ties loosely around her neck. With one more check of the kitchen to see if she'd forgotten anything, she let out a breath she hadn't even realized she'd been holding.

It was hard to go to the Fourth of July celebration. Harder than she'd thought it would be. She hadn't gone last year, and the year before that she'd been with the Brownings in California. Generally, she had stayed home during celebrations, and neither Grace nor Mercy or even Alex had tried to force her to do otherwise. This year she'd only planned to go because Grace intended to be there and Hope had promised Alex to watch over her. Now, however, Grace would remain home and Lance Kenner would round out their party. No doubt people would talk.

"There's nothing to be done about it now," she said to the empty room.

When she made it back to the wagon, Mercy was already seated in the back with the food, and Lance waited to hand Hope up to the wagon seat. She accepted his help and settled herself on the seat, and he climbed up and took his place beside her, as if this were how it had always been.

He took up the reins and turned to her. "Do you mind if I drive?"

"Not at all."

The ride into town was pleasant, even more pleasant than Hope had anticipated. The sun was peeking out from the clouds, and the day looked promising. Mercy chattered on about some of the games being sponsored for the younger children. She had volunteered to help with one game where the children would try to toss coins into jars. Apparently the prize was a cookie.

Hope directed Lance to park the wagon at the sawmill. It reminded her of the day of the hanging, and she couldn't help but glance in the direction where the gallows had stood. It was gone now, but Hope would never forget what she saw that day or the mood of the people.

Lance jumped down from the wagon. As Hope began to climb down, he grabbed hold of her and swung her to the ground.

He let go of her and stepped back, grinning. "See, you lived through it."

"What?"

He laughed. "You lived through me driving the wagon, having to sit next to me, and then enduring my help getting down."

She hated that he knew just how uncomfortable she'd been. "Yes, I suppose I'm no worse for the wear."

"Hope, I need to get to my station," Mercy said. "I'll see you at the picnic." She hurried away without waiting for Hope to reply.

"Well, I guess we'll get no help from her."

"What do you need me to do?"

Hope looked back at the wagon. "Uncle Edward has a small pen on the side of the mill. We can put the horses there."

"Yes, I'm familiar."

"Of course. Well, once the horses are tended, we need to deliver the food to the Methodist Church. I suppose we could try to drive it over, but with the crowds and some of the streets being roped off, I wasn't sure it would be worth the effort."

Lance walked to the back of the wagon. "Is this all you have?"

She smiled and shook her head as he hoisted the wooden crate as if it weighed nothing. "I figured we'd have to carry the items without the crate. It weighs quite a bit, but you make it seem an easy thing to bear."

"I've lifted a lot heavier things during my time in the army and even working for your uncle." He put the crate aside. "Now you stay here and guard the goods while I see to the horses."

It took Lance no time at all to turn the horses loose. He bounded back to her, looking for all the world like he'd just won a grand prize. When he reached the wagon, he hoisted the crate up on his shoulder.

"You lead the way."

Hope did just that, and once they'd turned over the food to the ladies at the church, she found a place for Lance to leave the crate of dishes they would use at the picnic.

"I never thought to bring dishes," Lance said, frowning. "I've done well just to get the cabin back in shape for proper living. Tomorrow your uncle and I plan to start laying the new floor. As for food, well, I've either been eating with your uncle's family or grabbing what I could in town. I'm not even sure I have dishes."

Hope couldn't help but smile. "Don't worry, I brought some for you. I figured since you were going to be with us, it was only right."

He looked relieved. "So what now?"

She shrugged. "I suppose we could walk around. I see some displays of woodworking that might interest you." She started them in that direction.

"You seem much happier today," Lance said, surprising her.

She looked up at him. "I suppose I am. I'm no longer afraid of Tomahas finding me, so that alone gives me relief. The trial is over and done with, and hopefully I'll never be expected to speak on the massacre again."

"Not unless you want to. And if that happens, I'm more than happy to listen. That's what friends are for."

Hope looked at him, wondering if he had any idea how difficult it had been for her to agree to accompany him to this celebration. Being in town was difficult, and it was made worse by the fact that there was no concrete purpose for her being there other than to have fun.

"I'd just as soon bury the past along with Tomahas."

"I understand, but forgive me for asking—has his death put an end to all of your fears and worries?"

If anyone else had asked that question she would have put them in their place, but with Lance it was surprisingly different. Still, she wasn't sure how to answer it. All around her were happy, laughing people, including women who had been with her at the massacre.

"Sometimes I don't understand why the other women can move on with their lives and I can't."

Lance nodded and took her arm. "It's been my experience in the army that no two wounds heal the same. One man might be laid up for weeks, even months with swelling and misery, while another is up and fighting the next day."

She let him lead her down toward the river. "I suppose that makes sense."

They passed a group of men who took off their hats and made themselves known. "Morning, Miss Hope. You gonna be at the dance tonight?" one of the men asked while the others nodded and awaited her answer with great expectation.

"Miss Hope is my date for the day, fellas," Lance said. "You'll have to find another."

The men muttered and replaced their hats atop their heads, looking utterly downcast as Lance and Hope passed them by. They were well away from the group before she could no longer suppress a giggle.

Lance looked at her in such surprise that it only made the situation funnier. "I'm sorry." She fought to control her laughter. "It's just that . . . well, the look on their faces and the look on yours . . . it just reminded me of a bunch of little boys being reprimanded by their father."

This made Lance smile. "I didn't want them crowding in on my fun."

Hope shook her head. "I doubt they'll even try to dance with me now."

"Good. That means I can have all your dances."

She sobered. "I don't know that I want to dance at all, so if you have your heart set on it, you may have to find another partner. Mercy might be willing to help you out."

He shook his head. "Like I told you before, I don't have to dance to have a good time with you, Hope. That's the joy of being friends. We can always just sit and talk about everybody else and how badly they dance."

A sense of relief washed over her. "Thank you."

"For what?"

She spoke before thinking. "For being my friend. For not expecting anything else. For understanding why I feel as I do."

He stopped, and from the look on his face, Hope momentarily thought she'd somehow offended him.

"I'm not sure I do . . . *exactly* understand. I don't think it's possible for a man to understand the feelings born out of a situation like what you went through. But I do care, and I understand enough to know you still don't feel safe most of the time."

She turned away and looked out at the river. "That's more than anyone else understands. But even the death of Tomahas and the others didn't leave me with any real sense of . . . being settled. I wish it had. I suppose that's the thing that bothers me most. I thought his death would finally lay everything to rest, but it hasn't. I'm not sure I'll ever feel safe in this territory." She continued to look out at the water until she sensed Lance's presence beside her.

"I figured his death would give you a sense of satisfaction. Didn't it help in that way?"

"Why do you ask?" She turned to look at him. His face looked pained.

"A long time ago, a man caused my family a great deal of pain and suffering, and that led to the utter destruction of our family. My father and my two older brothers and I were all that was left after we lost my mother and little brother to yellow fever. Then a series of events happened, and this man whom I've long considered an enemy did something that led to the death of my oldest brother. Shortly after that, my other brother died too, and ironically enough that too was connected to the same man. That left just my father and me. I was filled with anger and hatred toward the man who had destroyed my family. I often thought that if I could just make him pay for what he'd done, then somehow it would negate all the misery. But when I hear you talk, I doubt that it would."

Hope looked up at him. "I suppose it comes down to this. Revenge or even justice won't undo what happened. It won't bring the dead back to life or restore what was stolen, and while it might satisfy the requirements of the law, it satisfies very little for the heart."

He nodded, and it was his turn to stare off at the water. He gave a heavy sigh. "My father would have said the same. In fact, before he died, he did say as much. He was able to put the past behind him—to see that what happened to my brothers was a tragic turn of events that no one could have foreseen. He told me he'd given so many years of his life to questioning how he might even the score or how he might have done things differently, and all he'd accomplished was losing those years of his life when he might have done something far more productive."

"Was this man who wronged you sorry for what he'd done?"

Lance said nothing for a moment. He gave another heavy sigh. "My father says he was. Right after he killed my brother, which he claimed was purely accidental, the man sent my father a letter of explanation and apology. Father said he barely read the words before throwing the letter in the fire. He said apologies wouldn't give him his son back. Of course, at that time there were doubts about my brother's death. The perpetrator said it was an accident, but others said it was murder."

"I'm sorry you lost your brother." Hope felt as if this were yet another part of their lives that somehow intersected. "But I doubt you'd feel better, even if you were able to seek out that man and kill him. Grace says only God can heal a hurt like that, and only God can make you feel truly protected—safe. I've come to think she's right. Although I have to admit my faith is very weak."

"Mine too," Lance admitted.

She looked into his eyes and saw the pain there. It was more than she could bear, and without thinking she put her hand in his. There were no words for the thoughts in her heart. She wasn't a wise woman who could offer profound counsel, nor was she intellectual enough to reason it out through logic. All she could give him was her friendship.

~

Mercy enjoyed dancing with Toby Masterson more than she'd anticipated. When she was handed off to another partner, all she could do was think of him. Toby had captured her fancy, to be sure, but Mercy wasn't sure what to do about it. She was only fourteen. Where she had found his attention intriguing and fun before, now she found her thoughts toward him tangled in knots.

Feeling a stitch in her side, Mercy begged off the next reel and made her way to the refreshment table. She picked up a cup of punch and turned back to watch the dancers. Toby had partnered with Beth, and it appeared from their smiles and laughter that they were enjoying themselves.

Mercy now knew that Beth was sweet on Toby. She hadn't realized it at first, but little things throughout the evening clued her in. Several times she'd caught Beth staring up at Toby with such a look of adoration that it was almost brazen. Then during the musicians' break, Mercy was surprised to see Beth actually flirting with him. She touched his arm and batted her eyelashes in a practiced fashion that left Mercy no doubt of her friend's intentions.

The music ended, and Beth made her way to where Mercy stood. She grabbed a cup of punch and gulped it down. "Oh, my," she gasped, "I don't know when I've been happier. Toby is a wonderful dancer and he . . . well, he's so sweet." She looked at Mercy and smiled. "Don't you agree?"

"He's very kind and a great dancer." Mercy saw Toby crossing the room to join them. He looked at her through the sea of people and winked.

"Oh!" Beth said with a giggle. "He winked at me."

Mercy started to correct her but knew it wouldn't matter. Beth was clearly smitten. Rather than say anything, she sipped her punch. The last thing she wanted was to get into an argument with her best friend, especially over a boy.

Chapter 14

That evening as Lance sat with Hope, watching other people dance, he couldn't help casting sidelong glances at his date. The day had proven to be a quiet and comfortable time—one he'd enjoyed very much. Hope had comported herself in such a manner to receive well-wishes from the townspeople and offer them in return, but she never opened herself up to anyone. Not even to him—not truly.

He knew she was still wounded by the past and wished he could somehow alleviate her misery, but he was doing well to figure out his own haunting memories. How did a fellow go about undoing years of anger and mistrust?

"Mercy dances very well," Hope commented, looking at him momentarily. "Don't you think?"

Lance watched the young girl swinging on the arm of the pastor's son. The square dance seemed to delight her, and Lance thought he'd never seen her look so happy.

"She does. It's good to see her having fun. She's a very deep thinker, that sister of yours."

Hope picked at a piece of cookie and nodded. "She is. She's always been like that. Where other children were fidgety and noisy, Mercy was always quite still. She likes to think about things, and she feels things quite deeply."

"I had an interesting talk with her at your house the day I came to tell you about the trial. She's going to make an amazing woman. I wish I had the depth of understanding about God that she has."

"I know." Hope looked back at her sister. "She takes God at His word without question. I try, but I find myself constantly trying to look for something more."

"More?" Her comment intrigued him. "What do you mean?"

She shrugged and eased back in her chair as she looked at Lance. "I don't know exactly. I suppose in some ways I'm trying to figure out if God is really who people say He is. I'm trying to prove or disprove Him, I suppose."

Lance could understand that. "When I was little, faith in God was just a matter of daily living. My mother oversaw our religious training, and she was fixed in her own faith. After she died, it was hard for the rest of us to hold on to our faith when God had taken the heart of our family. It was far easier to be angry and bitter toward Him and everyone else."

"Yes."

The music ended, and Mercy came to join them. "I'm dying of thirst, and the refreshment table is overrun with parched dancers," she declared.

"Here, have my lemonade," Hope offered.

Mercy downed the half-full glass just as another young man came to claim her for a dance.

Lance watched Hope as she followed Mercy with her gaze. There was something of regret in her expression, as well as love.

"Would you like to dance?" he asked.

"No." She continued watching the dancers. "I don't feel comfortable with that idea. I'm sorry. You can certainly go ask someone else."

"I'm not a huge fan of dancing. I just thought maybe you'd changed your mind. You looked rather regretful just now."

She turned to him at this. "I suppose I am." She said nothing for a few moments then added, "Mercy is so sweet and carefree. I regret the loss of innocence in my life—of being able to believe that everything and everyone was basically good. A part of me wishes we'd never come west. I can't help but wonder what life would have been like for all of us had we remained in St. Louis."

Lance had wondered the same thing about his own life in New Orleans. His father's friends had advised him against joining the army. They'd encouraged him instead to focus on running the plantation and his interest in law, but Lance had known that getting away from all that was familiar was necessary for him to heal. For whatever reason, he knew he would never be the man he needed to be if he remained in New Orleans. Thinking about it now, he wondered if it was wise to return. Perhaps it needed more thought.

"Do you regret coming west?" Hope asked, jarring him out of his thoughts.

"No. Not at all. I think leaving home was good for me. Joining the army was an experience in maturity that I think every man needs. There's something about facing death that causes a man to evaluate his choices in life. It taught me not to waste time on foolish arguments, and it gave me a better understanding of human nature."

Hope considered this. The slight frown she wore made him wonder if she disagreed with him, and when she didn't speak, he felt the need to press the issue.

"You look as if you think me wrong."

She shook her head. "No. I had just never thought about how much those life-and-death experiences changed me. I mean, I knew it made me grow up and changed me from a frivolous flirt, but everything about me is different than it was prior to the massacre."

"How so?"

"It's made me more . . . more honest—more real. I think before, I was wearing a false front like people put on buildings when they want them to look like there's more to it than there is. I wasted a lot of time and energy on foolishness."

"I find that hard to imagine."

"You shouldn't. You can ask Grace or even Mercy. I was self-centered and childish, but everything changed that day at the mission." She fell silent and gazed at the dancers.

Lance got the distinct feeling she wasn't going to say anything more on the matter, so he didn't press her further. He cared about her feelings and wanted her to know that, as his friend, she could be at ease. If that meant they sat in silence for a time, he would happily comply.

The next day at work, Lance was still pondering all that he and Hope had discussed the day before. He remembered his father's dying words to him.

"Don't spend your life seeking revenge. If you do, you'll find you're left with nothing when death comes for you. Seek God's mercy and understanding instead, and we will see each other again in glory."

The words were hard to hear, especially as they were his father's last. Lance had stood at the casket and wondered if Alex Armistead would be happy to know that all of the Kenners, save one, lay cold in their graves. He had always imagined

Alex dancing a jig and offering his friends a round of drinks in celebration at the news. Now that image didn't seem to fit. And yet he hadn't met the man to know that for himself.

"Are you all right?" Edward asked, eyeing Lance with concern. "You've been staring at that saw blade for at least ten minutes."

"Sorry about that. I guess I have a lot on my mind." Lance picked up a file to sharpen the teeth of the blade.

"Son, if you have something you need to discuss, I'm happy to lend an ear."

"I find myself wrestling with the past." Lance shook his head. "I don't seem to be able to make sense of it all."

"God alone can help you with that. He's the only one who can take the messes we make and turn them into something worthwhile. Have you taken this matter to Him?"

"Not exactly." Lance looked at his employer and saw the face of a friend. "I want to, but I'm not exactly sure how."

Edward took a seat on the stool across from Lance. "Can I ask you a personal question?"

"Sure." Lance put down the file and waited for Edward to speak.

"Have you put your faith in God? Have you accepted Jesus as your Savior?"

Lance shrugged. "I went through all the training that the church gave. I always supposed I was as much a Christian as anybody else."

"Sitting in a church doesn't make you a Christian any more than being in a doctor's office makes you a doctor. It's more than that. The Good Book says it's about believing and confessing."

"I believe in God."

"That's good, because even the Devil does that much. Always makes me wonder about those folks who deny the existence of the Almighty. That makes them dumber than the Devil. See, the Devil not only knows God—he knows that God is in control. He knows he's under God's authority, and even though the Good Lord is giving him enough rope to hang himself with, the Devil just keeps trying to best God." He chuckled. "But I'm gettin' off on a rabbit trail.

"Believing in God is the first step, but believing that He sent His Son Jesus to die for your sins is the next."

"I believe that. My mother and father did too. It's only natural that I believe it."

"But you can't be saved on your parents' faith. It has to be your own. See, you can't save yourself. Jesus already did that by dying on the cross. But you aren't without responsibility. You have to accept His gift of salvation."

"And how exactly do I do that?"

"Confess your sins—your worthlessness without God—and ask God to forgive you. You have to humble yourself before Him and admit it's too much to handle on your own."

"And that will eliminate the pain of the past?"

"Maybe not at first, but God will ease that away—if you let Him. I've seen folks wrestle God for their misery, however. I think some folks just like being unhappy. They've been wallowing in it for so long, it's become a part of them—makes them who they are."

"I've never wanted that. It just seems hard to break away."

Edward smiled. "We've all been where you're at now. Just don't stay there. Take it to God. He can relieve you of that burden. He's the only one who can. Meanwhile, I need that blade sharpened." His smile broadened. "And then, if you're of a mind, you can follow me home for supper."

"Will Hope and her sisters be there?"

"Not this time. Why do you ask?"

"No reason." Lance smiled. "I guess I'm just getting used to seeing them."

"I think maybe you're used to seeing one more than the others." Lance couldn't hide his surprise, and Edward chuckled. "I've seen the way you look at Hope. You have feelings for her. I'm figurin' you may even have changed your mind about going back to New Orleans."

"We're just friends," Lance said quickly. "She only wants to be friends."

Edward sobered and nodded. "She's been through an awful lot, but I think you know that."

"I do. She's shared some of it with me."

"I hope you won't push her for more than friendship until she's ready for it. Going through the massacre at Whitman's and enduring everything afterward has left a deep mark on her. Grace gave me the details as she knew them, and Hope will be a long time healing."

"I know, and I don't want to do anything that will cause her more pain."

Edward smiled. "Glad to hear it. With her pa dead and gone, I feel the need to watch over her. All of them, for that matter. You do anything to wrong her, and you'll answer to me. Understand?"

Lance nodded, his expression serious. "Understood."

Later that night, Edward's words were still echoing through Lance's mind. Not so much what he'd said about Hope—that was nothing new to Lance. He already handled her with caution.

It was Edward's words about God that held Lance captive. He sat on the edge of his bed and pondered what to do. Edward made it sound like a simple matter of admitting he was lost in sin without Jesus. But that seemed much too easy. Wouldn't God require more of a man?

Noting the time, Lance blew out the lamp and stretched out on his bed. His body needed rest, but his mind seemed inclined to continue working. Maybe he would talk to the pastor on Sunday and see what he had to say about it.

~~~

"I just wish Alex would send me a message and let me know that he's all right," Grace said as she sat at the table, grinding herbs.

"It's not like he can run to the post office." Hope brought Grace the glass jars she'd asked for earlier. "It's not even that easy to get to one of the forts. Not from the areas he's visiting."

Grace nodded. "I know, but I'd still like to hear from him. It's been weeks."

Hope went back to measuring out the ingredients for a cake. It was Uncle Edward's birthday, and they'd invited the entire family for a celebratory meal. At the last minute, Grace had suggested they extend the invitation to Lance as well, and Hope thought it would be nice to see him again. She'd noticed him at church on Sunday, speaking with Pastor Masterson, but Grace had wanted to get home, and there hadn't been time to exchange pleasantries.

She hadn't spoken to Lance since the Fourth of July dance, but that didn't mean he hadn't been on her mind. It was strange to find him constantly there, in fact. She supposed it was because he was kind and undemanding. Other young men seemed to have only one thing on their minds—marriage. Women in the territory, although more plentiful now than they had been even two years earlier, were still scarce. Hope found complete strangers asking for her hand. For that matter, she'd heard them ask Mercy as well.

"Have you talked to Mercy about love and marriage?" Hope asked, glancing at Grace.

Grace looked up in surprise. "What brought that question to mind?"

"She and I are both proposed to all the time. I just wondered if you had ever talked to her about such things. Mama talked to me, but I was given to flirt and think myself in love from the time I was twelve. Mercy's never been like that."

"No, I suppose she hasn't. I doubt Mama ever spoke to her about it and probably thought she was too young. When I look at her I still think her too young."

Hope nodded. "So do I, but that doesn't stop men from thinking otherwise. Toby Masterson certainly isn't thinking of her that way. You should have seen the two of them at the dance."

Grace's expression grew serious and she frowned. "I suppose you're right. I should talk to her."

Three hours later, the family shared a lovely lunch. Grace had put Lance beside Hope at the table, making it hard to focus on anything but his presence. Throughout the meal, he asked her questions and told her about cleaning out the cabin. After a while, she found herself relaxed and enjoying the meal as if the past had never happened. When she realized she hadn't thought of the massacre at all that day, it surprised her.

When everyone seemed to have eaten their fill, Hope brought out the birthday cake for Uncle Edward. "Did you save room for this?" she asked.

"Well, if that don't beat all." Edward smiled and elbowed his eldest son. "Looks good enough to eat."

The boy looked at him oddly. "Of course it does. That's what cakes are for."

Edward chuckled. "I knew me a fella once who sat on a cake."

"Sat on one?" Phillip's eyes widened. "Why would he do that?"

Hope watched as her uncle's expression took on a mischievous edge. "Because I didn't see it sitting on the chair."

Everyone laughed, and Hope reclaimed her chair beside Lance. In Alex's absence, Edward made their days much brighter.

Lance smiled and leaned closer. "When's your birthday?"

"March tenth. How about you?" She had wondered about this since she and Grace first discussed having a celebration for Edward.

"September fifteenth."

"Mine's September twenty-second," Mercy offered from Lance's right.

The children all piped up to announce their birthdays as well.

Hope committed the date of Lance's birthday to memory. Perhaps she could talk Grace into throwing a party for him too. After all, Lance really had no one in Oregon City to care about him but Hope and her family.

After cake, the boys went outside to play while Edward and Lance played a game of checkers. Mina and Grace sat near the fireplace, talking. Mina gave some baby clothes to Grace, and they were giggling as they held them up and talked about the baby. Hope watched from afar while they spoke. She felt a twinge of sadness, remembering her own pregnancy. There had been no laughter and sharing of baby clothes. There had been very little discussion on the matter, given her condition and how she'd gotten that way. Unable to keep watching, Hope finally slipped outside, praying that no one noticed.

The day was beautiful. The sun was warm on her face and the breeze gentle. Off in the large fenced acreage, the sheep casually grazed. It seemed everything was right with the world.

"Except for me." She hadn't meant to speak the words aloud and quickly looked around to make sure no one had overheard. No one had. Uncle Edward's boys were busy playing tag near the barn, much to the frustration of little Thomas, who found himself constantly "it." They dodged in and out of a dozen or so hens that clucked in protest.

Hope smiled. Oh, to be young and free of cares. The world seemed so much nicer when she'd been a little girl. She leaned against the split rail fence.

"Penny for your thoughts."

She jumped. She hadn't heard nor seen Lance approach.

"How did you manage to sneak up on me?"

He shrugged with a smile. "My secret. Had to learn to be quiet when I was fighting the Mexicans and Indians."

"You're certainly good at it."

"I'm sorry I gave you a start. I assure you it wasn't my intention."

"I believe you." She felt her heart slowing to a normal pace.

Lance eased back against the fence post. "How about telling me what you were just thinking about? You looked . . . well, not quite sad, but almost."

Hope shook her head. "No, not really. I was just watching the boys play and remembering how simple life was when I was a little girl. I never felt afraid. My da was the biggest man in the world—or so I thought—and I never feared anyone when he was around."

"Are you afraid now?" His voice was soft . . . tender.

Hope trembled but would never admit her fear to him, because right now her fear was . . . of him. Not of what he might do to her, but rather of how she felt when he was nearby.

"Why should I be afraid now?" She shook her head. "It's a beautiful day, and everything is calm and peaceful. Even the sheep are happy. See how they graze without worry?" She turned toward the pasture.

"You're a terrible liar. You know that, don't you?"

Hope squared her shoulders and turned back to look him

in the eye. She was set to tell him he was wrong, but he raised a single brow and grinned as if daring her to deny the truth of what he'd said.

The words stuck in her throat, and for a minute Hope could only gaze into his eyes. Finally, a loud shout of protest from little Thomas shattered the silence, and Hope took a step back as the boys came racing past them.

She decided not to give Lance the satisfaction of answering and began to walk toward the house. This only caused Lance to chuckle and follow her.

"Some folks just can't stand the truth."

Chapter 15

August brought the full warmth of summer and days of sunshine. Hope enjoyed the warmth as she washed the last of the wool. She had spent many an hour washing, dyeing, and carefully arranging the wool to dry. As the colder, wet weather would soon be upon them, she wanted to have the wool ready for carding—something she could do indoors throughout the winter. For weeks she had worked on spinning yarn in light yellow and green as well as powder blue and pink. There was also an abundance of white, and all of it met with Grace's approval. Together, Grace and Mercy were spending their evening hours either knitting or sewing for the baby.

Grace had started to show, so most of their friends in town knew the truth of her condition. It was happy news to all, but Hope knew that Alex's absence weighed heavily on her sister. The joy of her pregnancy was tainted by the worry she held for her husband. There had been no word from him, and while Hope knew that Grace hadn't anticipated any, she longed for it. They all did.

Alex had thought he could be home by September, and Hope prayed it might be so. She knew that only his return would allow Grace to relax and breathe a little easier. Frankly, it would allow Hope the same sense of relief. She didn't like bearing the weight of responsibility for her sisters. Of course, she wasn't bearing it alone. Grace had always been the mothering type and still made certain everyone had their morning vinegar and that they never drank water unless it had first been boiled. Mercy too occasionally took charge. She had, for instance, taken over all the garden duties, telling Grace and Hope that she could manage quite well and needed to feel useful.

The summer had passed in an abundance of chores, each met one at a time and in a general spirit of unity. Hope had even found her faith growing slowly but steadily. She didn't dread the Sunday trips to church and had started reading her Bible each morning. She also enjoyed seeing Lance from time to time. He and Uncle Edward had the mill back up and running at full capacity.

Upon hearing about Grace's delicate condition, Uncle Edward had declared he would move ahead on building the house he and Alex planned to build. Lance had pledged his help as well. For weeks, additional logs were cut and prepared, and finished lumber for the interior walls and floor was set aside. Uncle Edward had even put together plans to have a house-raising.

"Are you nearly done there?" Grace asked.

Hope glanced up from the outdoor caldron where she was washing the wool. "This is the last batch, I'm happy to say. I'm rinsing it now, and once I get it spread out to dry, I'll be finished. Why?"

"Well, given that Uncle Edward has planned the house-raising for Saturday, I thought we'd best lay in a supply of food. It's only right that we feed the workers. I've been baking bread all morning. I thought tomorrow I could make pies and cookies. You know what a sweet tooth Uncle Edward has. I can't imagine the other men will be much different."

"No, I don't suppose so." Hope finished rinsing the wool and began to pull it from the water. "We still have plenty of ham and smoked fish, and I could go into town and buy supplies. I sold quite a bit of yarn on credit to the Brick Store, so I could definitely load us up with sugar, flour, cornmeal, and whatever else you think we need."

"That sounds good. I know some of the wives will accompany their husbands, and most likely they'll bring food. Still, I think it's only right we supply the bulk of it. We'll definitely need more tea, and I heard Mrs. Masterson say there was a supply of lemons just brought up from California. We could make lemonade for the men and cool it in the creek."

Hope nodded and spread the wool out on the drying table. "I can go to town in half an hour, if you like."

"Good. I'll come too. I need to purchase more flannel to make diapers." Grace pulled off her apron. "I'll go speak with Mercy and see if she'd like to come along as well."

Oregon City felt crowded compared to their country farm. The streets were filled with animals and people alike and more traffic than Hope had ever seen. New people were always arriving, and houses were being built on city lots as fast as the mills could supply lumber. There were still repairs being made to some of the mills, but otherwise life was back to normal. With the addition of steamships coming to town, the place was starting to take on the feel of a large eastern city. Before long, they might even have that railroad everyone talked about.

Hope parked the wagon outside the Brick Store then helped Grace down. The trio made their way inside, where Grace was immediately set upon by a couple of women from church.

"How are you feeling, Grace?"

Her sister smiled and answered their questions, while Hope moved away to look at some of the new fabrics that had come in. Within minutes it seemed the store had filled up and the noise of chatter swelled in the air. The gossip and news of the day kept most of the customers occupied, and Hope couldn't help listening in on some of the conversations.

"Did you hear about the body they found in the river?" one woman asked another.

"Who was it?"

The first woman announced that the body was identified as Dr. Prigg, a man who'd disappeared the previous fall.

"Did he fall into the river and drown?" the other woman asked. "Perhaps he'd been drinking."

"No," her friend replied. "I heard from my husband that there were obvious blows to the head, so it was murder."

"No! Oh my! Do you suppose it was Indians? Do you suppose they're starting a war?"

Hope frowned. Murder was unusual, but arguments were known to get out of hand. No doubt this was one of those situations. Surely it didn't signal an Indian uprising, as the second woman suggested. Dr. Prigg had disappeared nearly a year ago, and if there were some sort of Indian war planned, it would have materialized before now.

"Hope, are you all right?" Mercy asked, coming alongside her. "You look upset."

Shaking her head, Hope forced a smile. "I'm fine."

"Did you hear that Judge Pratt has sailed for the States? I wish I could sail on the ocean. It sounds like great fun."

"It would take a long time, and I'm sure you'd tire of it soon enough."

Mercy shook her head. "Pastor Masterson said that they can get from San Francisco to New York in little over a month if all goes well. They take the freight and passengers across New Granada and the Isthmus of Panama. I learned about that in school. And there's going to be a railroad built there so it will be even faster. Just imagine it."

Grace approached. "The stock boy is loading our wagon, so let's go. I'd like to stop by the post office and then check in with Uncle Edward at the mill."

Hope drove them to the post office and waited while Grace went inside. It wasn't likely that mail would come this way from Alex. If he managed to send a letter, it would have to go by Indian runner or trapper to one of the forts and then get passed along to someone coming to Oregon City. Although, as Grace pointed out, with the official postal service available now, the forts were more inclined to use them.

When Grace returned to the wagon with a letter in hand, Hope couldn't contain her surprise. "Is it from Alex?"

Grace took her seat and shook her head. "No, it's from Eletta."

Hope tried not to react. Eletta and Grace exchanged letters regularly, but it always caused Hope a bit of discomfort. She knew Eletta would write about Faith, and in spite of herself, Hope couldn't help wanting to know how the little girl was faring.

"Will you read it to us?" Mercy asked from her perch behind the seat.

"I will, if Hope will drive us over to the sawmill," Grace replied, smiling.

Hope released the brake and snapped the lines. The horses began plodding down the street while Grace began to read.

"*My dearest friends, I wanted to write to you as soon as possible, given the Indian troubles in our area. I wanted to assure you that we are doing fine. There has been a great deal of strife between the settlers and the Indians. In many cases, however, rather than the Indians being responsible for the attack, it is instead the white miners. In some cases, the white men have been most brutal, killing Indian women and children. I think they're inclined to remember Dr. Whitman and all that happened at the mission. Still, it is hard to see God-fearing men act no better than heathens. Of course, the discovery of gold has brought that attitude about even without the help of the native peoples.*"

Hope listened as Grace continued.

"*But while the fighting goes on around us, our own Indians are quite happy to have us in their midst. Still, the violence makes Isaac question the wisdom of moving to the Rogue River area. I point out something that he has often said to me at such times: we came to do God's work and must go where He leads. Isaac agreed.*

Faith grows bigger every day. She is such a smart baby and will soon be two. She talks a storm, and I've even started teaching her to read. Perhaps it's because she is around adults who talk throughout the day. She's quite a pretty baby with her dark hair and blue eyes. The natives here love her and spoil her. They have all but made her one of their own."

It was hard for Hope to conjure an image of the child without remembering Tomahas. She realized she hadn't thought much of him lately. There had been so much to keep her busy that she'd fallen into bed exhausted each night and hadn't dreamed of much of anything. During the days, she had been focused on other things. Perhaps she was truly starting to be rid of the past.

"Faith babbles on with other children, and I believe she's learning their language as well as teaching them English. I've set up a little school for the Indians, and Faith, of course, accompanies me. She loves taking a seat and sits so quietly as I teach. She's such a dear little creature."

Hope found the news more interesting than she'd expected. Faith's accomplishments surprised her. Hope had never been one for book learning.

Grace finished the letter just as they reached the mill. Uncle Edward and Lance happened to be outside talking and immediately came to the wagon.

"Well, ladies, are you ready for Saturday?" Uncle Edward asked as Hope set the brake.

"We were in town for that very purpose," Grace replied. "I wanted to stop by and check with you as to whether we needed to do anything more than prepare food."

"Nope, we have everything else under control," their uncle assured her.

Lance said nothing, but Hope couldn't help glancing his way. He smiled, and she returned it with a nod. She hadn't seen much of him except at church, and his absence only seemed to make her think of him all the more.

"We'll be out there as soon as the sun's up," Edward said. "I figure we'll get the entire building up by nightfall if we keep at it all day."

"Goodness, I can't imagine that being possible, but I trust you know what you're doing."

"I do, and so do the others. I've gone over the plans Alex and I drew up with a couple of the men who work building houses. They're each going to head up a team and a specific part of the house." Edward grinned. "You'll see. It'll take no time at all to get the main structure up. By the way, why don't you come see what I have made for your kitchen?"

"May I come too?" Mercy asked.

Uncle Edward smiled. "Of course. Why don't you all come?"

He helped Grace from the wagon, and Lance came to assist Mercy. Once that was done, he turned to Hope.

"How have you been?" he asked.

"Busy. Summer is always busy, what with tending to the sheep, gardening, canning, and of course the added work related to the coming baby." She didn't follow the others into the mill, and Lance didn't seem to mind at all.

"You look very pretty in yellow."

His comment took her by surprise. Hope looked down at the blouse that had once been white. "I came by it quite by accident. I was dyeing wool and got some of the stain on my blouse, and I figured it was better to dye the rest of it than deem the blouse ruined."

"It's a pretty color, and it complements you nicely."

She wasn't used to such personal praise. "Thank you." The words were barely whispered, but she knew Lance heard them.

"Are you looking forward to the new house?"

She shrugged. "I suppose it will make things much easier on Grace. At least in some ways. She's never liked our current kitchen and cramped pantry. She wants a room all to itself where she can keep her herbs and vinegar."

"I can understand that. What about you? What kind of house would suit you?"

"Something small like we have now is just fine. Even smaller works for me. I liked the little cabin by the river. It was homey."

He chuckled. "If by homey you mean tiny, then I understand."

"It always felt . . . safe."

"I know that's important to you." He met her eyes. "I hope you feel safe with me."

She looked into his brown eyes and realized that truly was the difference with Lance. She felt a sense of security that she didn't feel with other men. Her heart seemed to skip a beat, and her voice was only a whisper. "Yes."

He grinned and stuffed his hands in his pockets. His chest puffed out a bit as he rocked back on his heels. "It's about time you admitted that."

Surprised by his reaction, Hope shook her head. "What are you getting at?"

"Only that we've got something special, you and me. Our friendship is . . . well, it's more."

"More than what?" she asked, her knees starting to feel weak.

His gaze never left hers. "More than friendship."

***

Hope kept thinking about what Lance had said at the sawmill. Throughout the night, she'd tossed and turned, trying to make sense of it all. Now it was Saturday, and people had been streaming onto the property since first light. Even with all her responsibilities, however, Lance and his comment weren't far from her thoughts.

She hadn't believed it possible to raise a house in a single day, but as the teams set to work, she began to see how it could be done. The logs were arranged for the exterior of the two-story house then carefully notched. As the height of the wall grew, the effort needed to raise the logs into place increased. The men created a system of ropes and pulleys, but coordinating it with the other walls of the house appeared daunting. The men, however, made the work seem almost easy.

With her sisters and the help of some of the other women, Hope served food and refilled glasses and canteens. She liked keeping busy with the food. What had started off looking like a feast big enough for an army quickly dwindled and sent Hope and Grace back to the kitchen throughout the day to retrieve or create additional fare.

The only real problem of the day came in the form of the men. When they weren't busy working, many of the gentlemen sought out Hope. Some just wanted to talk about their plans for the future. Others were more forward, asking her to marry them. The rumors of new land bills being put together by Congress included provisions for free land to be doled out in the territory. Married men would be given additional land, and this seemed to stir the men already desperate for a wife into a frenzy.

Hope dealt with each man in a polite but firm manner. She didn't feel it necessary to explain herself, but some of the men insisted on knowing why she was refusing them. They didn't think much of her response that she had no interest in marrying a man she didn't love.

"You look tired," Lance said as he came to get a quick bite of food.

"You too." Hope looked at the ever-growing structure that would soon be her home. "I can scarcely believe what you men have accomplished."

"Your uncle is a taskmaster, to be sure." He grinned. "But that's the only way to get it done. He's still determined the entire house and roof will be up before we leave tonight."

"I'm surprised he isn't insisting on finishing the interior as well." She smiled and held out a clean plate. "See anything you like?"

He paused for a moment and fixed his gaze on her. "I might. Seems like a lot of other fellows have found satisfaction at this table."

"Interest maybe, but not satisfaction," Hope countered. "We're not serving everything they're looking for." She marveled at the easy way she could banter with Lance. She hadn't been this lighthearted in years.

Lance laughed and took the plate. "Well, I just came for some of that roasted meat, a few thick slices of bread, and maybe some of that lemonade to wash it down."

"Then we can accommodate you just fine."

"Maybe you could come have a bite with me. I haven't seen you eat anything all day."

"You've been much too busy to see what I've been doing all day." But he was right, and Hope was getting hungry. She was about to accept his invitation when Mercy ran up.

"Hope, we're out of butter and Grace wants me to get some more, but I can't find it. Do you know where it is?"

She looked at Lance and shrugged. "Duty calls."

He looked momentarily disappointed then offered her a smile and a brief salute. Hope smiled in return, surprised at her own regret in having to go.

The hours passed by quickly, and Uncle Edward was as good as his word. By Saturday evening, after a day of continuous work, the new two-story log house stood about one hundred and fifty yards from the smaller house where they'd been living.

Workers, including Lance, were atop the roof, pounding away. The men were covered in sweat, as the day had been warm and sunny. The women and children were just as exhausted,

187

having fetched water and food throughout the day. The tables that had once been laden with food were now empty except for stacks of dirty dishes. Thankfully a good portion of the used silverware and dishes had been washed by some of the other women throughout the day.

"It's really something," Grace murmured, coming to stand beside Hope.

"It is. I can hardly believe it."

"Uncle Edward said that he and Lance will come by after work each evening to work on the interior. Toby Masterson also volunteered his labor whenever his uncle could spare him from his farm. I told them they could take their supper with us."

"I'm not surprised Toby offered to help. He's sweet on Mercy." Even now, Hope spied them across the field with the sheep. They had taken to walking out together whenever possible. She could only pray that Mercy would take time to grow up before making any big decisions.

"I did speak with her," Grace said, following Hope's gaze. "I cautioned her to take things slow and not be in a rush to marry just because the men around her are in a hurry. I reminded her of all the responsibilities we three share in our home and how, if she married, all of those duties would fall on her shoulders alone."

"And what did she say about that?" Hope turned to Grace. "Does she realize that marriage will mean an end to attending school?"

"She does. In fact, that was one of the things she brought up. She thinks she might like to attend college. Can you imagine it?" Grace smiled and shook her head. "I never figured we'd have a scholar amongst us."

By the time the light was nearly gone from the sky, Lance and Uncle Edward had finished the roof and returned to the ground. Most of the men and their families had headed home already, and only a handful of men remained. Hope was busy cleaning one of the tables when Lance approached.

"Where's your group of admirers? Or were they only here to fill their plates?"

Hope laughed. "I'll have you know I had four proposals of marriage and two requests to court." She noted the look of concern on Lance's face. "I thanked them kindly and told them no. I assure you, I know how to handle myself."

He relaxed a bit. "I've no doubt about that. I just think it in poor taste that a man would do such a thing, given the circumstances."

Hope stiffened. Her past, so often distant lately, seemed to rush back at her. "What do you mean?"

Lance didn't seem to realize her discomfort and laughed. "Well, given the event was to build a house, it just seems the wrong time to sweet-talk a woman with proposals."

Hope shook her head. "With you men, I've never known there to be a wrong time for such things. When I was a girl, I was once asked to court right after a funeral."

Lance smiled. "Well, given you were probably the prettiest one there, I can't say as I am surprised."

She thought it best to change the subject. Her feelings were starting to confuse her. "I appreciate all the work you did today. You and the others. I know it means a great deal to Grace. She and Alex have been planning and dreaming about this house for some time."

"Will you all live together in it?"

"I don't know. I suppose Mercy will. I've actually thought about staying in the smaller house and giving Alex and Grace some privacy. They haven't had much since marrying. The house we live in now is hardly bigger than your cabin. Speaking of which, do you plan to stay there? I thought you were bound for New Orleans."

"I've been contemplating my future," he replied, sounding almost distracted.

"And what conclusion have you reached?"

He shrugged. "New Orleans isn't going anywhere, so I don't need to rush back. Your uncle says I can stay as long as I like. It's a comfortable place."

"Until the river floods." She turned her attention back to gathering dishes. "I thought at first we might have too much food, but now I can see I was wrong. There's hardly even crumbs left."

"Hard work builds healthy appetites."

"Lance, you ready to head back to town?" Uncle Edward asked as he approached the table. "I sent Mina and the boys back with some of the others, but I thought I might borrow Grace's horse and ride back in with you."

"That'd be fine."

"Good. I'll go speak to my niece and get saddled up."

"Uncle Edward, thank you for all you did today." Hope walked around the table and stretched up on tiptoes to kiss him on the cheek.

When she pulled away, she caught her boot in the hem of her skirt and began to fall backwards. Lance quickly caught and righted her while Uncle Edward looked on in concern.

"Are you all right?" he asked.

"I'm fine. Just caught my boot."

"Well, if you're sure. I'll go speak with Grace. Good night, Hope."

"Good night." She watched him walk away, and only after he had disappeared from view did she realize Lance was still cradling her against his chest. She stiffened and stepped away in a hurry.

"Careful. You'll just end up on your backside," Lance said, grinning.

Hope felt her face flush and was glad that the evening shadows were too heavy to reveal her embarrassment. She thought about how nice it had been to be in his arms, and that only embarrassed her all the more.

"Thank you for catching me." She forced herself to look him in the eye.

He chuckled and gave her a little salute. "What are friends for?"

With that, he strode off toward the barn, leaving Hope to ponder his comment. She knew what most friends were for, but the thoughts she was having toward Lance were anything but ones of friendship, and suddenly she wasn't at all sure what Lance Kenner's purpose in her life might be.

Chapter 16

Word didn't reach Oregon City until September that President Taylor had died on July ninth from typhoid. Millard Fillmore was now the president, and it was said he would sign the bill making California a state, bypassing territorial status altogether. Lance knew this would only encourage the push to make Oregon a state as well. It was a good idea. A full-fledged state would have more say—more power.

"Hard to believe it takes so long to hear that our president has died," Edward said as he helped Lance finish an inventory of cut lumber.

"I remember when I rode to war with Mexico. We knew we were hundreds of miles from home, but a few days of hard riding would fix that. Then I came here, and it's like living on another continent—like being half a world away from all you know." Lance finished his count and tucked his pencil behind his ear. "Here are my figures." He handed a piece of paper to Edward.

The older man looked at the paper and nodded. "Looks

right. Thanks. The Schwartz brothers are bringing down a large number of logs tomorrow. I think we'll be able to make that California order without any problem."

"I'm glad. The men you've hired seem good. I've been impressed with their abilities, and they've taught me a lot."

"Two of them worked for me before. They know what they're doing, as they did the same kind of work back east. Fact is, they taught me a lot, too." Edward grinned and put the paper in his pocket. "I'm mighty pleased with you as well. You've picked up your duties as if you were born to them. I know you fancy yourself a lawyer, but you've proven yourself a decent mill man as well."

Lance chuckled. "It's harder work, to be sure. Law mainly taxes the brain. Mill work taxes the body *and* the brain. And if you're not aware of both, you could end up injured or dead. It's definitely a different challenge."

"Have you given any thought to staying on?"

Lance could hardly admit to Hope's uncle that he was having a lot of thoughts about staying in Oregon City, and all of them centered on his niece. "I'm thinking on it. It's a nice town, and as you said, the river traffic is picking up to such a degree that Oregon City is bound to become a bustling city before long."

"That's true enough." Edward pulled out his watch. "It's about time to call it a day. Want to follow me home for supper?"

Lance rarely turned down an opportunity to share one of Mina Marsh's meals, but he already had plans. "I'm actually having supper with your nieces. Grace invited me at church on Sunday. I figured I might even get some interior work done on the new house."

"I plan to go out there tomorrow. Toby Masterson said he could come too."

"I'll be able to help then as well." Lance rolled down his shirt sleeves. "I thought I'd swing by the post office and see if they had any mail for Mrs. Armistead. I know she's worried about her husband returning."

"Poor Grace. If she doesn't hear from him soon, I'll have to do something about it. Maybe I'll send you to Fort Vancouver and then upriver to Fort Nez Perce. At least they might have seen something of him on his journey from one Indian village to another."

Lance forced himself not to react. He was still struggling to let go of the past and all that Alex represented. For days, even weeks, he'd go along without even thinking about it, then someone would mention Alex, and Lance could feel his body tense.

"Come on. I'll walk with you to the post office."

Edward led the way, and Lance was forced to catch up. Edward Marsh was a big man—broad-shouldered and ham-fisted. Lance stood nearly six foot, but Marsh towered over him. He couldn't imagine getting into a fight with him. Size alone would give Edward the advantage, but he wasn't a brawler. His gentle nature made him a favorite of the area children and adults alike. Lance truly admired him.

"So have you given God any more thought?" Edward asked, surprising Lance.

"I have. I'm just not sure I have all the right answers."

Edward laughed. "Show me one man who does. Just don't make it harder than it has to be. People assume that because it's the Holy God of the universe, it has to be complicated." He shook his head. "But it's not. It's just a matter of heart, and when you put your trust in the Lord, everything else falls into place."

The words pierced Lance's heart. He wanted to believe them. Wanted to believe that being right with God was just that simple.

Edward said nothing more until they reached the post office.

"We've come to get the mail," Edward announced, "if you have any for us. For Grace Armistead as well. Lance here is riding out to their place and figured he could take anything that might have come for her."

"I do have a letter for Mrs. Armistead. Just came in the mail pouch from Fort Vancouver." The postmaster quickly retrieved it. "Nothing for the two of you, however." He handed Lance the letter.

"I don't know anyone who'd send me a letter anyway," Edward replied with a grin. "Sure glad to see something's come for Grace. No doubt it's a letter from that rascal husband of hers."

Lance pocketed the envelope, and together they headed toward the livery. "I'm glad he's finally written. Hope said Grace has been pretty much beside herself."

"That she has. I've never seen two people more in love, unless it's myself and the missus. Never thought I'd find me a gal like Mina. She's a treasure, to be sure."

Lance didn't reply. He was still guarded about his feelings for Hope, and even within his own heart, he was finding it hard to put them into perspective.

They came to a stop in front of the livery, and Edward gave a nod. "You'd best be on your way. Let Grace know I'll be out tomorrow to work on the house. Since you plan to go as well, what say you get Grace to let you bring her wagon back to town tonight so we can load it up with lumber before we come out? I'm sure she won't mind."

"I'll do it," Lance promised.

His ride out to the Armistead farm was easy enough. The roads were dry, but the air was considerably cooler in the shade of the tall firs that lined the road. When he reached the open area of pasture that signaled the start of the Armistead property, still well away from the house, he spotted Hope walking among the sheep. As he neared, the sheep began bleating and gathered around their mistress. Hope looked up and gave him a wave.

Lance climbed down from his horse and walked to where she stood. The light on her face gave her an angelic appearance. He chuckled to himself. Hope would have laughed at that thought and told him she was no angel.

"I see you made it," she said as he joined her.

"I did. I would have been here sooner, but I stopped at the post office to see if there might be any mail for you or your sisters."

"And was there?"

He pulled out the letter. "One for Grace."

Hope took the envelope and frowned. "It looks like a man's script, but it's not Alex's. He has a good hand and writes well." She looked up at Lance. "We should get back to the house right away. I have a bad feeling about this."

He frowned. He hadn't considered that the letter would be from anyone but Alex. "How can I help?"

"Just ride behind the flock in case one of them decides to go off on her own."

She handed him the letter then quickly rallied the bell ewe, offering a handful of grain as an incentive as she led the way to the house. Lance rode behind the sheep as Hope had requested, but none of the animals seemed inclined to leave the flock. Twenty minutes later, they reached the fenced pasture, and he rode ahead to open the gate. Once the sheep were safely inside the pen, Lance climbed down from his horse as Hope secured the gate. They walked toward the house in silence. Hope's concern about the letter had put a damper on any further conversation, and once Lance tied off his horse, they exchanged a brief glance.

"It'll be all right," he assured. At least he hoped it would be. He couldn't imagine what would happen if the letter bore word of Alex's death.

"Grace!" Hope called as they entered the house. "Grace, where are you?"

"You needn't yell. I'm in the kitchen."

Hope made her way through the house with Lance just steps behind her. He tried to keep a positive spirit. Alex might have been his one-time enemy but in the last few minutes, knowing he might be dead, Lance knew he didn't want Alex to come to harm.

Grace beamed at him. "I'm so glad you could make it. Supper is ready."

"Lance brought a letter for you from town." Hope looked to Lance. He handed her the letter, and she in turn extended it to Grace.

For a moment Grace did nothing but stare at the handwriting. Finally, after a long silence, she snatched the envelope from Hope's hand. Her hand was trembling.

She scanned the contents, turning pale and reaching out for the table for support. "Alex has been hurt. A bear attack. It happened after he and Sam parted company and Sam returned to his people."

Lance stepped forward. "Here, have a seat." He led her to a chair and helped her sit. "Does it say how bad off he is?"

Grace nodded. "It says he was near death for some time." Tears came to her eyes. "He's rallied enough to ask that they send me a letter."

"Where is he?" Hope asked, kneeling beside Grace's chair.

"Fort Nez Perce. He's too ill and wounded to move. The factor there assures me that he's on the mend, but it will be weeks before he's well enough to travel."

Hope took hold of Grace's hand. "He's alive, Grace. You must think on that. He's alive, and you know how determined he is. I'm sure he'll make it through."

"But I can't go to him. The baby . . ." She left the rest unsaid.

Lance heard the anguish in her voice. "I'm sure they'll take good care of him, Grace."

She shook her head. "I don't even know if they have a doctor."

"Grace," Hope said in an authoritative manner, "you've had a shock and should lie down for a rest. Lance will help me get you to your bed, and then I'll finish up supper while you rest." She got to her feet, took the letter from Grace, and put it on the table. "Lance?"

He stepped forward and offered Grace his arm. She looked at him for a moment then got to her feet. She was no more than a few seconds standing, however, when she fainted.

Lance easily lifted her into his arms. "Where's her room?"

Hope led the way and pulled down the covers on the bed before Lance deposited Grace.

"I'll get a cold cloth for her head. Would you stay with her?" Hope asked.

"Of course." He stared down at the petite woman lying before him. This was the wife of his enemy. He shook his head, determined to put the past behind him. He didn't want any enemies.

Hope returned and sat next to her sister. She wiped Grace's forehead and cheeks with the cloth. Grace began to rally and opened her eyes. For a moment she looked confused, and then she seemed to remember.

"Oh, I'm sorry. I must have given you all a fright."

"You owe us no apology," Lance assured.

Hope smiled. "Just rest, Grace. I doubt you've eaten much all day, so I'm going to fix you a tray." She got to her feet then waggled her finger. "Don't you even think of getting up."

Grace smiled. "You sound just like Mama used to."

"You aren't the only one who can administer tender but firm care." Hope motioned to Lance. "Come help me in the kitchen."

"Yes, ma'am." He answered her with no less respect than he would have given his captain.

In the kitchen, Lance watched Hope gather things for Grace's supper.

"She's been working at this all day," Hope said. "She wanted to serve you a decent meal. So much of the time we just catch a bite on the run. There's so much work to be done that sitting down to a meal seems a waste."

"I wish she hadn't gone to such trouble." Lance could see a roast of some sort on a large platter, surrounded by large potatoes and whole carrots. Rolls filled a basket, and a pie of some sort sat alongside this. "I wouldn't have accepted her invitation if I'd known."

"Well, she would have just kept nagging you. You've been so good, helping finish the house, that she wanted to do something nice for you." Hope finished arranging the tray. "There, I'll take this to her. Why don't you go wash up out back? Mercy will be just about done with her gardening, so you can let her know we're ready to eat."

Lance nodded and exited the room without another word. He didn't like the idea of Grace being indisposed on his account. Should anything happen to her or the babe she carried, he would never forgive himself.

Mercy was already at the pump when he arrived. "I saw your horse and knew you must be here and that Grace would be ready for us to sit down to supper," she said.

"Your sister has had a letter." Lance took the bar of soap Mercy offered and tried to think of how to break the news gently.

"From Alex?" she asked, unable to hide her excitement.

"About him."

Her expression quickly changed. "Is he dead?"

"No." Lance began to soap up his hands. "He was wounded

200

in a bear attack. It was severe, but they're hopeful of his recovery."

"Who is?" she barely whispered.

"The factor at Fort Nez Perce. Apparently someone found him and took him there."

"Grace must be so upset."

"She was. She's resting in bed now."

Mercy grabbed a towel from the hook near the pump. She dried her hands quickly. "I'll see you in the house. I want to check on her."

Lance nodded and finished washing. He considered just heading back to town, leaving the sisters to focus their energies on Grace, but then thought better of it. What if they needed something?

He made his way back into the house and found that Hope had laid the table and was bustling around the kitchen. "Can I help?" he asked.

She shook her head. "I think everything is ready. I just put the platter on the table." She motioned Lance to take a seat.

Mercy came to join them, her face serious. "She's still so pale."

"It's not easy to carry a child and work so hard, much less get bad news," Hope replied, taking her seat.

"How would you know?" Mercy asked.

This seemed to take Hope aback. For a moment, Lance thought she looked embarrassed. "Grace has taught me a great deal," she said then regained her composure. "You'd do well to let her teach you a thing or two."

Mercy said nothing more on the matter and instead bowed her head. "It's my turn to pray."

The trio said very little as they ate. The food was delicious, but Lance wasn't sure what he could offer in the way of comfort to either young woman, so he remained silent. This apparently suited Hope and Mercy, because they didn't attempt to engage him in conversation.

"Well, I've had my fill," he said after finishing off his second piece of apple pie. "I'm going to work on the house. Tomorrow your uncle and I are coming out, and Toby Masterson is coming too."

This brought a smile to Mercy's face. "When will you arrive?"

"Early. Your uncle wants me to take your wagon back to town tonight so we can load it up with lumber tomorrow."

"That won't be a problem," Hope said, getting to her feet. "I'll help you when you're ready to head back." She lit a lamp and brought it to the table. "You'll need this. There are others out there you can light."

Lance took the lamp, his fingers brushing hers as he did. She startled and jumped back, almost causing him to drop the lamp.

"I'm sorry," she said then hurried back to the stove. "I'm afraid I'm still shaken by the news of Alex."

"It's all right." He didn't think that was all there was to it but decided against pressing her for more.

The new house was coming right along, and Lance was proud to have been a part of its building. He'd never done this kind of work before, but he enjoyed it very much. He also found it rather healing. He knew it was the same as working for Alex Armistead, but even more, he was working for Hope and her sisters.

As Lance worked on the second-floor walls, his thoughts were ever on Hope and her sisters. He wished he could offer some help but had no idea what it might be. Perhaps once Edward knew about the circumstances, he could come up with something.

He also thought about Alex lying near death. There was no joy in the thought as there once might have been. In fact, just the opposite was true. Perhaps God had truly taken the desire for revenge from his heart.

"Lance, are you here?"

It was Hope. He smiled. "Where else would I be?"

"Where are you?" she called from below.

He laughed. "I'm upstairs."

He heard her footsteps as she climbed and waited near the top to get her reaction.

"Oh, my, you've done a great deal in three hours."

"Three hours?" He looked at his pocket watch. "The time really got away from me."

"I thought it might have. I've hitched the horse to the wagon and put your gelding in the pen with plenty of hay."

"Thank you. Let me put these tools away, and I'll be right down."

She didn't seem inclined to leave, however. Without another word, she wandered past him. He'd managed to put up the framework for two of the bedrooms and knew it had captivated her attention.

"The rooms look like they'll be big."

"They'll look smaller once all the walls are in place."

She smiled and stepped back. "I'm sure it's going to make Grace very happy."

"And what about you?"

"Me?" He could see the surprise in her expression.

"Will it make you happy? Are you happy?"

Hope glanced at the ground for a moment then raised her eyes to his. "I'm happier than I was a few months ago. I don't think about the massacre or . . . anything related to it very often."

Despite the large open area, Lance felt as if the space had

grown smaller. He wanted nothing more than to feel her in his arms again. "What do you think about?" His voice was low, almost inaudible.

She held his gaze. Surely she felt something for him. Something more than friendship. He wanted to press her for answers but knew it would only frighten her.

"I . . . uh. . . ." She shook her head as if to shake off the intensity of the moment. "I think about the sheep and about my spinning and of course the future." Her words came fast and without emotion. "I think I can support myself nicely by spinning yarn and selling it, so long as Grace allows me the wool. If I keep busy, it helps me forget."

Lance crossed his arms and leaned back against the wall. "Just so long as you don't forget your friends."

She studied him for a moment then turned for the stairs. "I never forget about people who are important to me."

He stood there as she made her way downstairs. It wasn't much, but it was something—something that offered assurance that she saw him as important. Maybe even important enough that he could play a role infinitely more intimate than a friend.

Chapter 17

A cold rain fell on the Saturday in September when Uncle Edward and his family, along with Lance and Toby Masterson, moved the last of the furniture into the new house. Hope was amazed at how quickly it had all come together. She followed the men, drying off pieces of furniture as they were set in place. Grace sat nearby with Baby John, directing everyone as to where she wanted things.

Hope had planned to remain in the old house, but Grace begged her to join them, at least until Alex returned, and given her promise to Alex, Hope felt she could do nothing else. She didn't want there to be any strain on Grace during her pregnancy. Learning about Alex's injuries had been more than enough.

The room Hope had chosen for her own was one of those Lance had been working on the night he'd asked her what she thought about. That conversation had stayed with her, making her more aware that her feelings for Lance had changed. She had been surprised that night by the longing that had revealed itself. She hadn't felt this way since her time with Johnny Sager.

We're only friends. Just friends.

But no matter how many times she reminded herself of this, her heart cried out for more.

"Cousin Grace said this trunk belongs to you," Phillip said.

Hope nodded and took the small trunk. "I'll take care of it."

She headed upstairs just as Uncle Edward declared from the foyer that everything had been moved. Entering her room, Hope looked around. The bed had been put in order along with her small dresser. The latter had been built by one of Uncle Edward's friends and given to her on her birthday last year.

Behind the door, her two other dresses and a skirt hung on pegs. They had been washed and ironed just the day before. In fact, all of their dirty clothes had been laundered. Grace said it would be nice to move into the new house with a fresh start, but Hope wondered just how far that concept should extend.

She put the trunk aside and sighed. She was troubled, but not for the reasons she once had been. Now her mind was consumed with questions about her future and what she wanted from it. The only thing she knew for certain was that she wanted Lance to be in it.

She sank to the edge of her bed. How had this happened? She'd guarded her heart so carefully. After the massacre, she had planned never to marry. After giving birth to Faith, she had vowed never to have children. Now her feelings were contradicting her plans.

Downstairs she heard the laughter of her family and wanted to join them, but she was afraid of how she might behave now that she'd allowed herself to understand the turmoil in her heart. Lance was down there, and she feared he'd immediately see through her façade of indifference. But she had planned a surprise birthday dinner for him and Mercy, and she needed to get the food on the table.

She went to the window and noticed it had stopped raining. The skies were still overcast, however, and no doubt more rain would come. She sighed. "I can't stay up here forever."

She made her way downstairs, admiring the smoothness of the railing. She wondered if Lance had been responsible for it.

"There you are," Grace said, appearing at the bottom of the steps. "I was just about to come looking for you."

"Did you need something?"

Grace laughed. "No, silly. I wanted you to hear the wonderful news." She pulled Hope along the hall and into one of two front sitting rooms. Uncle Edward and Lance stood by the fireplace, warming themselves. Both looked up when the ladies entered the room. Their uncle was grinning from ear to ear, but Lance looked more stunned than anything else.

"Uncle Edward is sending Lance to bring Alex home," Grace announced.

Hope looked at Lance and saw concern in his expression. "That's wonderful news and very kind of you, Lance. I know Grace will rest better when Alex is back under her care."

"That's what I figure," Uncle Edward replied.

"Isn't it marvelous?" Grace said with more excitement than Hope had seen out of her in some time. Even the new house hadn't brought this degree of joy.

"It is." She smiled at Grace then turned to Lance. "When will you leave?"

"They want me to go tomorrow. I'm to go by river. Should take me about two, maybe three weeks, depending on the weather and . . . any other complications."

He spoke in such a distracted manner that Hope watched him for a moment. He wasn't at all his usual jovial self. Was he worried about the trip? Perhaps he feared something might happen to Alex on the way back and he'd be blamed. There were all sorts of perils on the journey to and from Fort Nez Perce. She remembered how terrified she'd been.

"The girls have made lunch for us," Grace interjected. "Let's go eat and finish deciding all the details."

Hope hurried into the kitchen, and she and Mercy set the table as the others came into the dining room. Once the food was on the table and everyone was seated, Hope brought in the birthday cake. She had purposely seated Lance with his back to the kitchen so she could bring in the dessert unnoticed.

She set the cake down in front of him. "Surprise!" everyone declared at once.

Lance, who already seemed stunned by the trip he was to make, was rendered speechless for several moments.

"I don't know what to say." He looked up at Hope.

She smiled. "I'm glad I didn't wait until tomorrow, or we'd be celebrating your birthday without you."

He smiled, and for a moment Hope felt like they were the only two people in the room. "Thank you," he murmured then turned to the others. "Thanks to all of you. This was very unexpected."

"Good," Uncle Edward said. "That's the way we planned it. I'm glad we had the heavy work and talk of the trip as a diversion. Otherwise I was afraid I might slip up."

"But there's more." Grace nodded to Hope.

Hope went back to the kitchen to bring out another cake.

"Two cakes!" Oliver exclaimed, his eyes wide. "We get two cakes?"

"We do," Hope said, smiling. "We're celebrating more than one birthday. In a few days Mercy will be fifteen, so we thought we'd surprise her as well."

Mercy looked delighted as everyone wished her a happy birthday. "How did you manage to make another cake without me realizing it?"

Hope laughed. "That's a secret."

Mercy looked at Lance. "Did you know about this?"

He shook his head. "I didn't have a clue. I guess they've managed to surprise us both."

"Well, I'm glad to share my birthday with you," Mercy replied. "We'll have to pack some of the leftover cake for you to take on your trip."

Bringing up the trip immediately caused the conversation to head off in that direction. It continued that way throughout lunch, though Hope noticed Lance hardly said a word. Uncle Edward's boys gobbled down their food and two pieces of cake each, then hurried off to see what kind of mischief they could get into. As the adults finished eating, Mercy volunteered to move the sheep, and Toby offered to help her. The young couple quickly deserted, no doubt anxious to be alone.

"I'm going to pack a bag of medicinal herbs and tonics for you," Grace told Lance. "I'll show you how to use them and what each one does. I'm certain it will be better than anything they're doing for him at the fort."

"They could have one of the Nez Perce women working on him," Edward offered. "They know a lot about herbs."

"True, but most likely there's just a handful of men getting ready to head out trapping. I can't imagine any of them will give Alex much attention once they focus on their livelihood."

Hope said nothing, continuing to watch Lance. What was he thinking? He seemed so troubled.

Baby John grew fussy, and Mina said, "I think we should be going."

Uncle Edward nodded and got to his feet. "She's right. Tomorrow's Sunday, and that means baths for all. The boys like that about as much as they like sittin' through church." He smiled and took the baby from Mina, then helped her to her feet.

"I hope you have a very happy birthday," Mina told Lance.

"I nearly forgot," Grace said, getting to her feet. "We have a present for you." She disappeared then returned with a folded quilt. "The girls and I thought you might need this, since the days have grown much cooler." She handed the gift to Lance.

He looked at the quilt and then to Grace and Hope. "Did you make this?"

"We ladies did," Grace replied, nodding at Mina and Hope. "Mercy helped too. We almost always have quilting projects in process. I hope you like it."

"I do. Very much."

He still wasn't himself. Maybe he was tired, or maybe his mind was on the trip to come. No matter his thoughts, however, they were clearly weighing heavy on him.

"A good quilt is always a welcome addition to a house," Uncle Edward said. "Now, if you'll excuse us, we'll round up our boys and head home."

Grace followed them out, leaving Hope with Lance.

"All right, what's wrong?" she asked.

He frowned and looked at her oddly. "What do you mean?"

"I can tell something isn't right. You seem upset about something, and as your friend, I thought I would ask."

He shook his head. "I'm fine." His clipped tone betrayed the lie. "I'm just surprised . . . that's all." He got up from the table with his quilt in hand and moved into the front sitting room.

Hope followed him. He went to stand by the fireplace, still holding the quilt. The fire had died down considerably during their lunch, so she added more wood, saying nothing while she stoked up the fire. Finally, she had no reason to keep poking at the logs and straightened.

"You aren't fine. You're upset about something. You don't

have to talk to me about it, but maybe you should talk to Uncle Edward."

"It's all right. I just hadn't planned to head out into Indian country again."

"I imagine that's a daunting prospect. I certainly couldn't do it." She remembered the trip she'd made from Fort Nez Perce to Fort Vancouver. The whole way she had feared the boat would be attacked and they'd be taken hostage again by the Cayuse. She shuddered and forced the thought away. "Hopefully now that there are so many soldiers around Fort Vancouver and The Dalles, it won't be such a risk."

He nodded but continued to study the flames. Hope had never seen him like this.

"Lance, you aren't at all yourself. If there's something else, you should say so. No one will force you to go if you're . . . troubled by it."

"I'm fine!" he snapped. "Mind your own business."

Her eyes widened in surprise, but rather than silence her, his words only emboldened her. She planted her hands on her hips. "I am minding my business. My sister is my business, and this trip is to help her."

He shook his head, and his voice dropped low. "Then go help her. I'm neither your husband nor your beau, so you have no right to question me."

He stormed from the room and headed out the front door.

Hope marched right after him. "I'm glad you aren't either of those things to me. Frankly, if this is how you see friendship, I'd just as soon not have any part of your romance."

He whirled around and opened his mouth to reply, but then closed it and shook his head. "I'm going to saddle my horse. Tell Grace to have that bag ready for me so I can head back to town."

"Tell her yourself. She's just around the corner of the house!"

Hope knew she was being rude, but his attitude and words had hurt her.

She left him standing there and made her way toward the smaller house. She didn't want to see anyone in her current state of mind. Edward and the others would be near the barn and pen, and Mercy and Toby would be with the sheep, so the empty house would give her quiet solitude. If anyone came looking for her and asked why she was there, she could always tell them she was making sure they hadn't forgotten anything.

She entered the house just as the rain began again. The cold permeated the thin cloth of her gown, and she rubbed her arms to keep warm. Gazing around the empty room only made her feel worse.

"What purpose does it serve, Lord, for me to realize how much I care about him if he doesn't return my feelings?" She whispered the prayer, all the time shaking her head. "I'm so confused. I don't know what to do."

Indifference had served her well before, so perhaps that was what she needed. She squared her shoulders and strengthened her resolve. She wouldn't be moved by this.

"I don't care about him."

But even as she spoke, she knew it was a lie.

Chapter 18

Lance hated himself for the way he'd treated Hope, but how could he tell her that the past had risen up like a beast and destroyed his peace of mind? No one had asked him if he was willing to retrieve Alex. Edward and Grace had been talking about it one minute, and the next Edward was saying he would pay Lance to go to Fort Nez Perce and bring Alex home. Lance hadn't even had a chance to refuse, because Grace began to cry in gratitude.

Unable to make sense of the mess, he put the quilt aside. He grabbed his saddle and flung it atop his mount, muttering to himself the whole time. He thought his anger toward Alex was dead and buried. Why did he feel like this now? And why were thoughts of killing Alex in his head?

"I'm not a murderer."

He tightened the cinch, remembering the men he'd killed in the war. He'd hated it. Hated knowing that he'd ended a man's life, and yet now he was thinking how easy it would be to smother a sick, helpless man. If Alex died that way, no one would think anything of it. They'd simply believe he had succumbed to his wounds.

The idea disturbed Lance immensely. The fact that the thought was his own made it all the worse.

With the horse saddled, Lance stepped outside the barn to see if he could spot Grace. She and Edward were near the large pen, where Edward was wrangling his boys. Mina and the baby sat in the wagon near the side of the house. Lance knew he couldn't wait around for Grace to produce the bag of medicine. He had to get away before he said something he'd regret.

No, I've already done that.

Again Hope's hurt expression came to mind. It had been so fleeting that another man might have missed it, but not Lance. He'd learned to read her and knew just how much he'd hurt her.

He marched back into the barn to retrieve his horse. Just as he started to mount, he spied the quilt. Hope had gone out of her way to plan a birthday party for him, and she and her sisters had made a beautiful quilt for him, and this was how he thanked them. He picked up the gift and stuffed it as best he could inside his coat to keep it from getting too wet. He thought about seeking out Hope to apologize, but fear held him in place. If he went to her, something inside him knew it would be a disaster.

He mounted and made his way out of the barn, and no one threw so much as a glance his way. He knew he should wait, but he couldn't. He had to get away from this place and these people. He slapped the reins and kicked his heels against the gelding's side, causing the horse to spring into a trot. That wasn't enough, however, and Lance pushed the horse to go faster and faster. The rain soaked through his coat, leaving him cold and uncomfortable, but he didn't care. He was barely holding his own in a war between his heart and his mind.

"If you ever have a chance to make Armistead pay for what he did," his brother Marshall had said as they led him off to prison, *"do it. Do whatever you can to end his life."*

Until now, that had been nothing more than the angry words of a man about to face several years in prison. Alex had disappeared from New Orleans and no one knew where he'd gone, so challenging him to a duel or even murdering him in his sleep hadn't been a possibility the then-twelve-year-old Lance could consider.

Then there was his father begging him to make peace with the past.

"I thought I had made peace."

He looked at the rainy skies overhead. Edward had told him that peace only came through God. Hope had said Grace gave her the same advice.

Hope.

He'd treated her abominably and would have to rectify that before he left. He supposed part of his reaction had been his own pent-up frustration. He had fallen in love with her and didn't know how to win her over. He had promised he only wanted friendship, but now he wanted so much more.

Once he reached Oregon City, Lance forced himself to slow the horse. He had no desire to bring attention to himself, nor did he want to stop and speak to anyone. Thankfully, because of the rain, there were few people out. Beyond a nod here or there, no one seemed at all interested in where he was headed.

The rain was falling harder by the time he reached the cabin. Lance saw to the horse, then made his way into the house, soaking wet. His first order of business was to start a fire. After that, he draped the damp quilt over a couple chairs, then shed his wet clothes and hung them around the living room to dry.

He dressed in the only other pair of long underwear and

trousers he had and found dry socks and a shirt. The comfort of the fire and dry clothes settled his temper somewhat. He pushed the worn settee closer to the fire then plopped down onto it, shaking his head.

"What's wrong with me? Why did I act like that? I was determined to put aside the past and make peace with Armistead, and now everything has changed." It made no sense, and Lance wondered if this was the way it would always be.

Only if you want it to be.

Lance looked up, expecting to find someone there, but the room was empty. Still, the words had seemed almost audible.

"But I don't want it to be that way. I'm in love with his sister-in-law. I can't hate him or cause him harm and expect to win her love. Then again, given the way I just treated her, I can't expect to win her love at all now."

He pounded his fist against his thigh. The turmoil was overwhelming. He sat in front of the fire, adding a log from time to time and trying to sort through his heart. Finally, he felt there was no other choice but to turn it over to God. It was much too great a burden to keep carrying himself.

"God, I don't know if I'm doing this by the book or not, but I'm sick and tired of myself, and I need Your help. Edward said it started with believing and confessing, and I guess that's what I'm trying to do now. I have all this hate and anger inside me. I thought I left it back in New Orleans after Father's death. I thought I could just make peace with the past and all that happened, but I don't seem to be doing a very good job of it."

A log rolled off the burning stack of wood and onto the stones around the fireplace. Retrieving the poker, Lance pushed it back into the hearth. He stared into the flames and thought of the fire that Marshall had set—the fire that had killed Alex's parents. He put himself in Alex's place. How would he have handled the matter? Had Alex been able to forget the past, or would he want to exact revenge on Lance once he knew who he was?

"I'm a hateful man, Lord. Ungrateful and full of anger. I confess that. I know I've made a lot of mistakes and bad choices, but I need to be forgiven. I need to find peace, Lord, or I can't make this trip tomorrow. Please forgive me and set me free. I want to please You and live by Your Word. I don't know exactly how to do it, but I remember my mother telling me that I should honor You above all else, and that's what I plan to do. I'll get a Bible and start reading it, and I'll be faithful to pray. Just please—please take away this ugliness from my heart."

Lance slept amazingly well after his time of prayer. He couldn't say that everything had come around right, but a definite peace had washed over him. When he awoke that morning, Lance knew he had to write Hope a letter and pray that she'd forgive him.

With only a few minutes to spare before he needed to head down to the dock, Lance took up his pencil and a piece of paper.

Hope, please forgive me for the way I acted. I can't explain in this letter, but I promise I will upon my return. I can't bear that I hurt you, and I don't offer any justification for my temper, because there is none. Just know that I hold our friendship very dear and would rather drown in the river than hurt you like that again.

He read over what he'd written. It seemed so little to counteract all the pain he'd inflicted. For now, however, it was the best he could offer. He signed his name, then folded the paper three times and dripped wax on it to seal it. He'd stop by Edward's and ask him to take it to Hope. He'd also apologize for leaving without saying good-bye last night.

Before he could gather his bag and leave, however, a knock sounded at his door. Opening it revealed a frowning Edward Marsh.

"I meant to come over here last night," Edward said without preamble, "but the baby was colicky, and Mina needed help with the boys."

"Is Baby John all right?"

Edward's expression relaxed a bit. "He is. Some of Grace's tonic fixed him right up." He held up a carpetbag. "Speaking of Grace, that's why I'm here. She sent these things and wrote instructions for how to use them. She was mighty upset that you'd taken off without waiting for them."

"I'm sure. I'm afraid I was in an ill temper last night, and I apologize. In fact, I was just on my way to your house. I'm sorry for the way I acted. I guess there was just a lot boiling up inside me. Hope and I argued, and I knew I had to leave before I lost my temper in full. I hope you won't hold that against me."

"Of course not," Edward replied. "You know you can always talk to me if you need to."

"I do. Fact is, I spent a good deal of time talking to God about it. I heeded your advice about believing and confessing."

Edward's face broke into a smile. "Well, if that don't beat all. That's good to hear, Lance. Real good."

Lance took the bag from Edward. "I need to hurry, but I wonder if you'd do me a favor and deliver this letter to Hope. It's an apology."

The older man took the letter and stuck it in his coat pocket. "I'll take it out there this morning. Can I help you with your things?"

Lance picked up his bag and shook his head. "I'll be fine."

And for maybe the first time in his life, he honestly felt the truth in that statement.

Grace walked out of the new house toward the chicken coop. She pulled her shawl close against the damp chill and prayed for the hundredth time that morning for Alex's swift recovery. She'd had no other letter from him since the one that informed her of his injuries. It had been hard not to defy sense and reason and jump on the first boat to Fort Vancouver, but she knew that would be foolish.

She put her hand on her protruding stomach and tried to reclaim the joy she'd felt when she first realized she carried Alex's child. So much had happened in the last four months, and all of it seemed unimportant except this. The baby was more important than anything else, and Grace knew she would do whatever she had to in order to reach a safe delivery.

Gathering eggs, she prayed for Lance to bring Alex home safely. She asked for Alex to have a miraculous healing—the same prayer she'd prayed since hearing the news of his condition. She prayed too for her sisters. Hope had been troubled after Lance's rapid departure. Grace thought Hope had feelings for Lance, but her sister declared them only friends. Still, friendship was the very best place to start a journey toward falling in love.

"Grace?"

She straightened and saw Hope standing in the doorway. "I'm just getting the eggs."

"I could have done that. You should have stayed in bed where it was warm."

Grace smiled and joined her sister, careful to keep the still-warm eggs safe in the fold of her apron. "I'm perfectly healthy and able to do my share of the work around here."

Hope nodded. "I know you are, but I . . . well, this baby . . ." She let the words trail off.

Grace looked at her sister and realization dawned. Hope had carried a baby too, but that pregnancy had been unwanted. Hope had desperately wanted to lose the child—to be rid of that final reminder of the wrong done to her and the others.

"Hope, I worry that my condition might be too hard on you."

"It's not that," Hope said, shaking her head. "That is, well, it's something to do with that, but not in the sense that it bothers me or makes me wish to be elsewhere. I just know that as much as I didn't want my child, you want yours. And I want it for you. I don't want anything to happen to you. I promised Alex I'd take care of you."

Grace smiled. She held such admiration for her sister. "Hope, you have changed so much from that silly, flirtatious girl who came west. So many times I've chided myself for ever forcing that move on you and Mercy, but you've turned out to be an amazing woman of strength, and I know Mama and Da would have been proud of you."

Her words seemed to take Hope by surprise. "I'd like to think that's true. I know Mama used to worry about me being flighty and full of nonsense." She smiled. "And I was."

Grace laughed. "Yes, but everyone has the ability to change— with God's help."

"I've thought a lot about God lately," Hope admitted. "I want you to know I'm on the right path where He's concerned. I know I pushed Him away at one time, but I know too that I was wrong. You've helped me see that more than anyone, and I know Mama and Da would be proud of you as well. You've done so much to keep us all together. I just want to return the favor."

Grace shifted her hold on the apron and leaned sideways to

give Hope a hug. There were tears in her eyes when she straightened back up. "No matter what, we're going to have a good life here."

Hope nodded. "Yes. I believe that too. I couldn't always, but I do now."

"There you are," Mercy declared, coming into the coop. "I was looking all over for you, Hope. Uncle Edward stopped by and brought you this." She held out a letter. "He said it was from Lance."

Hope hurried to Mercy and took the letter from her sister's hand. Grace saw the look that passed over Hope's face as she read the note. She was in love with Lance, of that Grace was certain. Her expression betrayed it, but so did her quick response to the letter.

"Hope, is everything all right?"

Hope looked up and nodded with the hint of a smile. "Yes, everything is going to be fine."

Chapter 19

The damp October air did nothing to discourage Hope. It had been a week since Lance went to retrieve Alex, but his letter of apology made her feel certain that things would work out when he returned.

Grace had arranged for the butcher in Oregon City to buy all the wethers, the male lambs. The agreement was that he would butcher them at the farm and leave the fleeces for them to use. Hope had taken on the duty of washing the hides. It was dirty, smelly work, but it would have been shameful to let them go to waste. Lamb's leather was some of the softest to be had when prepared properly.

At noon they paused, and Mercy and Grace served lunch to everyone. Clarence Ford, the butcher's son, managed to seat himself beside Hope and throughout the meal tried to keep her attention with stories about his life. When he started talking about how busy they were at the butcher shop and how he was making more than enough money to support a wife, Hope excused herself from the table and went back to work.

They had been at it all day and were finally reaching the end. Hope's back ached from the work, but she felt satisfied. There would be plenty of leather for gloves and slippers for each of them.

"Miss Hope, I wonder if you might talk with me for a few minutes."

Hope looked up to find Clarence Ford, hat in hand, grinning from ear to ear.

"We can talk right here, Clarence."

He looked around and nodded. "I reckon so. We've known each other for a long time, and like I was sayin' at lunch, I'm making enough money now that it's time I took a wife."

"That's nice." Hope knew where this conversation was headed. Clarence was one of those who proposed marriage at the house-raising the month before.

"Well, you know how I feel about you. I asked you to marry me last month, but there were so many folks around that I figured you didn't have time to think it through. Now you've had some time to get your mind around the idea, so I figured to ask again."

Hope turned back to her work. "I'm flattered by your interest, Clarence, but I cannot marry you."

"Why not?"

She shook her head. "There are a lot of reasons, but the biggest is that I don't love you."

He laughed. "Aw, Miss Hope, that ain't hardly a reason for not marryin' a fella. Not out here."

"Of course it is. My mother told us to settle for nothing less."

"Well, my ma says that love comes around in time. She married my pa because her pa told her to. They did all right."

Clearly he wouldn't be easily deterred. "That may be, but not everyone's loveless marriage turns out that way. My sister married a man she didn't love because the mission board wouldn't allow him to come west to preach unless he had a wife. That didn't end well at all. If he hadn't died, I've no doubt they would have remained loveless."

"You can't know that for sure. Besides, you've been around here long enough to know that we got a shortage of women-folk."

"So you only want to marry me because of that shortage?" She smiled and shook her head. "Clarence, I'm honored, but I can't marry you."

He cast his gaze to the ground. "If it's on account of me being homely . . . well, I can't help my looks, but—"

"Clarence, I would never call you homely, and I wouldn't refuse a man based on his looks . . . if I loved him."

He perked up at this. "Well, it shouldn't be on account of my financial situation either. My pa made me a full partner, and I've been putting money aside. I can afford a wife."

She shook her head. "Money has nothing to do with it."

He smiled. "Then besides your worry about love, there's no reason for sayin' no to my proposal."

She sighed and straightened. Meeting his hopeful expression, she knew she'd have to resort to desperate measures. "It's not my only reason, Clarence. I'm interested in someone else."

He frowned. "Who is it?"

"Lance Kenner. You remember him, don't you? He was here at the house-raising, and he used to be in the army."

"I recollect him."

For a moment he said nothing more, and Hope allowed herself to relax. She hadn't wanted to bring Lance into it, but given the way she felt about him, she knew she couldn't give false hope to another. She started back to work on the last of the hides.

"Well, bein' interested in somebody ain't no reason not to get to know me better." Clarence's disappointed look was replaced by renewed joy. "A lot of folks take an interest in each other, but that don't mean somebody else can't take an interest as well."

Hope's frustration built. "I'm not like that, Clarence. When I take an interest in someone, he's the only one for me."

This seemed to silence him for a moment, but then he shook his head. "You can't know for sure he's the one for you unless you give other fellas a chance."

"I have given other fellas a chance."

"You didn't give me a chance."

Hope drew a deep breath. "That's not true, Clarence. I've known you for two years now. If I'd taken to you in that way, I would have let you know."

He still wasn't deterred. "Well, I don't reckon unless a gal's engaged that she can't still change her mind."

"But I am engaged." The words were out of Hope's mouth before she could think them through.

With a crestfallen expression, he nodded. "I didn't know that."

"Yes, well, it was rather sudden." More sudden than he knew.

Clarence kicked at the dirt. "That is different. I don't reckon to come between folks who've made a pledge betwixt them. I'm sorry I bothered you, Miss Hope." He walked away, shoulders drooping.

Hope felt sorry for him but breathed a sigh of relief. She knew Clarence to be a quiet and reserved young man in crowds, so she prayed he'd keep her so-called engagement to himself. She didn't want to have to explain to Lance or anyone else what she'd done.

"I'll be eighteen next month," Toby told Mercy. "And with the new land bill, I can apply for land of my own."

"That's wonderful." Mercy smiled up at him. She had agreed to take the sheep to the farthest pasture while the butchering was going on. Toby had happened to come for a visit, and she'd welcomed his company.

"I've long wanted to be a farmer on my own," he continued. "My uncle has taught me a lot, and now that I've finished my schooling, I figure it's time to move forward."

"It's a big decision, to be sure, but I know you'll be up to it."

He smiled. "I figure to be. But there's something I want to discuss about it with you."

"Oh, what's that?" She looked across the field at the sheep. They seemed to be content for the moment, so she gave Toby her full attention and smiled.

He turned a little red. "Well, I . . . you know how I feel about you, Mercy. I figure we'd make a good team. I . . . ah . . . I want you to marry me."

Mercy couldn't have been more surprised. Her mouth fell open and she could only stare at him as he hurried to say more.

"I know this might seem kind of sudden, but we've been walking out together, and most folks know we're a couple. Marrying just makes sense. Not only that, but once I have my land, I'm gonna need a wife to help me, so I want us to get married right away."

The shock began to wear off, and Mercy found her voice. "Toby, I'm only fifteen and barely that. I haven't even begun to think about getting married. Maybe in three or four years I'll be ready, but right now I just want to get through school and learn all I can. I've even thought about going to college. Women are doing that now, you know."

"But you don't understand, Mercy. If we're married, I can get more land." He took her hand. "Besides, lots of girls get married at your age. Some even younger. Remember last year, when Susanna Wagner up and married and moved off to California? She was only thirteen."

Mercy remembered it very well. Susanna married a widower who already had two young children. Her parents had pushed her into it due to the other eight children they had to feed and clothe.

"I just don't think it's the right thing to do, Toby."

He frowned. "Don't you care about me?"

"Of course I do! This isn't about how I feel toward you. It's such a surprise to even think about getting married. I mean . . . I want to marry one day, but—"

"Just hear me out." Toby took hold of her shoulders and turned her to face him. "I don't know for sure how the law works, but I know that a man can get three hundred and twenty acres. If he has a wife, then he gets another three hundred and twenty acres. That's six hundred and forty acres of free land, Mercy. That's more than I could ever hope to buy."

Mercy shook her head. "So you just want to marry me to get an additional three hundred and twenty acres of land?"

"No. You know that isn't how I feel. We've been friends for a long time, and I have feelings for you. I love you, Mercy."

"I thought we were just friends." She looked at him warily. "Now all of a sudden you're declaring you love me."

"Well, it's not so sudden. I wouldn't spend so much time with you if I didn't enjoy your company. Now that I'm a man, I need to think about the future, and this land deal is going to get a lot of attention. Folks are coming here all the time from back east, and I don't want to miss out on getting as much acreage as possible."

She pulled away from him and started walking toward the sheep. She had to clear her mind and keep her heart in check. She did care for Toby, but as for love, she couldn't say. Besides, he seemed far more concerned about the land than her heart.

"Look," Toby said, catching up with her, "we wouldn't have to get married until next year when you're sixteen. The law just says it has to happen before December of 1851. Surely that would give you enough time to get yourself ready to be a wife. Won't you at least think about it? You could give me your answer tomorrow at the church dinner."

She sighed and nodded. "I'll think about it, Toby."

He grinned. "Good. You'll see that it's a good idea. I know you will."

Fort Nez Perce was nothing more than a few collections of buildings along the river. As a Hudson's Bay fort, its purpose had been taking in furs from the area trappers and selling them supplies. Other than that, its main benefit was offering them a bit of communal diversion and a sense of protection when the tribes along the Columbia decided to kick up a fight.

However, after ten days on the river with only a brief stop-over at the Vancouver fort, Lance found it as appealing as any other place. He didn't care much for river travel, and having his feet on solid ground again—even for an hour—was welcome.

The fort factor was more than glad to receive Lance once he heard that Lance had come to take Alex home. His Indian wife had been caring for Alex, and she was needed for other jobs, not the least of which was helping with the furs. He happily directed Lance to the building where Alex was recovering and promised to supply anything they needed for their journey home. Just before parting company, he reminded Lance that the boat would leave in less than an hour.

Lance made his way to the room where Alex Armistead was recovering and prayed for strength to handle whatever he might face inside. He knocked on the door and opened it. "Alex?"

"That's me," Alex said, struggling to sit up.

"Don't get up on my account." Lance crossed the room to see just how bad the situation was. The factor had told him Alex was in much better shape and had even started using a crutch to get around. "Your wife sent me to bring you home."

Despite Lance's concern, Alex sat up with a moan. "Grace sent you?"

"Yes. You might remember me from the Cayuse trial. I was a lieutenant in the army posted to guard the defendants. The name is Lance."

Alex nodded. "I do remember you. Grace said something about a soldier helping Hope. Was that you?"

Lance smiled. "Yes. I can tell you all about it later, but for now, we've got a boat waiting to take us to Fort Vancouver."

"Thank the Lord. I've been trying to get them to let me travel at least as far as Fort Vancouver, but they've been too afraid I'd die on the way or be too much of a fuss. I'm not sure which."

"Well, I know your wife is anxious for your return. It was all I could do to keep her from coming herself. Now, I can collect your things for you if you tell me what's what." Lance glanced around the sparsely furnished room.

"There isn't much for you to gather." Alex swung his legs over the side of the bed, grimacing the whole time. "What little I had with me is gone. The boys here arranged these clothes for me. The others were pretty shredded."

"So all I need to worry about is getting you on the boat?"

Alex nodded. "That alone will be tough. I'm not so steady on my feet yet."

"Where are your injuries?" In the dim sunlight, he could see that Alex had a healing cut running along his neck, but no other wounds were visible.

"Mostly my back and legs. The right leg was the worst."

"I have a bag of medicinal tonics and salves sent by your wife."

"And vinegar?" Alex asked, chuckling.

Lance smiled. "Of course."

An hour later they were settled on the boat and making their way down the Columbia. It wasn't a very big vessel, but it served the need, and Lance made Alex as comfortable as possible with a pallet of extra blankets he'd purchased.

Lance knew that sooner or later he'd have to tell Alex who he was. He felt a remarkable peace about the other man, in spite of their past. In fact, he liked Alex. That in and of itself left Lance little doubt that God had miraculously interceded in his heart. Not so long ago, he had contemplated how to exact revenge on this man, but now he felt nothing but admiration after hearing all that Alex had gone through.

Once he explained to Alex who he was, Lance felt certain there'd be no more obstacles to offering Hope a proposal of marriage. Unless he counted the woman herself as an obstacle. Which might well be the truth of it. Still, he knew she felt something stronger than friendship for him. He could see it in the way she looked at him—the way she felt at ease with him.

"So how did you meet Hope?" Alex asked.

Lance chuckled. "Your sister-in-law is quite a woman. She showed up at the jail on Abernathy Island to—" He sobered. "To kill Tomahas, the man who . . . hurt her during the captivity after the massacre. I walked in to find her pointing that little Colt revolver of hers at his heart."

There was no shock on Alex's face. Instead he nodded. "That doesn't surprise me at all. Hope is a quiet one, but a great strength runs deep in her."

Lance sat down beside Alex's pallet. "She is strong. Stubborn, too."

Smiling, Alex tried to sit up a bit. "That she is. Her sister is the same way. I could tell you stories, but that can wait. Tell me more about what happened. How'd Hope even get into the jail unnoticed?"

Grabbing a rolled blanket, Lance put it behind Alex to better support him. "She snuck by my guards when they were arguing about something. I was making my rounds and heard them fighting and went to intervene. Once I had them quiet, however, I heard a woman's voice coming from inside the jail. I walked in and found her confronting Tomahas. He was trying his best to intimidate her. I think he wanted her to pull that trigger. You know how the Cayuse feel about being hanged. After the sentencing, they begged us to shoot them instead. Anyway, Hope was plenty scared and angry. I told her he wasn't worth the effort and got her out of there. I've little doubt that if I hadn't shown up, she would have pulled the trigger."

"I can't say I blame her. Tomahas tormented her. It wasn't just the rape, it was the constant humiliation and threat of harming Mercy." Alex shook his head. "Hope endured far more than any woman should have to, and I suppose she was afraid he'd go free. That thought, coupled with all she went through bearing his child, probably put her over the edge of reason."

Lance couldn't hide his surprise. "She had a child?"

Alex grimaced. "Please keep that to yourself. Few people know about it. She gave the baby to a preacher and his wife who are good friends with Grace. It was a real nightmare for her. Grace told me Hope begged her to rid her of the pregnancy. She even contemplated killing herself."

The truth came like a blow. How she must have suffered. Lance felt an overwhelming desire to take Hope in his arms and tell her how sorry he was—how he would see to it that nothing ever hurt her again.

"I can't imagine the pain and humiliation she endured. She told me once that no decent man would ever want anything to do with her, and I told her she was wrong." Lance shook his head. "I almost wish she'd pulled the trigger on that beast."

"You love her, don't you?"

Alex's question was no less a surprise than the news of Hope's pregnancy. The truth was, however, undeniable.

"I do. I think I did from that first moment. I offered her friendship, and she told me it could never be anything more." He smiled. "She told me in no uncertain terms that she wasn't looking for a husband, and I told her I wasn't looking for a wife. And at that time I wasn't."

"But now?"

"Now I can't imagine life without her."

One of the crew members approached. "Mr. Kenner, do you have everything you need?"

Lance had avoided using his last name. He had hoped to have a little more time with Alex before springing the truth on him. "We're fine. Thank you."

The man left, and Lance turned to face Alex. The look on Alex's face was one of recognition.

"I thought you looked familiar."

"I was going to tell you." Lance felt suddenly tense, like he did before going into battle. "I didn't know you were in Oregon City until sometime after I'd met Hope."

"Were you looking for me?" Alex's tone held a bit of apprehension.

"No. I just happened to be in the right place at the right time." He hurried to explain. "I want you to know that I don't hold a grudge against you. Neither did my father. In fact, it was my father who, on his deathbed, told me I needed to let the past die. He knew you hadn't killed my brother on purpose.

He died knowing you were the one who'd been wronged, and for that he was deeply sorry."

The tension eased from Alex's expression. "The duel was a mistake from the start. I should have walked away when Justice challenged me, but things happened so fast and just got out of control. When Justice fired at me before the full count, I figured it was over. I didn't want to fire my shot, but the judge demanded I do so. I fired wide, having no intention of killing your brother, but . . . well, you know the rest. I've felt bad about it ever since, but feelings don't bring a man back to life."

Lance looked out across the vast expanse of the Columbia River. "I was angry for a long time. Marshall told me to hunt you down and kill you, but he's dead now too. Still, that need for revenge seemed unwilling to die. My father begged me to let it go, but it took coming to Jesus to help me put those thoughts aside once and for all. And as far as I'm concerned, it's a good time to bury the past. Especially since I intend to ask Hope to marry me."

Alex smiled and shifted his weight to sit up a bit more. "You don't know what you're getting yourself into with these Flanagan gals. They're a handful, and when they get a notion to do something a certain way—well, that's just the way it's going to be done."

Lance thought about that for a moment. A strong breeze blew across the boat, bringing with it a damp chill. Clouds on the horizon suggested it would be raining by nightfall. "I know you're right, but I also know Hope's going to need me. Especially now with your baby on the way. Once Grace gives birth, it might be hard for Hope to deal with, given the past."

He looked at Alex, whose mouth had dropped open. He looked stunned.

"Are you all right?"

234

"Grace," he breathed. He looked at Lance, his eyes wide. "Grace is going to have a baby?"

"I thought you knew." Lance felt like a heel. He smacked his forehead. "I honestly thought you knew."

"When?"

"December."

Alex was silent for a moment. It was his turn to gaze out over the water. "She knew before I left and didn't tell me. She knew I wouldn't go if I knew about the baby."

"Like you said, when these ladies get a notion of doing something a certain way, that's all there is to it. I'm sure she thought it was for the best."

"Is she all right? Is she healthy? Have there been any problems?"

Lance nodded enthusiastically. "She's fine. Learning about you hit her hard, but as far as I know, it did her no harm. Your wife's uncle decided to move ahead with building the new house. A lot of folks came from town, and we got the outside up in one day. We were another month finishing the interior, but the day before I left, we finished moving the ladies in. Grace looked very pleased, but not nearly so much as when Edward said he'd send me to fetch you home."

"I'm obliged for all you've done." Alex still looked stunned as he leaned back against the pillow. "A baby. I'm going to be a father." He chuckled. "If that doesn't beat all."

"Gentlemen, we'll be making camp in an hour," one of the hands announced.

Lance nodded. He'd slept on the shore on the way to Fort Nez Perce. It was a strong reminder of his days in the army. Then and now, he longed for a real bed and a warm fire. Another reminder of his days in uniform was the threat of attack. The tribes in this area were known to be hostile at times.

"You look concerned. I assure you I'm stronger than I look. I moan and groan a bit, but I'll make it just fine," Alex said.

"I wasn't concerned about you. I was wondering about the Indians in these parts. I mean, I know there's always a threat." He sized up the passing shoreline. High cliffs rose on the left and sloping hills on the right. Someone could easily stand atop and shoot down at them.

"The tribes in this area are pretty peaceful for the time being. There's been no report otherwise," Alex said. "Except for getting a sore back from sleeping on the ground, I think we'll be fine."

Lance met his gaze and smiled. "Yeah, I'm definitely concerned about the ground and the damp cold. I'm not getting any younger."

They shared a laugh, and Lance had little doubt that a strong friendship had begun.

There was no further discussion about Lance's family or the past. From here on out, it was all about the future, and for that Lance was grateful.

Chapter 20

They were late for church, so Grace suggested they just sit in one of the back pews rather than parade up front to their regular place. The congregation was standing and singing when they entered the small church, which made it much easier to take their place without too much commotion. Hope was grateful for this. She had been restless all night, worrying about whether Clarence had said anything about her supposed engagement. That morning at breakfast, she'd almost told Grace and Mercy. She didn't want them hearing about it from someone else and wondering what was going on.

A few people nodded and smiled as they continued singing. Hope easily joined in. Since she'd been going to church all of her life, she knew most hymns by heart, and this was her favorite part of the service. As the song concluded, Hope helped Grace sit. It was nearly November, and to Hope, Grace looked as if she might give birth any day rather than have six or eight more weeks to wait.

Hope remembered how it felt to be that large with child.

Her movements were clumsier as the baby grew. Nothing fit right, and no matter how hard she tried, she could never get comfortable, whether she was sitting or lying down.

Pastor Masterson made several announcements, including one pertaining to the dinner after the service. Once a month, everyone brought food and shared a meal together, and today was that day. Hope always dreaded the dinners and avoided them if possible. She didn't like having to make small talk with people, and today it would be even worse if Clarence had told anyone about her supposed engagement.

Pastor Masterson finished the announcements and moved into his sermon. "I'm reading today from Proverbs. This book offers us many guidelines for daily living and gives wisdom for handling all manner of problems. Open your Bibles to chapter twelve, verse twenty-two."

The rustling of pages filled the sanctuary.

Because she was seated between Grace and Mercy, Hope held the Bible. Alex had gifted it to Grace the previous Christmas because their mother's old Bible had been lost during the massacre. Hope always thought of the massacre and of her mother when they read from the new Bible. The Cayuse had taken so much from her . . . from them.

"'Lying lips are abomination to the Lord: but they that deal truly are his delight.'"

Hope felt the wind go out of her. Had the pastor somehow found out about her lie? It was bad enough that she'd been tormented by her conscience. Surely Pastor Masterson wasn't going to make an example of her.

"Lying is an abomination to the Lord," the pastor repeated. "There's only one reason for lying, and that's to avoid the truth."

The words pierced her heart. He was absolutely right. She had lied to Clarence to avoid the truth. She hadn't wanted to listen to him beg her to marry him. She had no interest in knowing him better. But she shouldn't have lied.

"Some folks tell lies thinking that by avoiding the truth, they'll avoid punishment for wrongdoing. They think they can hide the truth, but God always knows and will reveal the deceit."

Hope squirmed a little, nearly dropping the Bible. Grace eyed her with concern, but Hope just smiled and returned her gaze to the front of the church.

"Some folks tell lies thinking they'll make themselves seem more significant. They want to avoid the truth that they aren't quite as important as they wish they were. They tell tall tales about how much they know, when in fact they know nothing."

Forcing herself to draw a deep breath, Hope wondered what she should do. Certainly she should apologize to Clarence and explain her lack of interest in him—that her heart belonged to another. And it did. That part hadn't been a lie. Still, if she went to Clarence, it would only hurt him to learn that she so disliked the idea of courting him that she resorted to lying.

"Some folks even tell lies thinking they'll avoid a truth that will hurt someone else. They think they're lying to save that person's feelings. But it's still a lie, and most likely that person would benefit by knowing the truth."

Goodness, could the pastor read her mind? Hope felt over-whelmed. She knew that truth was always better than a lie. She could see Clarence and his father sitting several rows up on the opposite side of the aisle. After church, she would go to him and confess.

With that decision made, Hope breathed a little easier. She listened as Pastor Masterson spoke of the heart and how all that a man or woman did was based on the heart. She wanted to have a pure heart—a heart motivated by God. She had wrestled so long with Him, always seeking Him with her heart but holding back in case He disappointed her again.

Even as she thought these things, Hope knew she was wrong. Faith required boldness and a lack of fear.

But I'm full of fear.

There it was. The truth. The truth she'd worked so hard to avoid. Hope was afraid of life and all that went with it. She was afraid to trust God and afraid to get to know the people around her for fear of something horrible happening to them. She was even afraid to give her heart in love. In fact, when she got right down to it, Hope was afraid of almost everything, and that was a helpless feeling.

For so long she had tried to put her finger on what was wrong with her. Why she couldn't heal when everyone else seemed to do so. Why she continued to feel the need to carry a gun when Tomahas was dead. She had let fear control her life and eat away at her.

Being taken captive and used so abominably, Hope had survived by packing her anger around her like a wall. But that wall had been crumbling ever since she gave birth to Faith. Anger had given way to bitterness and regret, but that was motivated by fear, just as the anger had been. Even her response to Clarence had been born out of fear. It was a less intrusive fear, but it was wrapped in that emotion nevertheless.

This sudden revelation was almost enough to make her jump from her seat. She'd let fear control her thinking. She'd let fear make her decisions and choices. She'd let fear command her life . . . but no more. She would find a way to overcome this. She had to. Unless she did, she'd never be able to move forward.

The service concluded with a hymn and the pastor's prayers, but Hope was too consumed by her thoughts to even open her mouth.

"Hope, are you all right?" Grace asked in a whisper.

"I'm . . ." She'd nearly said she was fine, which would have been another lie. "I'm thinking about something. It's weighing heavy on me."

Grace nodded. "I can understand that. I'm laden with thoughts of Alex."

People started greeting each other, and as the conversations rose to fill the room, Hope felt less and less able to think. She needed to get back to the farm, where she could sit and work at her spinning and think, but there was the congregational dinner yet to happen, and that couldn't be avoided.

"Why don't you bring in our food and dishes?" Grace said, smiling. "Mercy can help you. I'm going to go help arrange things."

Hope nodded and gestured to Mercy. They went to the wagon and lifted the waxed cotton canvas covering the bed. "Can you take the big basket so that I can bring the two small ones?" Hope asked.

Mercy nodded and reached for it. "I usually like these dinners, but today I wish we were just going home."

"I do too." Hope took up the smaller baskets. She didn't know why Mercy was uncomfortable but didn't have time to prod her for information.

They returned to the church and made their way to the hall, where long plank boards had been placed between small tables. On top of these, the women were setting out pans and bowls of food. Hope and Mercy reached Grace just as another woman hurried up to join them.

"Oh, Hope, congratulations," Sally Cranston, Beth's mother, declared. "I heard just this morning from Abigail Ford that you're to be married."

Hope sucked in her breath. She would have to explain. But

before she could speak, several other women came to offer their congratulations while Grace and Mercy looked at her like she'd betrayed them. In the whirlwind of comments, Hope felt helpless to tell the truth. It would be far too embarrassing.

So instead of doing as she'd planned, Hope simply nodded and thanked everyone. Once again her fear was taking over. She knew she should simply take charge of the matter, but it was so much easier to let the women believe what they would. The congratulations continued through dinner, making matters all the worse. It became more and more clear how much easier it would have been to straighten things out when Sally had first commented.

As they were headed home, Hope felt the burden of guilt threaten to crush her. Fear had led her to lying, and that was a sin.

"Why didn't you tell us?" Grace asked. Her voice revealed the hurt she felt.

"Yes," Mercy added, "you should have told us first."

Grace continued. "It's not like it wasn't obvious that you and Lance were in love. I've known since he helped you when you were sick that you two belonged together."

Hope was driving the wagon to keep Grace from overexerting herself, but she took her eyes off the road long enough to confess. "I didn't tell you because it's not true."

"What?" Grace and Mercy asked at the same time.

"I'm not engaged. I lied. Yesterday, Clarence Ford was bothering me to marry him—at least to court him. He wouldn't take no for an answer, so I told him I couldn't because I was already interested in someone else. He said that unless I was engaged, he didn't see why I couldn't give him a chance to win me, so I told him I was engaged, and now I don't know what to do. I know it was wrong, but like Pastor Masterson said this morning, I wanted to avoid the truth. I didn't want to hurt his feelings, and I didn't want to have to explain my heart. Then today, I was afraid of being humiliated in front of everyone at church."

"But you do love Lance, right?"

Hope stiffened and turned her gaze back to the road. "That doesn't matter. I shouldn't have lied."

"No. You shouldn't have," Grace replied.

They didn't speak again until they'd reached the farm, and Hope felt even worse. "I'm sorry," she said as she helped Grace from the wagon. "I didn't want to hurt you or anyone else."

"You should have just said something at church. You know the women will have the news all over town by tomorrow."

Hope sighed. "Most likely by supper tonight."

"Well, what's done is done. Maybe we can put our heads together and figure a way out of it without there being too much fuss."

"Toby proposed to me," Mercy said matter-of-factly.

Grace and Hope both turned to her, surprised.

"You can't be seriously considering it," Grace said, shaking her head. "You're only fifteen."

"Well, it's not like it's my first proposal."

Hope was grateful the focus was off her for the moment. At least now she knew why Mercy had been preoccupied. "I'll see to the horse. You two go on inside." Hope didn't wait for a response but went to work unhitching the horse from the wagon.

"I know I'm only fifteen, Grace." Mercy jumped down from the wagon. "He said we didn't need to marry until next year when I turned sixteen."

"That's still too young." Grace looked as if she were about to cry.

Hope interceded. "Why the rush? You can take plenty of

time to court and get to know each other. It's important that you're certain you love him."

"That's just it. I don't love him. I like him very much and enjoy his company, but I'm not in love, and I don't think he really loves me either."

"Then you mustn't say yes," Grace said. "You know how terrible things were for us when I married the Right Reverend Martindale. That marriage was arranged purely to allow us to come west and find Uncle Edward. It was all a lie, and it was wrong. Had he not died on the trail, I would be stuck married to a man I didn't love."

"I know that," Mercy replied. "I don't intend to say yes. Toby only wants us to marry right away so that he can get more land. Apparently with the new land bill, a married man—one who married before December of next year—is entitled to an additional three hundred and twenty acres of land."

Hope finished unhitching the horse and pulled him away from the wagon. "That's certainly no reason to marry."

"No, it's not," Grace agreed. "I'm glad you've decided to refuse him."

Mercy shrugged. "I haven't given him my answer yet. He wanted me to at dinner today, but I told him I had to think some more. I know I should have said I couldn't marry him and leave it at that, but I didn't want him getting upset at church. Believe me, I understand why Hope did what she did. She didn't want to hurt Clarence or have to deal with his persistence. I feel the same way about Toby. I don't want to disappoint him or ruin his plans for land." She sighed again. "But neither do I want to deal with his pouting or anger at my refusal. I hate conflict of any kind."

Grace put her arm around Mercy. "Conflict is never easy, but sometimes it's best to face it and be done with it. When you see him next, you need to just come right out and tell him."

"I will. I won't like it, but I will."

Hope led the horse to the pen. She had told her sisters the truth, at least, but now she needed to figure out how to tell the rest of the town.

The fact of the matter was that she was very much in love with Lance Kenner and wanted to be his wife. She'd never thought to have feelings like that after what Tomahas had done to her. Only months earlier, she'd wondered why others had been able to move ahead with their lives while she was stuck in the past. Now, however, the past was all but dead, and she wanted to move forward. She wanted to declare her love to Lance.

Then a thought came to mind and with it . . . fear. Lance didn't know anything about Faith. Lance had always assured Hope that what happened at the massacre was not her fault and should never be held against her by any man. And she believed him. She believed he would never think her unacceptable because of that. However, she had given birth to a baby, and that was something entirely different.

There was no way of knowing how it might affect their relationship.

Hope already had most of their breakfast on the table when Grace made her way to the kitchen the next morning.

"I can't say I have much of an appetite this morning," Grace said, standing by the table. She looked down at the platters of food. "I'm not at all hungry."

"I figured with the colder weather, we need to eat a hearty breakfast. I'm frying up eggs as well."

"Well, none for me. I'll stick with a piece of toast."

"So long as you get proper nourishment," Hope replied over her shoulder. "Go ahead and take a seat."

Mercy came in with a pail of milk. "She didn't give much this morning." She put the pail on the counter.

"That's all right. Get washed up, we're ready to eat." Hope picked up the cast-iron skillet. She put two fried eggs on Mercy's plate, then two on her own.

When Mercy returned, Grace bowed her head and offered a blessing. "We thank You, Lord, for this meal and the hands that prepared it. I ask that You would be with Alex and Lance and bring them home quickly. I ask too that You would heal Alex completely and continue to grow this baby into a fine healthy child. Amen."

"Amen," her sisters replied in unison.

Hope began to dig in and Mercy followed suit, while Grace nibbled at the piece of buttered toast. They hadn't been long at it when a loud pounding sounded on the front door.

Grace looked startled. "Goodness, who could that be at this hour? It's only just after seven."

"I'll get it." Hope put down her fork and jumped up from her chair.

She opened the door to find Jed Drury, their closest neighbor, on the other side, hat in hand. "Sorry to bother you, but I need to speak with Mrs. Armistead."

Hope nodded. "Come on in. We were just sitting down to breakfast." He followed her into the kitchen. "It's Mr. Drury."

Grace looked up and smiled. "Good morning. What can we do for you?"

The man's brows knit together as his expression grew grave. "Sorry to bother you, Mrs. Armistead, but the kids have come down fearful sick. Sarah asked me to see if you might come take a look at them."

"Of course." Grace awkwardly maneuvered to her feet. "Let me collect my things. Hope, would you hitch the wagon for me?"

"I brought my wagon, ma'am. I can drive you."

Grace nodded. "Let me get my bag."

"Are you sure you're up to this?" Hope asked, following Grace into what she called her medicine room. It was a small, shelf-lined room just off the kitchen where Grace kept jugs of vinegar in various stages of development as well as the tonics and herbs she used for healing.

"I'll be fine, Hope. They probably just have the measles or mumps. I've had both, so it's not a problem."

"But you haven't had much to eat."

Grace continued to shove things into her bag. "I'm not hungry. The baby's put my stomach on edge this morning." She smiled, as if reading Hope's dislike of the situation. "Why don't you put some ham and toast together and wrap it in a dishcloth, and I'll eat it on the way over."

Hope still didn't like this. "But you've been awfully tired lately."

"I slept very well last night. Now go. Nothing ails me that a few more weeks won't cure. Once the baby is here, I'll be fit as a fiddle."

Hope returned to the kitchen and slapped a large piece of ham between two pieces of buttered toast. She wrapped the food as Grace had directed but couldn't shake the feeling that her sister should remain at home. If Alex were here, he would no doubt forbid his very pregnant wife from risking her own health.

Grace came out of the medicine room, bag in hand.

Jed quickly took the bag from Grace and headed for the door. "We should hurry."

Grace turned to Hope and Mercy. "I don't know how long I'll be, but don't worry. If I need to stay through the night, I'll have Jed come let you know."

"I don't think that would be wise, Grace." Hope frowned. "I'll come over to check on you in a few hours."

"I'll come too," Mercy declared.

Grace laughed. "You two have turned into a couple of mother hens. Go back to your breakfasts. I'll see you soon."

"Here's your food," Hope said, pushing the wrapped sandwich into Grace's hands.

"Thank you. This is perfect."

Hope watched as Mr. Drury helped Grace into the wagon and then took his seat. She felt a strange sense of dread settle over her and started to call out to her sister, but Jed had already slapped the reins, and the horses took off in a hurry.

"God, please keep her safe."

Mercy and Hope busied themselves with routine work. Mercy took the sheep out to pasture. She was becoming a regular shepherdess, and it made Hope smile. Her spinning was coming along too. It blessed Hope to know she had something she could teach her younger sister.

Hope rolled out dough for beef pie. Between her worried thoughts about Grace, she contemplated how she would rectify the situation of her false engagement.

"I wish I'd kept my mouth shut. I was such a fool, and now when Lance returns, he'll know just how stupid I've been."

She glanced around the room, grateful that Mercy wasn't there to hear her. But her sister's absence did nothing to soothe Hope's agitation. The truth was, she wished that what she'd said was true. She would very much like to be engaged to Lance. How strange that life had changed so much for her in the course of a few months. Since the massacre and even after the hanging, Hope had felt locked in a prison of her own making. Now, little by little, she was figuring things out. She knew that being afraid—feeling unsafe—was one of her biggest motivators, but she'd begun to pray about it. Last night she'd awoken many times, and prayer was the first thought that came to mind. She would overcome this so she could look forward to her future. So long as that future included Lance.

"But how do I let him know how I feel? I promised him I wasn't looking for a husband." She sighed. Maybe it was best to say nothing about her feelings. Maybe it was better to bury them deep and then have a good laugh together at the absurdity of her telling others they were engaged to be married.

The hours went by slowly, and when the sun began to set in the western skies, Hope decided enough was enough. Grace needed to be mindful of her own condition, and laboring over that sick brood of children wasn't wise.

She pulled off her apron. "Mercy, I need you to watch the oven. The beef pie comes out in twenty minutes."

"Where are you going?"

"To get Grace." Hope shook her head. "We should never have let her go."

"I don't suppose we could have stopped her," Mercy replied. "She's always done just as she likes."

"Well, for once she can do what I like."

Hope headed for the barn. A light drizzle dampened everything and made the coming night feel heavy. In the pen, the wagon horse stood head-to-head with Alex and Grace's riding horses. The trio seemed unaware of the weather and looked as though they were conversing on something important.

She was about to open the gate when she heard the unmistakable sound of a wagon coming up the drive. Hope hurried to the front of the house just as Jed Drury drove up with Grace. She could see that Grace was exhausted.

Jed helped Grace from the wagon then climbed back up to take his seat. He handed down her bag. "Thank you for what you've done. I guess it's in the Lord's hands now."

Grace nodded. "Don't forget what I said. Keep them drinking

fluids but don't give them anything solid to eat. Use only boiled water, and add the medicines I gave you when the water is still hot. Wash everything thoroughly—especially your hands and . . ." She let the words trail off and swayed on her feet.

Hope wrapped a hand around Grace's arm and took the bag from her. "I'm sure Mr. Drury can manage. Let's get you inside before you fall down in the mud." She pulled Grace along with her as Mr. Drury turned his team to head home. "I was just about to come after you. You must be exhausted. Did you have anything to eat?"

"I wasn't hungry."

Once they were in the house, Hope called for Mercy. "Put some water on for tea."

"Is Grace all right?" Mercy asked, looking doubtful.

"I don't know." Hope looked at her older sister and saw the weariness in her eyes.

Grace shook her head. "Don't worry, I'm fine. Just really tired."

Hope led her to a chair and helped her sit. "Well, you're going to do nothing but rest from now on. No more gallivanting off to heal the sick. There are town doctors for that."

When Grace didn't protest, Hope grew even more concerned. "What was wrong with the Drury children?"

Her sister looked up, her face ashen. She barely breathed the single word.

"Cholera."

Chapter 21

Grace's condition grew worse after her return from the Drurys'. Cholera was a deadly sickness, and Hope remembered only too well how it had struck the wagon train when she and her sisters were coming west. Fortunately, neither Hope nor her sisters had taken sick, but it had killed Grace's husband, the Right Reverend Martindale.

"I don't know what to do to help you." Hope looked at Grace, who had been sick all night.

"You have to make me drink liquids. No food. The water must be boiled, and you must wash your hands in boiled water with lye soap every hour."

Hope studied Grace's pale complexion. She feared for the life of her sister and unborn baby. If they died, it would devastate everyone.

"I don't understand how this happened." Hope finished cleaning Grace up and washed her hands in the basin once again.

"I can't be sure. The only thing we've done out of the ordinary was the church dinner." Grace moaned and clutched her stomach. "It might be something I ate there. The Drurys were there too."

"So were Mercy and I, but we're not sick."

Grace looked up with eyes that betrayed her misery. "You might not have eaten the same things we did. Grammy Marsh always said that some foods take on poisons from the air. Cholera steals away the body's fluids and dries out the organs, so drinking is important—especially with the added herbs and salts."

"I'll get you more." Hope quickly exited the bedroom.

She met Mercy in the hallway and could see she was just as worried as Hope. "She says we have to keep her drinking fluids, but she can't eat anything. It would be too hard on her system."

"Is she going to die?" Mercy asked, her gaze never leaving Hope's face.

An overwhelming sense of dread had settled over the house, and Hope could only shake her head. "I don't know. I think you should go to town and get Dr. McLoughlin or Dr. Barclay. I don't trust myself to be able to do enough in this situation."

Mercy nodded. "I'll go right now."

"Thank you."

Hope went to the medicine room and gathered ingredients as Grace had directed. She added peppermint and chamomile to sugar and salt. Next she mixed these into boiling water and let it steep. A million thoughts raced through her mind as she stirred the concoction.

How had this happened? Had someone brought contaminated food to the church dinner? On the wagon train west, Grace had been meticulous with Hope and Mercy, making them drink only boiled water and take their daily doses of vinegar. Grace had also insisted they eat nothing but food they could be certain of.

Hope tried not to think about Alex and Lance coming home

to find Grace gravely ill or dead. Poor Alex was already recovering from wounds, and Lance . . .

Only then did she remember the engagement issue. There was no time now to make things right. If others in Oregon City were sick with cholera, they wouldn't be overly concerned with whether Hope and Lance were truly engaged anyway.

Making her way to Grace's bedroom, Hope whispered a prayer for her sister's recovery.

I feel so inadequate, Lord. Please guide me and heal her quickly.

~

Mercy didn't return until nearly three hours later, and when she came, she came alone. Hope looked at her sister's crestfallen expression and knew things weren't good.

"There's a lot of sickness in town, and Dr. Barclay is quarantining everybody until he can figure out what it is. He doesn't know yet if it's typhoid fever or cholera. I tried to get him or Dr. McLoughlin to come, but neither one could. Dr. Barclay said he had his hands full there, and Dr. McLoughlin was too ill, according to his wife. He doesn't have the sickness, though."

Hope bit her lip. What were they going to do without real medical help? Grace was accomplished in herbal remedies, but Hope had never felt called to that particular gifting. Grace also knew about the symptoms and dangers that accompanied each disease and disorder. Hope wouldn't know what to watch for or even how to gauge if Grace was doing all right. And then there was the issue of whether it was typhoid fever or cholera. Were Grace's remedies different for each? What if Hope was giving her the wrong things?

"We've got soiled bedsheets to wash. They have to be rinsed off first and then washed in lye soap and boiling water, then rinsed in boiling water. I need you to set a fire under the kettle outside and fill it with water. We have to get on top of this."

Mercy nodded. "I'll take care of it." She headed for the back door then stopped and turned. "I'm sorry that I couldn't get help."

"It's not your fault. With so many others sick, we can hardly expect the doctor to drop everything and come running. We'll just do what we can."

The expression on Mercy's face told Hope that her words held little comfort. She wished she could say something to encourage her little sister, but frankly, Hope was in need of her own encouragement.

Reaching Grace's bedroom, Hope noticed how pale and small Grace looked. She had always been so strong, always the one who got them through their illnesses and trials. What would happen if they lost her? The thought was too terrible to even consider.

Grace opened her eyes when Hope put a hand to her forehead, and Hope smiled with what she prayed was a look of reassurance. "How are you feeling?"

"No better."

Hope sat on the bed. "I sent Mercy for a doctor, but no one can come. She did talk to Dr. Barclay, and he said he wasn't sure if this was cholera or typhoid fever. Several people in town have taken ill with it."

"It's cholera. The Drury children had no rashes." Grace closed her eyes. "My treatments would be similar anyway."

"I'd feel better if we could have a doctor look at you. Maybe I should take you into town."

"No. The doctors would just bleed me and give me opium. I don't want their help. It would be too dangerous for the baby."

"All right." Hope looked down at her sister, fearing she was making the wrong choice in agreeing with her.

The hours ticked by, and Hope continued her vigil. She forced liquids into the expectant mother every hour on the hour and then cleaned up the messes that followed. Grace tossed and turned in pain for a long time, then seemed to settle and grow less and less responsive. She had told Hope when she'd first fallen ill that there were four distinct stages of cholera, and this appeared to be the second stage, where the sickness was in full force.

Around noon, Mr. Drury came by to see if Grace could come to the house. One of his children had died in the night, and two of the others were near death. Hope informed him of Grace's condition, and his shoulders slumped as he moved away without another word. He climbed back into his wagon and headed home. No doubt he felt just as discouraged and afraid as Hope.

When she wasn't nursing Grace, Hope washed clothes and directed Mercy to keep boiling water as she cared for the animals. Once the laundry was washed, it was nearly nightfall, but because there was no rain, Hope told an exhausted Mercy to hang the clothes and bedding on the clothesline.

"I know you're just as tired as I am, but I can't leave Grace for much longer."

"I don't mind," Mercy said, her lower lip quivering. "I'm just so scared."

Hope pulled Mercy into her arms for a long hug. "I am too."

Lance breathed a sigh of relief once they reached Fort Vancouver. They could be back in Oregon City within a day or two, depending on available transportation. Alex was feeling stronger, although Lance could see he tired easily after walking even a short distance.

"The fort looks busy. A lot of people coming and going."

Alex nodded. "I see a friend of mine. Give me a minute to talk to him."

He limped off in the direction of a tall, broad-shouldered man while Lance wondered who he should speak to in order to arrange a meal and a place to rest.

To his surprise, one of the first people he ran into was Eddie Wilson. "You're a sight for sore eyes, Sergeant."

The redhead flashed his former lieutenant a smile. "I never thought to see you here. You re-enlisting?"

"No. I'm helping a friend get back to Oregon City. We've been on the river. Came down from Fort Nez Perce."

"Well, you won't be going much farther for a while. Oregon City is under quarantine."

Lance frowned and glanced across the room to where Alex was speaking with his friend. "Quarantine? For what?"

"Cholera. There's not a boat captain here who'll be willing to risk breaking quarantine."

This presented a whole new list of problems. When Alex heard about the quarantine, he was going to be hard to hold back. He would insist on immediately returning to his expectant wife, and Lance couldn't blame him. His own worries about Hope made him want to risk the journey. He couldn't imagine what Alex would feel once he learned the truth.

Lance decided not to try to think it through right now. He was tired and hungry, and it was best to put first things first. "We need a good hot meal and a place to sleep."

"The Hudson's Bay folks have everything you need."

"I thought they were long gone from here."

"Nah. They moved their headquarters north, but there's still some agreement with them and our government for using the fort. I'd rather they just cleared out so we can make this a regular army fort, but as I hear it, that's going to take a while. But enough about that, I want to hear all about your life as a civilian."

Lance followed his friend but wasn't in the mood to describe his exploits. He kept wondering about Hope and how he might help her. He prayed she wasn't one of the sick. Now that he knew how much he loved her, he couldn't imagine life without her.

"You still working for that sawmill?" Eddie asked.

"I am. I find it satisfying."

"Does that mean you've given up on being a lawyer and going back to New Orleans?"

"I'm not sure. I've fallen in love and intend to marry a local girl."

Eddie threw him a mischievous grin. "Another good man lost to the shackles of matrimony."

"Well, if I can talk her into it. As for going back to New Orleans, I plan to do that after we wed. She hates this place. I'll pick up my law practice again once we're there. You should come look us up when you muster out."

"I'll have to do that. Maybe you'll even have a job for me."

Lance smiled. "I'd have to have references."

They both laughed.

"Well, here you go," Eddie said, stopping at a desk where a thin, bearded man sat. "This is one of the Company's men, and he'll see that you and your friend are well cared for."

"Thanks, Eddie. Awfully good to see you again."

Eddie grinned. "You too, Lieutenant. I'm sure we'll meet again. Now, if you'll excuse me, I'm late for duty."

Lance smiled and turned to the Company man. "I'm in need of a hot meal and bed for me and my friend. A doctor too, if one's available. My friend was badly wounded by a grizzly and laid up for some time at Fort Nez Perce."

The man nodded and got to his feet. "Ah, you must be talking about Alex Armistead. We know all about the attack."

"Yes. He's talking to one of his acquaintances over there. I figured I'd get things squared away."

"No problem. I'll arrange a room for you. You two can take a seat in the dining area, and I'll have someone bring you something to eat."

Lance nodded and went to fetch Alex. When he reached the two men, however, he could see that something was wrong.

"What's going on?"

"Oregon City is quarantined for cholera," Alex replied as his friend departed. "Bart says no one is going in or out of the town."

"I just heard the same."

"Well, if there aren't any boats, then we need to get a couple of horses."

"You can hardly stand on your own two feet. How in the world are you going to ride a horse for hours in your condition?"

Alex's dark eyes quickly glanced around the room. "I'll manage. You need to go ask about borrowing horses. Bart's going to see about a boat that would at least get us close without going into town."

"Alex, you're being unreasonable."

Alex fixed him with a hard look. "My pregnant wife is sitting in the middle of a cholera epidemic. She's one of the first people others seek when they're ill—especially if they don't believe in doctors. I'm not going to sit by while she's in danger."

Lance heard the desperation in Alex's voice. There was no point arguing with him. "I'll go ask around. Meanwhile, they're arranging a meal for us in the dining room. Why don't you wait for me there?"

"Just be quick about it," Alex replied.

"I'll do my best."

Lance went in search of Bart. He didn't know him, but if Bart knew Alex, he surely understood the gravity of the situation.

"I'm Lance Kenner. I'm traveling with Alex Armistead," he said when he finally caught up with Bart outside. The clouds overhead were dark and heavy, and the temperature was steadily dropping.

"I'm Bart." He was bearded and tall and looked like a brute of a man. "What can I do for you?"

"Alex has it in his head to get to Oregon City despite the quarantine. He wants me to secure horses or find someone with a boat willing to take us close enough to walk in. He said you might know someone."

Bart nodded. "I told him it was impossible, but I know a fella who lives where the Willamette and Clackamas Rivers meet. He's heading home this afternoon with a stop in Milwaukie. He might be willing to take the two of you on."

Lance nodded. "If you don't mind, I'll come with you to find out. I'm afraid if I don't arrange something soon, Alex will walk out of here, crutch and all."

Bart laughed. "Yep. He'll do just that."

Grace was slipping away. She had expelled everything that went into her body, and still Hope continued pushing fluids into her. Her sister was far too weak to sit up on her own, so Hope had propped her up with rolled blankets and pillows. This made it easier to spoon water into her mouth, although Grace didn't want it. Thankfully, so far neither Hope nor Mercy showed any signs of the sickness.

Grace said very little. Mostly she slept. Throughout the night, Hope had done whatever she could to make her sister comfortable. It was clear that Grace was fighting with all her will to live, but the sickness refused to abate.

259

Hope kept reminding herself that people lived through cholera. She'd seen it on the wagon train. It was possible—if God willed it.

Mercy showed up at the bedroom door just after the sun began to rise. "Pastor Masterson is here."

Getting to her feet, Hope nodded. "Send him in." When he entered the room, Hope couldn't keep the tears from spilling over her cheeks. "I've done everything I can."

He put his arm around her. "I'm sure you have. You're a devoted sister, but cholera is a terrible illness."

"Grace told me what to do before she got too bad, but I keep worrying that I've missed something. I feel so helpless and afraid." She sobbed as he patted her back.

"There now, you can't allow this to overtake you. God is still with you and will never leave you to bear this alone."

Hope pulled away. "I want to believe that. But just when I think I'm getting my heart right with God, something happens and the doubts return."

He smiled. "It's hard sometimes to hold on to our faith. The things that happen around us seem to have no purpose or reason except to exhaust and discourage us. Still, you have to hold on and remember that God is in control. After all, what is the alternative?"

She shook her head. "I suppose . . . nothing." She sniffed back tears and tried to get a hold on her emotions. "If I don't put my faith in God, then there's nothing worth putting faith in at all." She sank down onto the bed. "But if He's truly in control, then why does He allow these things?"

Pastor Masterson pulled up the chair that Hope had used in the night. He sat down and shrugged. "I've often asked myself that. Why did God allow the serpent a place in the Garden of Eden? Wouldn't it have been simpler if He had kept temptation out of the garden altogether?"

"Exactly." Hope nodded. "He's all-powerful and all-knowing. He can do anything."

"Including heal a body when death seems to have a grip." He smiled. "But sometimes healing comes in the form of death."

She shook her head. "Grace must not die. Nor the baby. It's important she live. So many people depend on her, love her. If God must take one of us, let Him take me."

"But God doesn't work like that, Hope. He's not waiting for you to suggest a barter. I don't know why this sickness has come upon Grace, but I do know that my trust is in the Lord. I will pray and ask Him to heal your sister, just as I know you are praying." He took her hand. "But, Hope, you mustn't be afraid to trust Him whether things go your way or not."

"I know. I've let fear be my constant guardian since the Whitman Massacre. I hate it. I don't want to live in fear."

"That's good, because fear doesn't come from God. The second book of Timothy in chapter one tells us that. 'For God hath not given us the spirit of fear; but of power, and of love, and of a sound mind.'"

It was the key Hope had been searching for. "So fear is the Devil's doing?"

The pastor smiled. "Exactly. Fear is what gives life to doubts, to lies, even to murder."

She thought of how she'd wanted to kill Tomahas and nodded. "But how do I overcome fear? How do I stop being afraid?"

"Believe that God is more powerful than Satan. You do, don't you?"

"Of course." She considered the ease with which she'd answered. Did she really believe that, or was she only saying so because it was expected? "I'm . . . well, I know in my head that it's the truth, but . . ."

"In your heart you have doubts?"

"I suppose I do." She nodded. "Can God still love me when I feel like this?"

"Hope, God loved you before you were even created." He squeezed her hand. "God doesn't stop loving us when we do wrong or make bad choices. He loves you, and though sometimes we cannot see it or feel it, His love is constant and will never leave us. Grace knows that. She has a strong faith. I've heard her speak of God. She has put her life in His hands, and now you must do the same."

Hope let out a long breath. "I know." She straightened and wiped away the last of her tears with the edge of her apron. "Sometimes I feel as if I'll never learn the things God is trying to teach me."

Pastor Masterson smiled. "That's why He gives us a lifetime."

Chapter 22

Lance felt sorry for Alex. He was desperate to reach his wife, but the only means of transportation available was much slower than he desired. Even with Lance helping the boat owner, Patrick Smith, and his sons row, it was an extremely slow process to make their way upriver. Thankfully the skies had cleared, and they weren't having to contend with the rain.

If the boat had been larger, no doubt Alex would have been pacing. As it was, he offered more than once to help with the rowing. When they stopped for the night in Milwaukie, Lance did all that he could to encourage his friend.

"We'll be home tomorrow."

"I know." Alex stared off at the dark waters of the river. "It feels like I've been away for a lifetime. I never meant it to be this way."

"Everyone knows that—especially Grace."

Alex walked as best he could from one end of the bedroom to the other. Lance had gotten them a room at the hotel nearest the dock, but he doubted Alex would sleep much. Lance, experiencing the soreness of muscles unaccustomed to rowing, knew he'd have no trouble sleeping, even on the floor.

"Are you sure your soldier friend will get word to Edward?"

Lance smiled. Eddie had told him just before he and Alex departed the fort that he and a dozen soldiers were headed to Oregon City to evaluate the situation and whether additional help was needed. When Alex heard this, he gave Eddie a letter to take to Edward Marsh. They would need help getting from their stopping point to the Armistead farm.

"Eddie's a good man. We served together for several years, and there's not another man I would want by my side. He'll get the message through."

Alex nodded and finally sank into a chair by the window. He dropped his crutch and began massaging his thigh. "I wish we'd gone by horseback. We could be there by now."

"Not necessarily. I know you're determined, but you're barely off your deathbed. Grace would have my hide if I let you die on my watch."

Alex met his eyes. "I know. I just wish I knew if she was safe."

"Well, they're out on the farm away from town. Maybe they've managed to avoid the sickness."

"You don't know Grace like I do," Alex replied with a hint of a smile. "She'll be the first one out there helping folks. Even expecting a baby, she would feel it was her duty to help heal folks."

"I know that much about her." Lance wished he could offer something more consoling.

"I've been praying, but it's so hard to wait. I know God is with Grace—with all of them—but I want to be there too."

"Still, we wouldn't be any help if we came down sick too. You're in a weakened state of health, and it would probably be deadly if you took on cholera."

"I realize that, but I can't stay here. I've been away too long as it is."

Lance completely understood. He hadn't been away from Hope very long at all, and yet he felt it had been months. "We should probably put out the lamp and get some sleep. Morning's going to come soon enough, and Smith wants to leave at first light."

"I doubt I could sleep. I keep thinking about everything. I know God knows what has happened—that He allowed it. He knew about the bear that would attack me and the damage it would do. I remember Grace once talking about how she thought being spiritually saved would keep you from any evil harm. We talked about how the Devil goes around looking to do his worst. We came to the conclusion that only by leaving this world could we be completely safe from harm."

Lance thought about that for a moment. "It is hard to face. What's the sense in asking God to intervene or keep us from harm if it means nothing?"

Alex shook his head. "I don't think it means nothing to God. I think He hears and honors each prayer. I think sometimes, however, we go through things to learn from them. We learn, and then we can help others when they go through the same thing."

"So you got attacked by a bear so that when someone else gets attacked, you can offer them consolation?"

Alex actually smiled. "Or tell them before they get attacked not to let their guard down even for a moment when they're cooking in bear country."

"I think it'd be a whole lot nicer if He just kept us from all the troubles of the world. Just imagine how quickly folks might come to Him if they knew that once they did, nothing bad would ever happen to them again."

"Yet that wouldn't be coming to Him out of a desire to be

with Him—to know Him and love Him. I look at it like this. I love Grace and want Grace to be with me because she loves me. But if Grace only married me because I promised her a big house with all the food and clothes she could ever want . . . well, that would be a hollow victory. She wouldn't be there because she loved me but because I could give her something."

"Makes sense when you put it that way. But on the other hand, when Grace came to you as a wife, you set yourself up to be her protector and provider. You were determined to keep her from harm."

"Yes, I want to keep her from harm. But Grace still makes her own choices, and sometimes those choices take her into situations that can cause her harm. I see all of us that way. We could come to God and then live in a cave somewhere, waiting to die, but that wouldn't make us very useful. We can also choose to go places or do things we know are dangerous—that might even cost us our lives—but what did the Apostle Paul say about 'to live is Christ and to die is gain'? I think it's in Philippians. Anyway, I suppose that was his way of saying that so long as we live, we do so with Jesus, and we further God's Word and help folks get to know Him. And when we die, we gain living in His presence where nothing will ever hurt us again." Alex yawned and motioned to the bed. "I think I am going to try to sleep."

Lance nodded, glad he was finally willing to rest. "Morning will be here before we know it."

"It can't come soon enough for me," Alex replied.

⁓

Lance felt like he'd only slept for a few minutes when he was woken by the Smiths. Despite his injuries, Alex was up and ready to go within a matter of minutes while Lance lagged behind, fighting to clear his head. There wasn't even time for coffee, which he would have paid ten times the normal price to have.

The rest of the trip upriver passed quickly despite the rain that fell. Lance did his part to help row, but he found himself nodding off from time to time. Just as he relaxed his grip on his oar, however, the river would stir violently and either pull or push it against him, waking him up.

"You think we're gonna have trouble with flooding, Pa?" one of the Smith boys asked.

"Can't be sure. River's definitely higher than it was a few days ago."

It was the most Lance had heard Smith say since they'd begun their journey from Fort Vancouver. None of the Smith men seemed bent toward conversation.

When they finally reached their destination, Lance was relieved to see Edward standing on the Oregon City side of the river beside his wagon. He waved his hat in greeting. It was a welcome sight, and Lance felt that he could finally relax his vigil. Edward could take responsibility for Alex now.

"Alex, you look a little worse for the wear," Edward said, coming down to the dock. "I'm glad that bear didn't hurt your handsome face, or my niece might have decided to send you packing." He chuckled and embraced Alex. "I thought we'd lost you."

"I thought you had too—for a time, anyway. How's Grace? Lance told me about the baby."

Edward frowned. "She's sick, Alex. Caught the cholera, but Dr. McLoughlin says she's going to pull through. The baby too."

Alex sank against the side of the wagon. "Get me home. Please. Just get me back to her."

Edward nodded. "That's my plan. Let me help you up, and we'll be on our way."

Together, Lance and Edward got Alex comfortably arranged in the back of the wagon.

"Now you just sit tight," Edward said. "Won't take much time at all to get you home."

Climbing up and taking a place on the driver's seat, Lance yawned and fought to stay awake. He was glad when the horses finally started down the road.

"How do you plan to get back into town?" Lance asked.

"Quarantine was lifted this morning. Lost some folks, but after that first bunch took sick, nobody else came down with it. Dr. Barclay decided it was an isolated cholera and we could go about our business."

Lance nodded and lowered his voice. "Did anyone else in your family become ill?"

"No, I'm happy to say. Dr. Barclay has some thoughts on what caused it. Seems the sick folks all attended the church dinner last Sunday. Even then, some in the same family took the illness and others didn't. After reading up on some eastern doctor's writings, he figures it might have come from bad food or water."

"So Hope and Mercy are all right?"

Edward laughed. "They're just fine, but that reminds me. I understand congratulations are in order."

"For me?" Lance couldn't imagine what he was talking about.

"Yes, for you . . . and Hope. I understand you're engaged to be married."

The words hit Lance like a blow. He lowered his head so that Edward wouldn't see his shock, and apparently it worked, for the older man began to talk about how he knew Lance and Hope were perfect for each other from the start. He didn't seem at all concerned that Lance had nothing to say.

But what could he say? He knew nothing about the engagement—not that he hadn't planned to talk to Hope about how he felt. The entire matter was puzzling, however. Hope had told him she didn't want anything but friendship, and while he knew she cared for him, he couldn't imagine why she'd declared them to be engaged.

But maybe she hadn't. Maybe someone else had speculated about them being engaged, and the gossips had taken over. He thought about saying something to Edward, but they were only a few blocks from Lance's cabin.

It was growing dark, and Lance needed time to think. He didn't want to approach Hope amidst the reunion between Alex and Grace. Especially if things took a bad turn and Grace died.

"Edward, just let me off here. I'm done in. You can tell the others that I'll be out tomorrow to see how everyone has fared."

"Are you sure, son? Don't you want to see that gal of yours?"

Lance had already jumped down from the wagon. "I'll see her soon enough, don't you fret."

～

Hope straightened from her bedside vigil. Every muscle in her body ached. Outside a steady rain fell, and the skies grew dark with nightfall. Inside, however, Hope felt a sense of joy. Grace had made it through the worst of the sickness and was now resting comfortably. Dr. McLoughlin, despite his own physical troubles, had come to visit that afternoon. He had examined Grace and declared her to be past the point of crisis. He felt the baby move, so they knew the unborn infant was still alive.

Tears had come to Hope's eyes when Dr. McLoughlin commended her on helping Grace survive. He said he couldn't have done a better job himself, and that Grace owed her life to Hope. But she knew it had been God's doing. She looked at the Bible on Grace's bed. It was still open to Second Timothy, chapter one. She had committed verse seven to memory. God hadn't given her the spirit of fear. That was the Devil's doing, and it was to his benefit that she go on being afraid.

Hope smiled. "I won't give the Devil that kind of power over me." The Bible verse had finally given her the answers she needed.

Looking at her sister sleeping peacefully, Hope felt a relief that left her completely exhausted. All she longed for was a hot bath and sleep. Hours and hours of sleep.

"Uncle Edward's coming in the wagon," Mercy said, entering the room. "He's got someone with him."

Hope yawned and got to her feet. "Maybe he's brought Dr. Barclay to follow up on Dr. McLoughlin's visit. Send them in, and I'll wait here."

Mercy nodded and left the room as quickly as she'd come. Hope straightened Grace's cover and then felt her forehead. It was dry and cool.

"Hope?" Grace opened her eyes then closed them again.

"I'm right here." She touched her hand to Grace's cheek. "You're on the mend, so don't fret about anything."

"The baby?"

"Dr. McLoughlin was here earlier today. Do you remember?" Grace nodded. "I think so."

"He said you're past the worst of the sickness. He also said the baby was moving quite a bit, and that was a very good sign. Your remedies impressed him."

"What about Alex?" Her voice was so soft that Hope could barely make out the words.

"I don't know about Alex."

"Don't know what about me?"

Hope whirled toward the door and gasped at the sight of Alex hobbling into the room on a crutch. His return was the very best thing for Grace. "I don't know why you took so long

270

to come home." She went to him and kissed him on the cheek, surprising them both.

He smiled. "Me either." He went immediately to Grace's side and sank onto the bed. "Grace." He drew her hand to his lips. "My treasured Grace."

Her sister's eyes opened again. She looked into the face of her husband, and for the first time since she'd fallen ill, Grace smiled. Hope thought it the most marvelous sight in the world.

"How's my girl?" Uncle Edward asked, coming up behind Hope.

Hope turned to face her uncle. "She's much better."

He smiled. "I meant you." He put his arm around her shoulders. "You look exhausted."

"I am. I've never been so tired, but I've also never been so relieved. Dr. McLoughlin came by earlier today and said that Grace was past the worst of it and that she and the baby would be just fine."

"I know. I saw him in town before heading out to pick up this scallywag."

"Did a lot of people get sick?"

"About twenty," Uncle Edward replied. "Twelve died, including the Drury children."

"Oh, I am sorry for that."

"We can talk about it later. You're swaying on your feet. You go on upstairs and get some sleep. Mercy and I can manage to take care of these two."

"But won't you be needed at home?"

"I already squared things there. We didn't catch the cholera, thank God. Mina sent some food and her love. I told her I would plan on staying here all night."

Hope nodded and covered her yawn. "I'll go clean up and rest then. Just for a little while."

"No, you go ahead and sleep all night. We'll be just fine."

Alex looked up from where he sat. "Hope, thank you for what you've done for Grace."

She smiled. "Just stay away from grizzlies, and we'll all be a lot happier. Oh, no solid food for her. She told me it would kill her at this point. Something about her stomach being too thinly stretched or something like that. If she's hungry, there's chicken broth on the stove."

She stepped into the hall and made her way to the kitchen for a pail of hot water, and it was only after she was halfway up the stairs with it that she thought of Lance. Where was he? Hadn't he returned with Alex?

Setting the pail down on a step, she went back downstairs and sought out her uncle. He was still in Grace's room.

"Uncle Edward?" She motioned him to come out into the hall.

"I thought I told you to go to bed."

She nodded. "I will, but I wanted to know about Lance. Did he make it back safely?"

"He did. He's at his own cabin. Said he'd be out here to-morrow."

"Thank you. I just wanted to make sure."

Edward smiled and turned her toward the stairs. "Of course you did. Now, go on. I don't want to see you again until morning."

Chapter
23

Hope woke with a start the following morning. She threw back the covers, desperate to see if Grace was all right. Only after she'd pulled on her robe did she remember that Alex and Uncle Edward were here.

"Grace is going to be fine," she murmured aloud to reassure herself.

She relaxed and took her time dressing. The room was chilly and so was the day. Keeping that in mind, she pulled on warm wool stockings and a flannel petticoat. Over this she wore a linsey-woolsey dress that a lady from church had given her. The blue plaid suited her and enhanced the blue of her eyes.

She tied her long brown hair back with a blue ribbon, completely unconcerned about how she looked. She had no plans to go to town anytime soon. At least not until she could explain everything to Lance.

Poor Lance. By now he might have heard that they were supposedly engaged. She flushed when she imagined how he might have reacted to the news, but she was no longer afraid. She could only hope that he'd get a good laugh out of it.

Hope went to the window and looked out at the fenced meadow where the sheep grazed. Mercy must have let them into the field already. There was something so peaceful about watching them. She knew every ewe and lamb, and they were each special and precious to her for different reasons. That brought a smile to her face when she thought of how Jesus had called Himself the Good Shepherd.

"'I am the good shepherd, and know my sheep, and am known of mine,'" Hope whispered, quoting John chapter ten, verse fourteen.

She thought of all that she and her sisters had come through since moving west. There had been so much to overcome, but she finally knew that God truly cared for her. Ever since Pastor Masterson had talked to her, Hope had been able to see things more clearly.

I know it's taken me longer than some, Lord, but I want to keep trusting You. I want my first thoughts in the morning and the last at night to be of You. I want to take possession of that Spirit of power and love and sound mind that the Bible says You've given us.

She thought again of Lance and prayed aloud. "I'm gonna need help with this, Lord. Forgive me for the lie, but please help me face the truth and be honest with Lance. Please don't let him hate me for what I've done." But even with that fear in the back of her mind, Hope wasn't going to let it stop her. God would give her the strength and the power to deal with it. She felt confident of this, and confidence was a new companion that she intended to keep by her side.

Hope headed downstairs and checked in on Grace and Alex. The bedroom door was open, and Uncle Edward slept in a chair by the door, his oversized body awkwardly twisted in slumber. Across the room, Alex and Grace slept peacefully. Alex had wrapped Grace in his arms as if to shield her from any more harm. Hope smiled at the scene. What a difference it made to have them back together. It seemed the entire house had settled into a calm that had long been missing.

Seeing there was nothing she could do, Hope went to the kitchen and found Mercy already hard at work.

"I couldn't sleep. I was so excited about Alex being home. I just know that everything is going to be wonderful now." Mercy beamed at Hope. "Finally life is just as it should be, and it made me feel that I couldn't sleep another minute. I got up before light and milked the cow and collected the eggs. I turned the sheep loose in the field and got feed to the other animals." She held up a cast-iron skillet. "And now I'm working on our breakfast."

"My, you've been busy."

"Being happy just gave me so much energy." Mercy stopped a moment. "Aren't you happy? Alex is home and Grace is much better."

"Yes. I'm happy about that, but I'm a little worried about what I'll say to Lance when I see him."

Mercy frowned. "What do you mean?" She put the skillet down on the burner then turned to Hope.

"Well, when he comes through town, someone is bound to congratulate him on our engagement. Since Grace got sick, I haven't had a chance to resolve that little matter."

She was surprised when Mercy giggled. "I don't think you have too much to worry about. Lance likes you a lot and maybe even loves you. He may be glad that you told folks you're engaged."

Hope shook her head. "I have no way of knowing until I

actually come face-to-face with him. I both long for it and dread it at the same time."

"Well, neither emotion is going to change anything." Mercy turned back to her work and put bacon in the frying pan. It sizzled and popped as it hit the hot pan, and almost immediately the aroma filled the air.

"No, you're right on that count. I'm still learning that God doesn't give us a spirit of fear." Hope sat down at the table and decided to change the subject. "I'm going to take the sheep to the far north pasture, so I'll be gone most of the day. I figure you'll be here, and if Alex or Grace needs something, you can help them."

"I'll pack you some biscuits and bacon to take with you, and a jug of water." She smiled over her shoulder. "And don't forget to take your vinegar. It's right there on the table."

"As if I could forget." Hope picked up the bottle and poured herself a large spoonful. She downed it and then another. She followed it with a swig of coffee from the mug Mercy handed her.

"You'd think we'd all be used to that flavor by now." Hope grimaced. "I'm not sure I'll ever be fond of it, but if it keeps us healthy, I guess I have to allow that it's good."

Mercy nodded. "I think if Mama were here she'd say it was, so that's good enough for me."

Hope smiled and took another sip of coffee. The hot liquid warmed her and stirred up her hunger. "Maybe I'll wait to move the sheep. I'm hungry."

"You stay put. You did so much for Grace, and you've hardly eaten since she got sick. Making you breakfast is the least I can do." Mercy fetched a bowl. She dished up some oatmeal and brought it to the table with a pitcher of cream. "The bacon will be ready in a few minutes. The biscuits too. Uncle Edward had me open a jar of cherries last night. If you want some of those, I can fetch them."

"No, this is fine. I'll have the oatmeal now and eat the bacon and biscuits when I'm out with the sheep. You might throw in a bit of cheese as well."

Mercy smiled and nodded while Hope whispered a quick prayer. She was so grateful for God's healing of Grace. Grateful too that her own faith was finally starting to take deep roots.

Half an hour later, with the rest of the house starting to stir, Hope bundled up in her wool coat and scarf and pulled on her old boots. She tucked her pistol in her coat pocket. Since first purchasing the piece, she had seldom been without it. There had always been that underlying fear of being helpless, and the pistol helped ease that fear. Now, however, Hope felt it was more a precaution than fear. Wild animals could attack without warning, so it wasn't foolish to be on her guard. After all, being wise about a situation and being afraid of it were two different things.

Outside, the breeze made the damp air feel all the colder. Hope pulled her scarf around her head as she made her way to the barn. She found her crook, then grabbed a handful of grain and put it in her empty pocket. She headed out to where the sheep were feeding, smiling as they gathered close to her.

"Hello, my dears." She leaned down and picked up a black-faced lamb. "I know it's rainy and wet, but I also know you're going to enjoy feeding in a new area." The bell sheep came to Hope, nudging her for the grain she knew Hope would have. Giving the animal a little feed, Hope smiled. "Come, little ones, we're off to greener pastures." She opened the gate and led them out.

As the day passed, the skies overhead cleared, and the sun

began to warm the air. This made the sheep all the more content. They fed off the grasses and vegetation while Hope kept watch. The ewes had been rebred and would hopefully give them another couple dozen lambs in the spring. Maybe even more. She tried to imagine what it would be like to have a large band of sheep—a thousand or more. They would definitely need a dog or two by that time. She and Grace were already considering getting a dog to help with the herd.

When several of the sheep started bleating in distress, Hope realized her thoughts had drifted and she hadn't been paying attention to her surroundings. She put her hand on her pistol and felt the fear rise in her, making her breath catch.

"No, I won't be afraid." She thought of another verse the pastor had shared just before he'd left her. "'What time I am afraid, I will trust in thee.'" She looked heavenward as she spoke the words of Psalm 56:3.

The sheep moved closer to Hope and knotted together in a tight group. Just as she sought her Shepherd, they sought theirs. Hope scanned the area beyond the open pasture. Tall firs and oak edged the field along with other trees she couldn't identify. The brush was thick, and she knew it was possible an animal lurked there.

Then she spotted the figure of a man coming up the same path she'd used hours before. She recognized Lance from a distance and felt her heart beat all the faster. Was he angry? Would he understand when she told him what had happened?

"How am I going to explain this?" She waved at him and felt her stomach clench. "I won't be afraid."

He waved back and smiled as he drew closer. Hope tried to relax. Maybe he hadn't heard yet.

"Mercy told me where I could find you," he said as he crossed the remaining yards between them. "I figured it was important to locate you right away." He paused and locked his gaze on her. "Especially since I understand we're to be married."

Hope felt as if her stomach did a flip. She gasped in a breath and held up her hand. "I . . . I can explain." At least she hoped she could.

Lance crossed his arms, and his expression became sober. He cut quite the figure in his dark wool coat. "I'm listening."

"Well, you see . . . it happened quite by accident." She turned away, uncertain she could continue if she could see his reaction. "Let me start at the beginning."

"That's always a good place to start."

She drew a deep breath and let it out slowly. "Grace sold the wethers to the butcher, and he and his son Clarence came out to tend to them. I was working with the hides, and Clarence had been making eyes at me all day." Her words came faster and faster. "You might remember him. When we were building the house, he was one of those who asked me to marry him, and of course I told him no." She paused, her gaze fixed on the sheep, but when Lance said nothing, she continued.

"Well, he cornered me and asked me to marry him again. He's a nice enough man, but I told him I couldn't marry him. He wanted to know why, and I told him I didn't love him. He said that didn't matter and kept pressing me, so I told him I was interested in someone else . . . you."

Lance remained silent, and Hope didn't turn around, uncertain what he might say or do. "But that still wasn't enough. Clarence said it didn't matter if I was interested in someone else. Apparently he thinks you can be interested in several folks at the same time. He said that if I wasn't engaged, it was only fair to give him a chance. And that's when I just . . . I sort of blurted out that you and I were engaged."

She turned, no longer able to stand his silence. His head was bowed, so she couldn't see his eyes. "I'm so sorry, Lance. I never meant to lie. I didn't want to hurt Clarence by telling him that I couldn't begin to imagine myself married to him. I thought it would be easier if he thought I belonged to someone else. I just wanted him to go away and leave me be.

"I figured he wouldn't say anything about it, but when I went to church Sunday and folks started congratulating me on our engagement . . . well, I just couldn't figure out how to tell them the truth. But I wanted to." Again her words came almost faster than she could consider what to say.

"It just got out of hand. I know we're only friends, but I also felt . . . oh never mind that. The point is, I tried to figure out what to do about it. I realized that fear has been controlling my life—that I said and did most everything out of fear. I just didn't know what to do. I had no idea that Clarence would tell his mother and she in turn would tell the whole town."

She felt horrible. He still hadn't said a word, and he wouldn't even look at her. If ever she had doubted her love for him, she no longer did. It hurt so much to imagine him walking away and never speaking to her again.

"Lance, please don't be angry with me. I know what I did was wrong, but I don't want to lose you as my friend. You're really the only one I have." She shook her head and tears came to her eyes. "I don't know what to do to make this right."

He looked up, his face serious. "You have made quite a mess, I must admit."

A tear slid down her cheek. If he told her they could no longer be friends, Hope knew she'd fall to her knees and beg him. The thought startled her. She had never felt this way about anyone—not even Johnny Sager. What she'd felt for Johnny paled in comparison to the deep, burning love she held for Lance Kenner.

She put her hand on his arm. "Please, Lance. Please forgive me."

His expression softened, and he reached out to wipe away the tear. "There's only one thing to be done in a situation like this."

She swallowed hard. "What's that?"

"We'll have to get married."

"We'll *what*?"

He grinned. "Hope, on this trip I realized just how much you mean to me. I already knew my feelings for you were more than just friendship. I think I fell in love with you when I found you pointing that gun at Tomahas."

Hope shook her head as if she hadn't heard right. *He loves me?*

"I know we promised that we'd just be friends, but if I'm honest, I already knew I wanted more when I made that promise. I just knew you weren't ready for it. I think from what you've been saying today that you want more too, but just because I'm in love and want to marry you . . . well, I know that doesn't necessarily mean you feel or want the same."

"But I do."

He took hold of her chin and tilted her head back. She couldn't look away from his searching blue eyes. "Are you sure about that?"

Her heart pounded so hard she was sure he could hear it. "Yes. Oh yes." She sighed. "When I thought I'd lose your friendship, I realized how much more I felt for you—that I'd fallen in love with you. I've felt that way for some time, but I wasn't sure what to do about it. After all, you didn't want anything more than friendship—at least, so you said."

He nodded. "Yeah, that was pretty dim-witted of me."

She shook her head. "No. Not at all. I wouldn't have had anything to do with you had you declared your interest in me. I would have run as far away from you as possible had I thought you loved me. I just couldn't face those kinds of thoughts or feelings then."

"And now?" He rubbed her cheek with his thumb.

"Now I can't imagine my life without you. You make me feel safe, cared for . . . loved."

He grinned. "Well, now that we've got that settled—will you make our engagement official and agree to marry me?"

Hope was so overcome with happiness that all she could do was nod.

"May I kiss you?"

Again she nodded. He took her in his arms, and just for a moment she had a fleeting memory of Tomahas. But when Lance's lips touched hers, thoughts of the mission faded away. Tomahas no longer had any power over her. Hope knew this was exactly what she wanted. She put her arms around Lance's neck and trembled as the kiss deepened. This wasn't like any of the kisses she'd stolen as a young flirt.

But then a terrible thought came to mind, and she pulled away. Turning from Lance, Hope felt as if she couldn't draw breath as the old fears took hold again.

"Hope?"

She couldn't face him. He knew nothing about the baby—about Faith. She couldn't expect him to marry her without knowing, but she was terrified that telling him would put an end to everything.

God, help me. I don't want to be afraid.

He turned her toward him, and she didn't resist. Instead she met his gaze, shaking her head. Her body began to shake. She had to tell him the truth and let him decide their fate.

"What's wrong?" He looked so worried—almost fearful.

"I . . . you don't know . . . everything . . . about me."

"What do you mean? I know what I need to know."

What she was about to say might cause Lance to walk away from her, but she knew her marriage couldn't be built on deception. "You know what happened to me at the mission. You know how Tomahas forced himself on me. But you don't know . . . you don't know . . ."

His expression changed to one of recognition, and Hope fell silent. He put his hand on her cheek and looked at her with such tenderness. "I do know. I know about the baby you had. I know, and it doesn't matter to me."

"It doesn't?" she barely whispered.

"No. If anything, it makes me love you all the more."

"But how? How did you find out?"

"Alex accidentally told me when he found out I was in love with you. Hope, I can only imagine the horrors you've gone through in your life, but that one act of sacrifice—of love— humbles and amazes me. I don't know that I could have ever done such a thing had I been in your place." He shrugged and smiled. "Frankly, I don't think there are many men who would ever go through what you women do to bring life into the world. You were very brave."

"I didn't want the baby. I wanted Grace to give me something that would . . . that would end the . . . situation. When she wouldn't, I decided to end my own life. I had nightmares about what was growing inside me. But then Grace's best friend begged me to have the baby and give it to her. She wanted a baby so much."

"And that changed your mind?"

"No. What changed my mind was when she reminded me that the baby was innocent of wrongdoing. That if I imposed my will on the unborn child and ended its life, it would be no different than Tomahas imposing his will on me. Thinking about that, realizing the baby was innocent . . . I couldn't kill her. So

I went to live with Eletta and her husband before anyone knew about my condition. I didn't want anyone to know for fear of what they'd say or think about me. Even Mercy never knew." She shook her head. "I've let fear take charge of me for far too long."

Lance took her hands in his. "As long as we're being completely honest, I feel the need to explain my anger the day I left here."

Hope gazed at him expectantly, ready to offer him the same love and acceptance he had just shown her.

"Remember I told you that a man had wronged my family?"

"Yes."

"That man was Alex."

Her eyes widened. "Our Alex?"

"The same. He had a duel with my older brother Justice, which ended in my brother being killed. We were told Alex had cheated—had killed my brother by shooting him in the back. Alex *had* shot him in the back, but he hadn't meant to. My brother was the one who cheated—he fired early. Alex refused to fire his shot, but the judge said he must. My brother turned to run as Alex shot wide. If Justice hadn't run, he wouldn't have been killed."

She nodded. "I'd forgotten about that. Grace had told me about the duel. I never knew who the man was."

"My other brother, Marshall, decided on revenge. He set fire to Alex's family's house since Alex lived there too. I think he wanted to strip them of all their possessions. I honestly don't think he intended for Alex's folks to die. He wanted Alex dead, to be sure, but I think he was honestly sorry for what happened. Even so, he always stirred me to revenge. I was just twelve, and since even my father believed it was all Alex's fault, I decided I hated Alexander Armistead."

"But you don't now—do you?"

"No."

"When Uncle Edward wanted you to bring Alex home—did you still hate him then?"

"I didn't know what I felt for sure. I'd been praying about it and doing my best to deal with it. I knew my brother's death wasn't Alex's fault. My father knew it too and encouraged me to let go of my desire for revenge. I thought I had until I came here and Alex became part of my world again.

"When your uncle and sister decided that I would bring Alex home, I found myself filled with doubts. I knew Alex only through the thoughts and feelings of others. My brothers' bad feelings and your family's good ones. Once I had a chance to think about it, I knew I wanted to know Alex for myself."

"And what do you think now?"

Lance chuckled. "I find I like him very much. He's got a good heart."

She nodded. "He does, and he loves my sister almost as much as I love you."

He wrapped her in his strong arms. "Hope, I love you, and nothing that has happened to you will ever change that. Not the attack, nor the baby, nor even the lies. I love you more than I've ever loved anyone, and I want us to spend the rest of our lives together."

Hope couldn't help the sob that broke from her throat. She buried her face against his wool coat and cried. She cried for the loss of her friends and her innocence at the mission. She cried for the baby conceived in bitter anger but born to the love of a different mother.

But mostly she cried because for the first time since that November day in 1847, she finally felt the chains completely fall away. She was free. The truth had set her free. Fear could no longer command her. She wouldn't let it. With God's help, she would never again fall prey to its power.

Chapter 24

Someone was knocking on the front door. Mercy gave an exasperated sigh and dried her hands. All morning she'd been working to can potatoes, and one thing after another had called her away. The knock sounded again, this time a little heavier.

"I'm coming," she called, crossing the room.

She dried her hands on her apron once more then opened the door. "Toby, what are you doing here?" She smiled and opened the door wider. "Come in."

He crossed the threshold and pulled off his hat. "I wanted to speak to you private-like. Is that possible?"

Mercy's smile faded. She knew what this was about. "The smaller sitting room is empty." She pointed to the left. "We could talk there."

He nodded, and Mercy stepped past him to lead the way. She was glad Hope had started a fire in the hearth. The damp cold combined with the unpleasant task at hand caused a shiver to wash over her.

"Please have a seat," Mercy said, taking the upper hand. "I need to ask Hope to look after the canning for me. I'll be right back."

She hurried from the room before he could protest.

"Hope?"

Her sister was just coming into the kitchen through the back door.

"Toby's here. Could you watch the potatoes for me?"

"Of course." Hope frowned. "Are you going to refuse him like you planned?"

Mercy nodded. "Yes." She sighed. "I have to."

Hope gave her a hug. "I'll be praying for you, and I'll be right here if you need me."

"Thank you."

Mercy drew a deep breath and made her way back to the sitting room. Toby jumped to his feet, but before he could speak, Mercy held up her hand. "I know what this is all about. I know why you've come."

"I'm glad you want to get right to the point," Toby said, sitting down on the settee.

Mercy knew he expected her to join him, but instead she took the wooden chair by the fireplace. "You should know I haven't changed my mind, Toby."

His eyes narrowed. "But why? I know you care for me. We get along so well."

"Toby, I'm your friend. We went to school together and go to the same church. I value your friendship, but Toby, I'm only fifteen and too young to marry."

"As I said before, a lot of gals get married young." She could hear the pleading in his voice.

"Yes, but that's often because there's a need for them to do so. Although some do marry for love, most marry because they have no other recourse. Either they're alone without anyone to care for them, or their folks push them out to lessen the financial burden on the family. In my case, neither is an issue."

"But you know how this would benefit us both." His pleading tone matched the look of desperation on his face.

"I know it would garner you additional land, but it wouldn't give you a happy life. I don't love you as a wife should love a husband. I saw my sister Grace marry a man she didn't love in order to get us all to Oregon. She was miserable, and so were the rest of us. I don't want that for either you or myself. You deserve true love, Toby."

He looked angry rather than hurt. "And nothing I say can change your mind?"

"No." She shook her head. "I'm quite certain that my decision is the right one."

At this Toby jumped up in a rage. "How can you possibly know what's right? Your decision is that of a child."

She knew he was just lashing out due to the pain of rejection, but she didn't care for his temper. "Then you should feel grateful that I've refused you. After all, you wouldn't want to be married to a child."

This irritated him all the more.

Toby sneered. "I am grateful. You're a stupid little girl, and I'm sorry I ever thought you'd make a good wife."

He stormed from the room, leaving Mercy to stare after him, mouth agape. She'd never seen him lose his temper like that. She heard him open the front door then slam it behind him.

Hope appeared in the doorway. "He's wrong, you know."

Mercy couldn't shake her surprise. "I . . . well, I don't know what to think. He's never been so angry with me. In fact, I've never known him to be angry at all."

"He's the childish one, Mercy. He didn't get the toy he wanted, so he's throwing a fit. Pay him no mind. You made the right decision, and I'm proud of you. Maybe in time he'll come to see the truth of it."

Mercy leaned back in her chair and caught her breath. "Thank you, Hope. It helps to hear that. I just feel so . . . foolish. Maybe I am being stupid."

Hope pulled up another wooden chair to sit directly in front of Mercy. "Toby will come around in time if he truly loves you, or he'll stay mad at you, but either way he's wrong to call you childish and stupid." She reached out and held Mercy's hand. "The opposite is true. Today you've made your first real adult decision."

"But he was my friend, and I didn't want to lose his friendship." Mercy bit her lip and shook her head. "I guess being an adult isn't always pleasant."

Hope shook her head. "No. Not always."

"How are you feeling?" Alex asked, coming to join Grace as she stood looking out the window.

She turned and smiled. "So much better. I can't believe the difference a couple of weeks can make. I feel that I have my strength back . . . mostly because I have you back." She put her hand atop her swollen midsection. "And I feel certain the baby is fine. He's moving a lot, and I figure he'll be like you."

"You're so sure it's a boy?" Alex grinned and put his hand on her stomach as well.

"I am. I don't know why, but I feel certain it's a boy."

"And have you come up with a name for this boy of ours?"

She smiled. "I've had a few thoughts on the matter."

"Just a few?" He raised a single brow and tilted his head slightly.

She laughed. "Well, I've had a long time to think about it."

He shook his head. "I wish you'd told me before I left."

"But you wouldn't have gone, and I know that you most likely helped secure peace. I couldn't hold you here, knowing how important it was. I knew you'd enjoy time with Sam too."

"But it was my choice to make." He curled a piece of her hair around his finger. "Please don't ever keep something this important from me again."

"I promise." She touched the scar on his neck. "I was so afraid when you didn't come back. When word came that you'd been hurt, I wanted to pack up my medicines and come to you. I knew I couldn't, but believe me, I tried to figure out a way to do it."

He smiled. "I've no doubt of that. I can just imagine you ordering a team of men to take you to Fort Nez Perce."

"Lance was so good to go instead. I still can't believe his connection to your past. I never even suspected."

"When he showed up at the fort, I thought he looked familiar, but I couldn't place him. I figured he was someone from Oregon City that I knew through Edward or even church. Then I remembered he was one of the soldiers in the courtroom, and I figured that was all there was to it. When I heard someone use his name, however, it was all too clear. He even looks like his brother Justice."

"Well, Hope seems to like his looks. You don't mind that they're getting married, do you?"

Alex laughed. "Of course not. Lance has proven himself to be a good man. The past isn't important, and even if it were, I would never be so petty as to stand in the way of Hope's happiness. God knows that poor woman has gone through enough."

Grace looked back out the window. "She has, and she deserves happiness. I'm glad they've agreed to marry for real.

I've felt for a while that they would be good together. Their friendship reminded me of ours when we first met."

"That bad, eh?"

She turned to face him, her stomach leading the way. "I didn't think it was that bad."

He laughed. "No, just bad enough that you were always mad at me for something I'd said or done."

"I don't remember being mad very often, but there were times when your stubbornness was very nearly my undoing."

"*My* stubbornness? What about yours? As I recall, you're the one who snuck off during the night to go back to a mission where Indians were killing people and taking hostages. I hate to think what might have happened if Sam and I hadn't caught up to you."

That thought sobered Grace. "I know what would have happened. I learned a lot that day." She paused to shake away that thought. "Alex, do you think the tribal leaders will keep this peace? Did they believe you when you told them that the government didn't want any more killing?"

"I can't say for sure. I'm not certain I believe the government is done killing Indians. Still, I told them it was to their benefit to live peacefully and avoid the whites if possible. If they aren't confronting or being confronted by us, then hopefully there will be no chance for violence."

"I hope you're right. Eletta tells me there's been trouble down south in the Rogue River area. She said the tribes there are given to fighting with each other all the time, but now the miners have laid claim to the river, and it's not boding well for either side. She said the miners are actually attacking the Indians without cause and doing so with the authorities' encouragement."

Alex let go a heavy breath. "Like I said, I'm not sure the government will ever be done killing Indians." He leaned forward and placed a brief kiss on Grace's cheek. "Enough about that. I thought we were going to talk about names for our son. What name are you considering?"

"I'd like to call him Gabriel."

Gabe had been Alex's mentor and dearest friend, besides Sam Two Moons. The trio had hunted and trapped together for years. Then Gabe slipped while cutting wood and put an axe into his leg. He died of infection and what Grace perceived as Dr. Whitman's interference.

"Gabe was such a good friend to you and a good man." The look on Alex's face told her he approved, so she continued. "I'd also like to give him your name."

"Mine?"

"Yes. I'd like to call him Gabriel Alexander, after two of the finest men I've ever known."

Alex pulled her into his arms as best he could. "I can't think of any name that I'd like better. But what if you're wrong and it's a girl?"

She shrugged. "That's easy. Gabrielle Alexandria."

Laughing, Alex hugged her close. "Of course."

"I think getting married on the thirtieth is a wonderful idea," Grace said as Alex helped her take a seat at the dinner table. The entire family had come together once again, and everyone was caught up in the plans for Hope's marriage to Lance. "A November wedding served me quite well."

Hope gave Lance a smile as he pulled out her chair for her. Grace had encouraged them to marry before the baby came, and to Hope's delight, Lance completely concurred.

Taking his hand, Hope looked at her sister and the other

guests. "We won't have the same anniversary date, since I think it's important we each have our own."

"I agree," Mina Marsh said. She looked at her husband and smiled. "It's too special of a day not to have it to yourself."

Edward chuckled. "There are no doubt plenty of other folks who married the same day we did."

"Yes, but I don't know them, so it doesn't matter." Mina gave Edward a sweet smile before turning her attention to Baby John, who was trying to work his way off her lap. "No, you don't, little man."

Hope enjoyed the moment. It was such a pleasure to have everyone together for the Saturday evening meal. She and Mercy had fixed a fine feast of roasted beef and gravy with potatoes and carrots. Added to this, Hope had baked several Chinook salmon Lance had caught and created a special concoction of mushrooms, spinach, and dried lemon zest to go with them. Rounding out the meal were deliciously scented yeast rolls, fresh butter, and three different kinds of pie.

"My mouth is already watering," Uncle Edward declared, taking his wife's and eldest son's hands. "Alex, I think you ought to bless this meal so we can dig in."

Everyone laughed and joined hands as Alex began to pray. "Father, we thank You for Your provision and blessings. We thank You that we can all come together under one roof to share in the love that is family. Bless this meal to our bodies, and bless the hands that prepared it. Amen."

"Amen!" ten-year-old Phillip declared, pulling his hand from Edward's. "Can I have pie first?"

Edward ruffled his son's hair. "Spoken like a man after my own heart."

Everyone laughed at this and began to pass the platters and bowls around the table. Hope couldn't remember ever being so happy. She had never really understood the importance of family until after the massacre. When she was young, her family had been more of an intrusion than anything else, but after all she'd come through, Hope could see how much she needed these people.

After dinner, Hope and Lance settled in one of the front sitting rooms while the rest of the family lingered around the table.

"I'm impressed," Lance said, rubbing his stomach. "A wife who is both beautiful and a good cook. What more could a man ask for?"

Hope smiled as he put an arm around her shoulders. "I'm glad you enjoyed it. I enjoyed making it. There's a lot of satisfaction in preparing a meal that everyone likes."

"So now, about this wedding of ours . . ." Lance let the words trail off.

Hope fixed him with a serious look. "What about it? I didn't think men liked to discuss such things."

He shrugged and tightened his hold on her. "If it involves you, then I'm happy to discuss it. Besides, I know you've been making plans."

She nodded. "I have. Grace and Mercy are so excited. They want me to have a nice wedding at the church with a special dress and a wedding breakfast afterward. The ladies of the church have all gotten involved too. In fact, I think the only person who isn't excited is Clarence Ford."

Lance chuckled and shook his head. "A number of bachelors are grieving the loss of another single woman. The men outnumber the women by at least twenty to one out here."

"Well, it won't be that way for long. In case you hadn't noticed, another group of settlers arrived a week ago, and it seemed to me there were plenty of pretty girls."

He shook his head. "Nope, never noticed that at all. I've only got my eye on one pretty girl."

Hope settled back against him and marveled at their exchange. "You know, I can hardly believe that when I first met you, I was ready to commit murder. It seems like a hundred years ago."

"You scared me to death that day."

She laughed. "I scared myself." She paused and shook her head. "But you didn't seem afraid. You handled it like the professional soldier you were."

"That was my training kicking in, I suppose. I guess it wasn't so much fear *of* you as *for* you. You put the fear of God into Tomahas." Lance chuckled. "The look of terror in his eyes was a complete betrayal of his suggestion that you go ahead and shoot him."

"I didn't think he was afraid. He just kept sneering at me, and I knew he wanted to hurt me. His hatred was what I saw, but if he was afraid, then I'm glad." Once she'd said the words, she worried what he would think of her. It wasn't a very kind or compassionate sentiment. "Does that shock you?"

"No. I can't say that I feel any differently. He took your peace of mind and had no regret for the ways he'd hurt you. Thankfully, you don't have to worry about that anymore."

Hope sat up and turned to look Lance in the eye. "There are still a lot of problems with the Indians, Lance. As happy as I am to marry you, that issue is always in the back of my mind. Not like it used to be—I'm not bound up in fear or memories, but I am mindful of the situation."

He pulled her back against him. "I know. I heard them talking in town today about the new laws removing title to land from the Indians. It will make for hostilities, but we can't live in fear about what might happen. It's dangerous country, but we only need stay until we can secure passage on a ship."

"What?" Hope shot up again. "What are you saying?"

"I thought I told you. I inherited my family's plantation just outside of New Orleans. I kept on the manager after my father died and I joined the army, but my plan has always been to return."

Hope shook her head. "I knew you were a lawyer there and planned to return, but that was before . . . us. I didn't know you owned property in New Orleans."

"You never asked," he said in a teasing tone. "It's a lovely place. I also own part of a shipping business."

"And you want us to live there?" Hope had never considered leaving her sisters. She could easily walk away from Oregon Territory, but leaving Grace and Mercy was an entirely different matter.

His eyes narrowed slightly as he studied her. "You sound as if that is unappealing."

"I've never thought about it. When we left St. Louis to come west, I knew it would be a one-way trip. It's far too expensive to return to St. Louis, and besides, we have no one there."

"I don't have any other family to speak of in New Orleans either. There are some cousins in Mississippi, but I can't remember the last time I saw them."

"I suppose the plantation has long been in your family."

"My grandfather purchased it in 1790. He passed it down to my father, and my father to me. We were all born there. In fact, we were all born in the same beautiful four-poster bed." He gave her a wicked grin. "Maybe we can carry on that tradition with children of our own."

Hope's feelings were completely jumbled. She hadn't given much thought to where they would live after their wedding. There was a time when she would have gladly fled this territory without a second glance, but now things were different.

"You seem troubled."

"I've just never thought about leaving."

"But I thought you hated it here. You told me you'd never feel completely safe here. Just a few minutes ago you said you're still uneasy about the situation with the Indians."

She nodded. "I don't know how to explain it. I suppose I have thought of leaving, but it never seemed a possibility. And Grace and Mercy are here."

"Well, now it is a possibility. It's one thing I can give you to help you continue to heal. I'm glad to be able to take you away from a place that represents only pain and sorrow. I know we'll be very happy . . . no matter where we go."

She nodded, barely hearing him. Her thoughts were consumed with how she could choose between the love she held for her sisters and the love she had for Lance Kenner. Why couldn't life ever just be easy?

Chapter
25

Besides planning her wedding to Lance, Hope now had the added concern of where they would live after they married. If they married. She hadn't wanted to discuss the matter with anyone before now, but as she sat at the spinning wheel while Grace sewed baby clothes, Hope felt she had to speak.

"I need your advice."

Grace looked up, surprised, and smiled. "Since when?" She went back to her stitching.

"Since now. I have a dilemma."

Grace looked up again, and this time she frowned. "What's wrong?"

"Lance expects us to move back to his ancestral home outside of New Orleans. He inherited a plantation there. It's been in the family since last century." She stopped spinning and leaned back. "He wants to return there as soon as possible."

"Well, that comes as a surprise."

"I know. It's completely overwhelmed me. I've never held

any great love for this territory. In fact, there was a time when I wanted to leave here. I wasn't sure where I wanted to go, but I knew it'd be anywhere but here. Now, however, I can't imagine life without you and Mercy." Hope shook her head. "You two and Uncle Edward are the only family I have left, and while I never thought that mattered much, I've come to see that it means a great deal to me."

"But Lance means a great deal too."

Hope nodded at her sister's soft words. "He does. I can't imagine my life without him either." She sighed. "I don't know what to do."

"Have you told him this?"

"No. I mentioned never having considered leaving, but I didn't explain further."

"Why not?" Grace's expression was so full of concern that Hope had to look down.

"I suppose because it was such a surprise, and I wanted time to think about it. We both agreed to pray about it, but I think Lance's mind is made up."

"When I fell in love with Alex, I knew he would never want to leave this territory. He hates the city." Grace smiled. "I think Oregon City is even too big for him at times. I can't imagine him wanting to go back to New Orleans."

"Lance has an entire life planned there. He wants to pick back up with his legal practice and perhaps even become a judge one day. He wants to run his plantation, although I have no idea what that entails. He told me I would never want for anything." Hope sighed. "I know he's planning all this on my behalf. He knows I don't feel safe here. I just don't know if I can be a part of it."

"But you love him."

"I do, and that's what makes this so difficult. I never thought

I could love another man after Johnny—especially given what Tomahas did to me. I fully expected to spend my life alone and never marry. Then Lance came along, and everything changed. He was so easygoing, never demanding." Hope got up from her chair and walked to the window. "I never really appreciated you and Mercy until these last few months. I always took you for granted—figuring you'd be in my life forever."

"Of course we will be, whether you're here or in New Orleans. We'll always be a part of your life."

Hope turned to face Grace and leaned against the windowsill. "I know that, but it wouldn't be the same. I want to be here to help you when it comes time for the baby. I want to continue working with the sheep. I want to see Mercy grow up and fall in love. I can't do that from thousands of miles away."

"So are you going to tell Lance you can't marry him?"

The question was so matter-of-fact, so simple. Hope found it hard to believe that everything she'd considered and all of her misery could be summed up in one question.

"I don't know."

"Let's call it a day, boys," Edward Marsh announced. "I've already sent the rest of the crew home."

Alex and Lance looked up from the invoices and purchase orders for lumber they'd been going over. All week the new orders had been pouring in, most of them from California. Alex arranged the production and delivery to the ships, while Lance took care of the logistics required to ship the lumber all the way to San Francisco. Overseeing in this capacity was all Edward would allow Alex to do as he continued to recover.

Alex pulled out his watch. "I didn't realize it was so late. Grace will wonder what's keeping me. Now that Mercy rides the horse to and from school each day, I don't have that reminder to tell me the day is nearly over."

Edward laughed. "If I stay too much past six, Mina will send the boys to fetch me. I'll see you fellas later. Be sure the fire's out in the stove."

Lance stacked his papers and put them in the drawer. "Will do, Edward. Alex, you go on ahead. I can see to all of this."

Edward gave a wave and headed out, but Alex tarried. Lance wasn't sure what was going on, but by the look on Alex's face, it wasn't good.

"Is something wrong, Alex?"

"I want a private word with you."

Lance nodded. "Go ahead."

"I'm not usually one to stick my nose in another man's business, but I feel the need to speak to you about your future."

Lance was crossing the room to the stove but stopped and turned to face Alex. "My future?" He grinned. "What about it?"

Alex crossed his arms. "Like I said, this is out of my nature, but you've really troubled Hope with your plans to move to New Orleans."

This took Lance by surprise. "I don't understand."

"A few days ago, Hope told Grace that you plan to move back to New Orleans after the wedding. That was something she didn't expect, and it's upset her. She doesn't want to leave Grace and Mercy, but neither does she want to end her engagement to you."

"End the engagement?" Lance knew he sounded riled and tried to calm his tone. "She's said nothing of this to me."

Alex nodded. "You haven't been around."

"Well, we've been busy with all these new orders. It wasn't for lack of wanting to be with her." Lance went to one of the tall stools they kept at the orders table and sat down, shaking his head. "Here I've been planning out our future together, and we may not even have one." He felt a heavy sense of dread. He'd never once thought he might lose Hope.

"Hope has gone through so much. I know you understand."

"I do. That's why I want to get her out of this place. She's only just begun to overcome her fears. I figured New Orleans would make her feel safe. I have a big place there, and she could have everything her heart desires."

"Except for her family."

Lance let out a heavy breath. "I never thought about it being a problem."

"Are New Orleans and the plantation that important?"

Without Hope by his side, his home would hold no joy for him. He finally shook his head. "No. Not unless Hope is there too."

"You might want to figure out what matters most and make your plans based on that."

"I wish she had talked to me about this."

"She probably will, but you need to remember that Hope isn't like most women. She doesn't talk much about her feelings. She's probably been more willing to discuss matters since meeting you and seeing Tomahas put to death, but even so . . . she keeps a lot inside."

Lance considered this. "I'll go to her and coax it out. I want to discuss this, and I never want her to feel put upon." He got off the stool. "Thanks, Alex. I appreciate that you care so much about Hope that you'd come and talk to me."

"I care about you too, Lance. It seems our families are destined to intertwine, and thankfully not just because of the tragedies that happened so long ago."

"I appreciate that, Alex. I feel the same about you and Grace. Mercy, too. You all seem like family to me."

"Because we are," Alex replied, heading for the door. "Now, shall I tell Hope you'll be out to see her later?"

"Yes, please do. Oh, and Alex . . ."

Alex turned. "Yes?"

"What are your plans for the old house on your property?"

Alex smiled. "Why, do you have a suggestion?"

Lance could see the amusement in his expression. He already knew the answer. "As a matter of fact, I do. I wonder if you might be interested in renting it to a newly married couple."

"Renting?" Alex grew serious and shook his head. "No. However, I would let the couple stay there in trade for help around the farm. Oh, and they'd have to be willing to share at least the evening meal with us."

Lance laughed. "Seems a reasonable price."

Chapter 26

Hope had come to a conclusion by the time Lance showed up after dinner. She sat at her spinning wheel in the large front room, working with finely carded wool. It was so soft and delicate that it would be perfect for a baby blanket. She hoped to surprise Grace with it once she had a chance to crochet it into the finished product.

Hope glanced up at Lance. "Alex said you were coming, but I was beginning to wonder if you'd changed your mind."

He smiled and came to help her up. "I would never change my mind where seeing you is concerned. It's too cold and windy for a walk, or I would sneak you off into the dark and—"

"Lance, it's good to see you again," Grace said, coming into the room. Her walk was much slower these days as the baby seemed to settle lower.

"Grace, you look beautiful." Lance left Hope's side and went to help Grace take a seat in the rocker.

"I don't feel very beautiful," she said with a smile. "I'm as big as a horse."

"For a very good reason. A most blessed reason," he countered.

Grace nodded. "I agree with that." She reached into the basket beside the rocker and took up her sewing. "Don't feel you have to sit here and make small talk with me. I know Hope would much prefer to have you all to herself."

"I would." Hope motioned across the hall to the smaller sitting room. "I have the other room prepared for us."

Lance nodded and gave Grace a sweeping bow. "Until later, milady."

She laughed and shook her head. "You Southern gentlemen certainly have a way about you."

"It would please my mother to hear you say so." He extended his arm to Hope. "May I escort you, my dear?"

She rolled her eyes but couldn't help laughing. "My sister may be completely drawn in by Southern charm, but I'm immune to it."

He arched a brow. "Oh, you might be surprised. I'm sure I can figure out a way to charm you."

She sobered. She loved this man very much. "You already have won my love. There is no need to charm me."

Hope and Lance crossed the foyer and entered the smaller sitting room. She pulled the pocket doors closed so they had some privacy. She had made up her mind about the future, but it wasn't without a price.

He took a seat on the settee and patted the place beside him. Hope smiled and joined him. "I'm not sure how much talking we can accomplish sitting so close."

"I'm chilled, and you can help warm me up."

She caught the teasing in his tone and put aside her worries. "I'll put more wood on the fire." She started to rise, knowing he would pull her back down and into his arms. He didn't disappoint her.

After much too brief a kiss, he pushed her away. "First we need to talk."

"All right. What is it you've come to say?"

"It's come to my attention that you actually might not want to leave this area once we wed."

Hope swallowed the lump that rose in her throat. Had Grace spoken to him? "It's not the area I would have trouble leaving."

"Yes. I was too thick-headed to consider your family when I told you I planned for us to move to New Orleans. I just assumed you would want to put miles between you and Oregon Territory. It was wrong of me not to consult you, and I want to apologize."

"You don't need to. I can understand you wanting to return to the home you shared with your folks. You have good memories of living there and a responsibility to your ancestors to keep the land and raise your family there."

To her surprise, he shook his head. "I don't have a responsibility to anyone but you. My dead ancestors hardly care whether I live in New Orleans or Oregon City." He reached out to touch her cheek. "But you care, and that is far more important. I have no desire to drag you somewhere you don't want to go."

Hope looked away and tried to focus on the flames of the fire. "I don't want to make you give up the life you planned for yourself. That was never my desire."

"And I don't want you choosing between your sisters and me. I'm afraid I might lose out."

She looked at him and shook her head. "No. You wouldn't have. I had already made up my mind after much prayer that I love you too much to give you up. I'll go wherever you ask me to go."

Adoration and joy lit his face. Hope would have known without any further words that Lance was pleased with her decision, and in truth she was pleased as well. It was the right choice despite being a very hard choice.

"I can't tell you what that means to me, Hope. One thing I've learned from all this is that we need to make decisions of this magnitude together. I was wrong to plan out our future without talking to you about it, and I'm sorry."

"Husbands make the decisions for their families. I can't fault you for that nor ask you to regret your actions. It's the way God has made you."

"It is, but He's also given me understanding, compassion, and wisdom. However, I don't have to be a wise man to realize that marriage works best when both parties are respectful of the other."

"Thank you, Lance. That means so much to me."

He wasted no time in continuing. "If it meets with your approval, I plan to sell my holdings there and use the money here."

"But you needn't sell. Couldn't you keep the plantation and have it go on as it has been, with someone else running the day-to-day operations?"

"I could, but I don't need to. I want to invest in my life with you. Besides, I can get new property through the Donation Land Bill, and since we'll be married, we can get a nice large piece. Then we can build a home of our own, though maybe not right away. After all, such things take time, especially when handled from a distance."

"You wouldn't go back to New Orleans to oversee the matter yourself?"

"No. Not for any amount of money in the world. I couldn't risk you getting away from me." He grinned. "I have friends there, and the lawyer who trained me can easily handle the sale. I'll notify my Mississippi cousins in case they'd like to buy the plantation and keep it in the family."

"But what of your things? Surely there are heirlooms you would want with us here."

"I've already thought about that. There are some pieces I want to keep in the family—paintings, handwork my mother did, books my father introduced me to, a few pieces of furniture. There is, in fact, a very large, ornate bed that has been passed down through generations of my family that I think will serve us very well. I mentioned it once before."

Hope felt her face grow hot and looked away, making Lance chuckle. "There's also a collection of lovely porcelain dishes you might like. My mother's family hailed from France, and the collection was handed down to her."

Hope was so overwhelmed with happiness that she felt close to tears. She bit her lower lip to keep from saying anything, lest she begin to cry. That he loved her more than his family holdings was no small thing to her.

"I'll make a list and arrange for all of it to be shipped here when the rest of the property is sold. How does that sound?"

She fought to control her emotions. "It sounds like . . . it's . . ." She let the words trail off and turned to look at him. For a moment, all she could do was study his handsome face. She put her hand on his cheek. Leaning toward him, she turned his face to meet her lips and kissed him, hoping he would understand her feelings without the need for words. He wrapped his arms around her and pulled her against him. The kiss deepened, and a sigh escaped Hope. He understood.

She leaned against his shoulder and put her head against his neck. For some time, neither one said anything at all. Hope imagined they would have many quiet evenings just like this in the future. She remembered her mother and father sharing moments before the fire. As a young girl, she had sat on the floor, playing at their feet, but from time to time she had glanced upward to see their shared whispers and looks of love.

"Does this mean you'll still marry me next Saturday?"

Hope smiled but didn't move an inch. "I'm thinking about it."

Lance surprised her by jumping to his feet, pulling her up as he stood. He scooped her into his arms and lifted her from the floor as he might a child. She squealed at his antics and clutched him tight as he gave her a little upward toss.

"You'd better think hard and fast, because I don't intend to set you back down until you give me an affirmative answer."

Hope wrapped her arms around his neck. "Well then, I must take pity on you, because I know your arms will grow weary under my weight. I will most assuredly marry you next Saturday."

The following morning, as Mercy dressed for church, she could hear Alex and Grace having an argument downstairs. It wasn't so odd that they would disagree, but Alex generally didn't raise his voice loud enough to be heard.

Mercy picked up her bonnet and gloves and hurried down the stairs to see what the commotion was all about. She found Grace seated at the table with Alex opposite her and Hope standing in between, as if keeping them from attacking each other. Mercy giggled as she imagined her very pregnant sister trying to take a swing at Alex.

The trio looked at her as if she were mad, and Mercy forced the smile from her face. "What in the world is going on? I heard you all the way upstairs." She moved closer to the table and looked at Grace. "What have you done to get him so worked up?"

"Me? Why do you suppose I've done something?" Grace asked, looking surprised.

"Because she knows how foolish you can be," Alex countered. He picked up his mug of coffee and downed it.

Hope took the opportunity to intercede. "Grace has been having some pains. Not true labor, but she's questioning whether she might be further along than she originally thought."

"Why should that make Alex mad?" Mercy looked to her brother-in-law for an answer.

"I'm not mad. I'm just frustrated that your sister won't listen to reason," Alex replied.

Mercy turned back to Grace. "What reason are you rejecting?"

Grace fixed her husband with a frustrated glare. "He doesn't want me to go to church. He feels I should be confined to the house."

"I don't think that's such a bad idea." All three fell silent and looked at Mercy in surprise. "Grace, you know as well as anyone that if this were any other expectant mother, you would advise her to stay home and rest. You can hardly walk across the room, much less climb into a wagon and then ride all the way to town. Remember how exhausted you were last week after we came home from church? You had to take a long nap just to recoup your energy."

Grace eased back in her chair with a look of defeat. "But what about Hope's wedding?"

"We can have it here." Mercy shrugged and looked around the room. "The folks who care about attending will drive the distance, and the ladies of the church will be just as happy to set up a wedding breakfast here as in town. You designed this big house for just such a purpose, so you might as well take advantage of it."

"For a girl of fifteen, you certainly have sound reasoning," Alex said, looking pleased at the turn of events.

"It just makes sense. Hope and I can announce it at church this morning. Everyone will understand, and I'm certain Lance won't mind."

"No, he won't," Hope assured. "He wouldn't care if we married at the sawmill, so long as we married."

Mercy nodded. "So it's settled. Grace, you know it's best for you and the baby, so don't sulk. And Alex, you go gentle on her because she's bearing a tremendous burden carrying your child." With that, Mercy sat down. She picked up her fork and speared a piece of ham, then added it to her plate. With that accomplished, she looked up with a smile. "Has anyone asked the blessing yet?"

Later, at church, Mercy stood nearby as Hope explained to Lance and Pastor Masterson about the need to change the wedding venue. Both men heartily agreed, and after that it was just a matter of making the announcement, which the pastor did at the end of the service.

"Along with that wedding-related announcement," Pastor Masterson said, "I have another more personal one to make. My son Toby has asked Beth Cranston to marry him, and she has said yes."

Mercy felt as if someone had delivered a blow to her mid-section. The wind was momentarily knocked from her lungs, and she might have gasped had Hope not squeezed her hand at that very moment.

There were smiles and murmurs of approval throughout the congregation, leaving Mercy with no choice but to force a smile. They stood and sang the closing hymn, but Mercy could only stare straight ahead. Beth was the same age as Mercy, but she was the eldest of six children—seven, if you counted the baby her mother was expecting the following year.

Mercy was relieved when half a dozen women encircled her and Hope after the service.

"Mother Cranston and I will be out just after dawn on Saturday to set up the wedding breakfast," Sally Cranston announced before anyone else could speak.

"Mother and I will also be there," Mary Fuestelle declared as her mother-in-law joined them. The two women were known for their competitive spirit. One was not to be outdone by the other.

"I'll make my cinnamon breakfast cake. Grace absolutely loves it, and it will bring her some joy," Bertha Fuestelle added.

"And I shall make a proper applesauce wedding cake with velvety white cream frosting," Mrs. Cranston declared with a challenging look in Mrs. Fuestelle's direction.

Mercy had no doubt there would be plenty of food to be had once these women began competing with each other. Other ladies came to offer their help, and Mercy edged away to let Hope deal with them. It made her smile to see Lance do the same thing.

"Were you surprised at our announcement?"

Mercy turned to find Beth Cranston all aglow. She swallowed the lump in her throat. She had to be honest. "I was. You're only fifteen, Beth. That's much too young to marry." She hadn't meant to criticize, but the words just poured out.

Beth frowned. "You're just jealous. I know you thought Toby would marry you because he was spending all that time with you."

"I'm not jealous, Beth. I just care about you. You're my best friend, and I want you to be happy."

The blond-haired girl smiled. "I've never been happier. I love Toby. I've loved him for a very long time, and I was so jealous because he only seemed to have eyes for you. But when I told him that, he said he was only spending time with you to get closer to me. He said you told him things about me when you two talked."

Beth's name had come up in their conversation at times, but Toby certainly hadn't shown any special interest in her. Mercy toyed with the idea of telling Beth that Toby had recently begged her to marry him, but she couldn't be petty and unkind. Hopefully someone would talk some sense into Beth before they set a wedding date.

But as if reading Mercy's mind, Beth smiled. "We're going to be married just after Christmas. Won't that be wonderful? I'm so excited, and Grandmother is going to make me a special dress. It's going to be lavender."

"Why rush this, Beth? Christmas is just a month away. That doesn't give you and Toby much time to really get to know each other."

Beth laughed. "It gives us plenty of time."

"But you need to be certain that he's the one God intends for you."

Her protest fell on deaf ears and only irritated Beth. "I thought you were my friend, Mercy Flanagan."

"I am." Mercy frowned. There was no way to help Beth see the truth. She was completely over the moon.

"My family approves, and everyone else is so happy. Why can't you be?"

Mercy gave a heavy sigh. "I just want you to be sure this is the right thing to do. What about school?"

"I wasn't going to attend past this year, anyway. I would have had to get some kind of job to help at home. Now I'll have a home of my own. Maybe when you're more mature, you'll understand." Beth flounced off, a defiant child with her nose in the air.

"Well, that was certainly less than pleasant," Hope said, coming to stand beside Mercy.

"Yes, it was. I tried to dissuade her from marrying Toby, but she just thought I was jealous."

Hope continued to glance in the direction Beth had gone. "Does she realize Toby asked you to marry him first?"

"No. That seemed cruel. I just pointed out that she's terribly young and they hardly know each other." Mercy shook her head. "I wish she wouldn't do this."

"She has to make her own choices, Mercy. Just as you do." Hope looped her arm through Mercy's. "But just so you know, I'm very proud of you. You could have created quite a scene by telling her about Toby's proposal, but I doubt it would have changed her mind."

They made their way outside, where Lance sat in the driver's seat of the wagon, collar turned up on his wool coat and hat pulled low. Mercy thought it amusing how he chose to be in the damp cold rather than endure the wedding plans going on inside the church.

As they approached, he jumped down and helped Hope up first, then Mercy. Mercy climbed into the bed and pulled back the duck canvas from where she'd placed it to keep her seat dry. She breathed a sigh as she caught sight of Toby and Beth talking to Pastor Masterson.

Well, Lord, I pray that you make them happy and keep them from harm. It isn't how I would see things done, but I know that it isn't my place to interfere.

Chapter 27

November thirtieth dawned overcast, and by eight o'clock, it was raining. Hope looked out the window of her bedroom and sighed. She would have loved for the day to be sunny and dry, but it was November, and the rain was expected. Thankfully there was no threat of flooding—at least not yet.

She looked at the new dress she and her sisters had made. It was a lovely creation, prettier than anything Hope had ever owned. She went to where it lay on the bed and touched the soft barege material. The pale blue silk-wool had come as a gift from the McLoughlins. From drawings of the new styles back east, Grace had helped Hope create a bodice that went from shoulder to waist in a dramatic V. The lines of the V had been trimmed in a darker blue pleating, and a lighter blue material filled the bodice to the neck. It was fancier than Hope's day-to-day dresses and would become her Sunday best after the wedding.

A knock at her bedroom door revealed Mercy. "Why aren't

you dressed? There are quite a few people here already, and the ceremony starts in an hour."

Hope nodded. "I just wanted to wait until the last minute so I didn't do anything to damage the dress."

"Well, it's the last minute, so let me help you get into it." Mercy picked up the gown.

Hope cast aside her robe and let Mercy assist her. She couldn't help but feel a little nervous. Everyone was there to see her, and the idea of being the center of attention was unnerving.

"It's funny," she said as Mercy did up her buttons in back, "I used to love having all eyes on me, but now I'd just as soon get married in private."

"You're going to be the most beautiful bride ever and you deserve the attention. However, I bet once you descend the stairs and join Lance, you'll completely forget about everyone else."

"I hope that's true and I don't throw up."

Mercy finished and came around to face Hope. "You won't throw up. Sit down, and I'll help you with your hair."

"Nothing fancy. This dress is more than elegant, and there's no need to worry overmuch about my hair."

"No matter what," Mercy said, brushing through Hope's long brown hair, "you'll be beautiful. You've always been the prettiest of us all."

"I have a feeling that will change. You've become quite pretty yourself. Now that you've grown a few inches taller and have started to fill out, I think there are going to be a bevy of men lining up to court you."

"I don't think I want to be courted. At least not for a long time. Does that sound terrible?"

Hope smiled. "Not at all. Since you have older sisters—both of whom are married, or will be in a matter of minutes—you needn't worry about it. You'll always have a home with one of us."

"I appreciate that. I don't know exactly what I want to do with my life other than continue my education, even though that's frowned upon for women. Especially out here."

"No matter what, Mercy, stay true to yourself. God will guide you. I never used to believe that or even think it important, but I do now. I know that prayer changes everything and that God really does care about the tiniest details."

"How do you know that?" Mercy put down the brush and started braiding Hope's hair.

"The Bible says He does, for one thing. It says He sees the little sparrows when they fall, and He knows the number of hairs on our head. I suppose that's how it is with loving someone. You take time to know everything about them. You want to know all the things that relate to them."

"That makes sense. I just don't know what I think about anything anymore. What Toby did completely surprised me. I feel confused about everything now. I don't know why."

"Understanding will come in time. I'm sure a part of your heart feels hurt because he so easily transferred his affections to another."

"I suppose so."

When Mercy finished, she handed Hope a mirror. Surveying the work, Hope smiled. "You've done a very nice job. I couldn't have asked for anything more lovely." Mercy had woven braids around and through a rounded knot of hair. "Thank you."

A knock sounded on the bedroom door, and Mercy went to answer it while Hope stepped into her new leather slippers. Now she was ready.

"I've come to escort the bride," Uncle Edward said, stepping into the room. He grinned. "You look beautiful, Hope."

"Thank you." She drew a deep breath. "I guess I'm ready."

Mercy led the way down the stairs, Hope and Uncle Edward following. When Mercy reached the bottom step, someone with a violin began to play. Hope didn't recognize the song, but it was lovely.

She saw Lance when they first entered the large sitting room full of people. Mercy was right. Everyone else seemed to fade away, and all that remained was the man she would marry. Lance's expression was full of reassurance and love, which gave Hope all the strength she needed. She had a feeling that for the rest of her life, it would be that way.

Uncle Edward handed her to Lance then stepped back as Pastor Masterson stepped forward. "Let us pray."

"I'm glad to have this day over with," Lance said, closing the door to the house he would share with Hope. "I hope you aren't offended by me saying as much. I know women set great store by such things as weddings."

Hope laughed and watched as her husband tossed his jacket aside and then unbuttoned his vest coat. "Hardly. You and I share the same love of formal affairs."

"It reminded me of being in the army."

He shrugged out of the vest and then pulled off the burgundy cravat he'd borrowed from Dr. McLoughlin. Next he unbuttoned the high-necked collar of his shirt and gave a sigh of relief. Then, motivated by that bit of liberty, he pulled the starched white shirt from the waist of his pants and unbuttoned it the rest of the way, revealing his chest and well-muscled abdomen.

Hope had never seen him in this state of undress and felt embarrassed. She went to the fireplace, thankful that someone had seen fit to ready it for their arrival, and held out her hands to the warmth. Without warning she was taken back to the first time Tomahas had attacked her. She shivered. Surely her married life with Lance wouldn't be that way. Surely when he touched her, she wouldn't feel the same revulsion.

Lance came up behind her and pulled her back against him. Hope didn't resist, but she couldn't shake the memories of what had happened at the Whitman Mission.

"Are you all right?"

"Honestly?"

He turned her in his arms. "Of course."

"I can't help remembering the massacre—or rather the aftermath." She swallowed hard and looked into his eyes. "I suppose I'm afraid that . . . well . . . "

He put his finger to her lips. "Don't be afraid. I don't ever want you to be afraid of me. I love you, and I will do whatever I need to in order to make you feel safe. I would never force you to do anything."

"I love you very much," Hope said, touched by his words.

"You're not sorry you married me, are you?"

"No!" She shook her head. "I just hope *you* aren't sorry you married *me*."

"I'm not. And so you know, I had already considered the past and how hard our wedding night would be for you."

"You did?" She shook her head. "I doubt most men would care."

"I'm not most men." His blue eyes twinkled in the glow of the firelight.

She shook her head again. "No, you certainly aren't."

He kissed her gently, without even taking hold of her. Hope wrapped her arms around his neck and held on to him even after the kiss ended. She buried her face in his neck and breathed in the sweet scent of the cologne he'd also borrowed from Dr.

McLoughlin. There was no odor of sweat or bear grease, as there had been with Tomahas.

Lance put his arms around her and held her for several long minutes. Hope knew that if anyone were going to make the first move toward something more intimate, it would have to be her. He would never force himself upon her nor press her for more than she could give.

Pulling away, Hope turned her back to him. "Would you undo my buttons?"

He didn't answer but began the task. When he'd finished, he stood back, and Hope turned to face him. Still he said nothing, just watched her.

Hope extended her hand and Lance took it. She gave him a slight smile and led him toward the bedroom.

Hope had barely fallen asleep in Lance's arms when a loud pounding on the front door roused them. Lance shot out of bed and pulled on his trousers before leaving the room to see who had come calling in the middle of the night.

Rising from the bed, Hope yawned and reached for her robe. She startled to hear Alex's voice and hurried from the room to see what was wrong.

No sooner had she joined them than Alex took hold of her shoulders. "It's Grace. The baby's coming."

Lance went to stoke up the embers in the fireplace, and Hope drew Alex toward the hearth. "Is Mercy with her?"

"Yes." His expression was full of agony. "I don't know what to do."

"Ride to town for Dr. McLoughlin, and I'll get dressed and go to her." She smiled and patted his arm. "Try not to worry. Women have been having babies for thousands of years."

"But not my baby and not my woman." Alex shook his head. "She's in so much pain."

Hope nodded. "I understand. Now go get the doctor. I really don't want to deliver the baby by myself."

This seemed to settle Alex a bit. "Yes. I'll go right now."

He left the house without another word, and Hope turned to smile at her husband. "You'd better come along and make coffee. I have a feeling it may be a long night."

Lance looked almost as bad as Alex had. "Are you sure I wouldn't just be in the way?"

She laughed. "It's a very big house, Lance. Now come help me dress."

They reached the main house ten minutes later, and Hope immediately hurried to Grace and Alex's bedroom. She found her sister sitting on the mattress, bent in the throes of heavy labor. Mercy stood beside her, wiping her face with a damp cloth. She looked at Hope with relief.

"How are you doing?" Hope asked, sitting on the bed beside her sister.

Grace panted against the pain. "This is happening so much faster than I expected."

"Has your water broken?"

"Yes, earlier. But I didn't feel any real pains, and since it was so late, I didn't want to alarm anyone. I figured there was plenty of time, but this little one doesn't seem to want to wait."

"Mercy, go make sure we have plenty of boiled water."

"I already did that. Grace told me to earlier. I brought in the wash basins and vinegar as well. And there's scissors and twine and plenty of clean towels." Mercy motioned to the table across the room.

"Good. Then I imagine we're fairly well set. I sent Alex for Dr. McLoughlin."

"Oh, you didn't need to bother that poor man," Grace said. "I'm sure we can manage without him."

Hope shook her head. "You may be sure, but I'm not. What experience I have with this kind of thing is limited."

The pain appeared to pass, and Grace leaned back against a stack of pillows. "How was Alex doing when he came to you?"

"Not well. He looked absolutely terrified."

The sound of something breaking came from the direction of the kitchen.

Hope looked at Mercy. "I believe that is my husband attempting to make coffee. Would you go help him?"

Mercy nodded and hurried from the room. Grace let out a heavy sigh. "She's been so good to help me, but I can see that she's afraid."

"She's never seen a baby born, has she?"

"No, I don't think so." Grace closed her eyes. "But you understand what has to be done. I take comfort in knowing that you've gone through this before and can help me."

Hope heard something in her sister's voice that made her offer reassurance. "I know exactly what you're going through and what must take place. Try to rest between the pains and not worry."

Grace opened her eyes again and met Hope's gaze. "Thank you. I'm so glad you're here. I wish I could have been there for you when you delivered Faith."

Giving birth had been a terrifying experience for Hope, not so much because of the pain or risk of complications, but because she feared the child would be something hideous and deformed. Instead, a beautiful little girl had been born. This time, the baby was very much wanted by its mother, and things would be so different. Grace also knew about the processes of labor and birth. She wouldn't face it with the same confusion and ignorance that had accompanied Hope with her delivery.

The pains started again, and Grace bent forward as best she could. Hope rubbed her sister's back and, to calm herself more than Grace, began to sing a hymn. She felt Grace relax a bit, and for the next half hour, when she wasn't asking Grace about her progression, Hope sang.

The mantel clock had chimed three when Alex returned with Dr. McLoughlin. Mercy joined them at Grace's request. She felt it was important for Mercy to learn what to do in case she was ever called upon to deliver a baby.

"I hope I'm strong enough to endure it," Mercy replied. Her face was filled with fear, but she remained nonetheless.

Hope knew it wouldn't be long until the baby was born. Already Grace was pushing against the pain and telling Hope that she felt the baby coming.

"Babies are no keepers of time," Dr. McLoughlin said, washing his hands in the basin. "How is she doing?"

Hope joined him at the washstand. "I can see the top of the baby's head." She picked up a jug of vinegar. "She'll want you to rinse your hands in this as well."

The doctor looked at her oddly for a moment, then nodded. Hope poured the vinegar over his hands, and he smiled. Hope returned his smile.

Mercy nodded and held out a towel. "She makes us use it for everything from cleaning wounds to cleaning house."

Dr. McLoughlin nodded in understanding and took the towel. He moved to the bed, where Grace lay writhing in pain, and began to check the position of the baby. "So, Grace, are you having a boy or a girl?"

"A boy," she said through gritted teeth.

Hope stood by to assist however she could but was totally unprepared when Dr. McLoughlin ordered Grace to stop.

"The cord is wrapped around the baby's neck, so you must stop pushing."

Grace's eyes grew wide. She knew the dangers even better than Hope. The fear that spread across her face tore at Hope's heart. She quickly sat down beside Grace and took her hand. Mercy, going to the opposite side of the bed, did likewise.

Hope wiped Grace's brow. "It's going to be fine. Dr. Mc-Loughlin has done this hundreds of times, and he knows what to do."

"Yes, but it won't be all that pleasant for Grace," the doctor replied. "Even so, you must not fight against me. I'm going to maneuver the babe so that I can release the cord. Whatever you do, do not bear down."

There was perspiration on Grace's upper lip and forehead. "I won't."

Hope felt Grace's grip tighten as her eyes glazed over in pain. "Grace, do you remember when we were little girls and got hurt? Mama would make us recite the alphabet and the Lord's Prayer and anything else that we knew by heart while she worked on the wound."

Grace nodded and barely whispered, "I remember." She grimaced. "I don't think that will work for me right now."

"But you never know," Hope said. "It's all about thinking on other things. I know the pain is still there, but you should at least try it."

Grace moaned and shook her head. "I can't."

Mercy spoke up. "Well, to quote Mama, '*can't* never did anything.'"

An expression of irritation crossed Grace's face before she let out a cry.

Alex's face went white at the sound of his wife's scream. Lance had no idea how to comfort or even distract him and so did nothing at all.

"Something must be wrong," Alex said, pacing the room. "She wouldn't just scream like that if something wasn't wrong."

"I don't know about that." Lance felt like joining Alex as he paced but forced himself to stay seated. "It can't be an easy thing to deliver a baby. I mean, when you consider the actual process, it must be quite an endeavor."

Another cry rang out, and Alex stopped and gripped the stone mantel. He said nothing, just stood there, staring at the clock.

Lance knew nothing he said or did was going to ease Alex's mind. Instead, he reached over to Hope's spinning wheel to marvel at the yarn on the bobbin. "I don't know how she takes wool off sheep and turns it into this fine yarn. It looks so simple when she's sitting here, but I don't think I could ever master it."

Alex looked at him, but Lance doubted he really comprehended what he was saying. Someday Lance would find himself in the same situation, and he knew that if Hope were the one crying out, nothing would keep him from her side.

After a few minutes, the house grew quiet. The silence was almost worse than the screams, however. Alex was absolutely tormented by it.

"Why don't you just go to her?" Lance said. "The doctor can hardly throw you out and deliver a baby at the same time. It might be comforting to her to have you there."

Alex shook his head. "No, she told me not to come. She said most men can't stand the sight and faint dead away."

Lance chuckled. "That doesn't surprise me. We can hunt

and clean game, even dress our own wounds, but watching a woman give birth sounds daunting."

The sound of a baby crying filled the air. Alex looked at Lance with such surprise that Lance had to laugh again.

"You knew this was going to happen, so don't look so surprised." He got to his feet and moved to Alex's side, then slapped him on the back. "It would seem that you've become a father."

Alex walked to a chair and slumped into it. He put his head in his hands and sat there, unmoving. Lance didn't know if he was praying or just trying to keep from fainting.

They waited for what seemed an eternity before anyone came for them. Finally, Mercy appeared with Hope right behind her. Both were beaming.

Hope went to her brother-in-law. "Alex."

He shot up off his chair. "Is she all right? Is the baby all right?"

Hope took his arm. "Come see for yourself." She glanced back at Lance. "You too. Grace said it would be fine."

Lance wasn't at all sure he wanted to go along. He'd never experienced anything as exhausting as this had been.

Hope sensed his hesitation and motioned with her head. "Come on."

He followed her and Alex through the house and into the bedroom. Grace sat in bed, sweat-soaked and worn. Her face wore a look of elation, however.

"Come meet your son," she said in a whisper.

Alex immediately left Hope's side and went to the bed. Grace held out a small bundle to him. Alex stared down in wonder for several seconds.

"Go ahead and take him. You won't hurt him," Grace encouraged.

He took the baby in his arms and looked back at Hope and the others. "It's a boy," he said.

"And a fine boy he is," Dr. McLoughlin added, standing next to Alex. "A feisty fellow who gave his mother a bit of a hard time, but who nevertheless is healthy and whole."

"And Grace?" Alex asked, glancing at his wife, who watched him with a smile.

"She's just fine, son. Just fine. She did a great job and now she needs to rest. I don't want to hear about her getting out of this bed for at least two days."

"I'll see she stays there even if I have to sit on her."

Hope laughed. "We'll all make sure she obeys doctor's orders." She looped her arm through Lance's. "I think we've done enough here. I, for one, am sleepy, and although the sun is soon to come up, I'd like to go back to the warmth of my bed. Someday I'm going to tell my nephew how very inconsiderate he was to choose the middle of the night—my wedding night, no less—in which to be born."

The others laughed, and Lance gave her a smile. He bid the others good night, then let her pull him through the house. Once they were outside, they could see the sky growing light. The clouds had cleared, and it looked like they might enjoy some sunshine.

"It was nice to be part of something as wonderful as Grace giving birth. I couldn't help but remember how terrified I was when I had . . . Faith," Hope began. "I hated Tomahas so much, and I was sure that hate and his violence would result in something hideous, but instead she was beautiful."

"I can't imagine you having anything but beautiful babies." Lance put his arm around her shoulders as they walked.

"I suppose it was neglectful of us, but we've never talked about children." Hope stopped and looked up at him. "Do you want children?"

He chuckled and brushed away a wisp of her hair. She had

gotten ready so quickly to go to her sister's aid that she'd done nothing more than tie her hair back, and now it was coming loose. "I'm not sure we get a choice in the matter, but I'll be happy with whatever happens so long as you're there."

"I didn't think I wanted children," she admitted. She gave a sheepish little grin. "But then again, I didn't want to marry either."

He smiled. "And now?"

"I rather like being married, and given that, I might also like to have your children."

Lance pulled her close. She smelled of vinegar and soap, but it didn't matter. "What I know for certain is that God will give us exactly what we need, when we need it. He's already given me more than I could have ever imagined by giving me you."

She nodded. "I feel the same. You kept me from committing murder and befriended me in spite of knowing what you did. You've helped me not to be afraid. I never thought all of this would be possible, and I'm so glad you chose me to be your wife."

He took her face in his hands. "There was no other choice. You are my beloved Hope. Surely by now you realize that a man cannot live without hope."

Tracie Peterson is the award-winning author of over one hundred novels, both historical and contemporary. Her avid research resonates in her stories, as seen in her bestselling HEIRS OF MONTANA and ALASKAN QUEST series. Tracie and her family make their home in Montana. Visit Tracie's website at www.traciepeterson.com.

Sign Up for Tracie's Newsletter!

Keep up to date with Tracie's news on book releases and events by signing up for her email list at traciepeterson.com.

More from Tracie Peterson

Emily Carver is tired of moving from one mining camp to another and longs for a true home. When a handsome geologist arrives in camp, the two are drawn to each other but fight the attraction for different reasons. Will these broken souls allow God to bring healing to their hurting hearts—and embrace love?

A Treasure Concealed
SAPPHIRE BRIDES #1

 BETHANYHOUSE